Portrait of Deceit

Paul & Lizzie ~
Congratulations!
Enjoy the read ~

Jerome H Mansfield

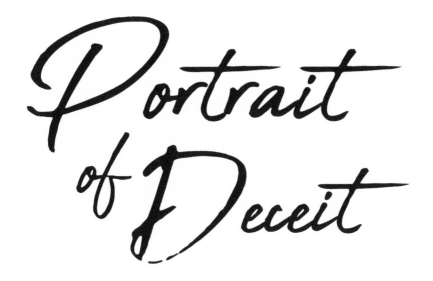

Portrait of Deceit

A Novel

JAYME H. MANSFIELD

ILLUMIFY
MEDIA.COM

Published by
Illumify Media Global
www.IllumifyMedia.com
"Let's bring your book to life!"

Paperback ISBN: 978-1-959099-15-4

Typeset by Art Innovations (http://artinnovations.in/)
Cover design by Debbie Lewis

Printed in the United States of America

Contents

Acknowledgments

If I hadn't stumbled across attending a lecture about art forgery in Denver eight years ago, this novel would not exist. Dr. Colette Loll, founder of Art Fraud Insights, a consultancy dedicated to art fraud-related prevention initiatives, exhibitions, lectures, training, and specialized investigations, was the stellar presenter.

It would be mild to say I was interested in her content. Instead, I was wildly captivated, and a story seed took root that I couldn't shake. Nearly two years later, I reached out to Colette. Little did we know that a literary collaboration, and even more cherished, a cross-country friendship, would blossom.

With her expertise and support, the story progressed. We shared time touring D.C. art exhibits, Modigliani archives, and Winterthur's Art Conservation Lab, and experiencing Colette's acclaimed exhibit, *Treasures on Trial: The Art and Science of Detecting Fakes*.

Colette—I am grateful for our initial chat several years ago as you power-walked through D.C. Perhaps it was the exercise adrenaline rush, but you decided to join me on this exciting literary adventure. Oh, my . . . what fun it has been!

Kelly Berger, artist extraordinaire and long, long time friend. Once again, your creativity and artistic talent grace my novel. Your cover art provides a heavenly gateway into my stories, and I can't thank you enough for continuing to share the journey with me.

To Illumify Media—Mike, Lisa, Larry, Jen, Greg—thank you for providing a highly professional and personal publishing experience. All hands on deck makes for smooth sailing and sunny skies!

And always, to my husband, James, it's climbing steep mountains like this that remind me how much I love you. Thank you for believing in my passions and purpose.

"With one eye you are looking at the outside world, while with the other you are looking within yourself."

Amedeo Modigliani

1884-1920

CHAPTER ONE

Olivia ~ Forged & Forever Friendship

We were an odd couple—Olivia and May—best friends since childhood and raised in the forested hills of Kennett Square, Pennsylvania. *Mouse*, we called her—shy and quiet, petite and quick—given the nickname by my father when she scurried through the cluster of trees and thick undergrowth between our homes when she needed to escape her mother's temper or fill her hollow belly.

I was a different animal—long and lanky. It served me well as a teenager and into adulthood. Long torso, slender legs and arms, the kind of body that makes swimsuit shopping enjoyable and attracts looks that should be discreet. May, the skittish and sneaky mouse. Me, the cat. Agile, curious, and wildly independent. Cat and Mouse. Logic would have it that we'd be enemies. But fate had another plan for two little girls, who many years ago found each other in the midst of despair.

*****

April 2017. Last month, May and I turned thirty-eight years old only days apart. I once thought it was fun to share March birthdays. *Spring chickens,* my father called us. But today neither of us felt spry and renewed. I was burying my biological father and May was saying goodbye to the only father she ever knew—no birthright necessary.

Only the two of us were in attendance. After all, not many attend the funeral of a recluse, especially since my father's best friends of late were his paints, brushes, and Jack Daniel. Now, the shoveled earth danced on top of his pine casket like rain in springtime, a grand symphony for a life that evaporated after Mother took her life when I was twelve.

If I were counting, the hunched groundskeeper made three, and the pastor from the nearby Presbyterian church rounded our party up to an even number. But the religious man had excused himself once formalities were spoken and the erratic spring wind lifted his stiff, combed-over hair. I didn't expect more. It must be hard to talk about someone's life when you don't know where a man's soul is headed. The church man didn't have much to offer me either—the absentee daughter, returned home only in time to watch her father buried.

Stray hair fell around my face and stuck to tears that fell too easily since May called me in the city last week. She found my father slumped in his recliner, positioned on the front porch so he could watch the cherry blossoms bloom. *Heart attack. Most likely fast. Probably didn't suffer much, much, much* . . . the word skipped across my mind like a stone cast on the silky surface of the pond behind my house. May and I swam in the sticky summers and ice skated when it was cold, pretending to smoke cigarettes when we breathed out tiny clouds.

The groundskeeper lifted another shovelful and moaned. I understood his agony. Not physical. But like his gnarled fingers, resembling willow twigs twisted around the wooden handle, my heart felt stiff and numb in a different way from when Mother died twenty-six years ago. Then, everything was confusing, and I locked my thoughts and heart in the pages of my diary. But time has a way of sneaking in and teasing out hidden memories—slipping around success, image, and perceived happiness—revealing that things aren't always what they seem.

Above us, branches from a 100-plus-year-old maple swayed, saying its own goodbye to the man who'd walked alone in the forests of southern Pennsylvania. It somehow knew Thomas Danford would never again rest against the sturdy trunk, catch spinning whirligigs in late summer, and breathe in the crisp autumn air. Instead, while my father's brushes lay still and his palette hardened with time, other artists would be beckoned by the same innate passion as his . . . to capture the area's beauty in art.

"May." Though no others were present to hear, I lowered my voice to nearly inaudible. "Do you remember your last conversation with my father? Did he say any final words?"

May seemed lost in thoughts and her silence voided any message, if any, my father had meant for me. I stood still, trying to recall his raspy baritone heard during my occasional calls or infrequent visits home. The memory seemed already faded, muffled by the earth now covering his grave.

May squeezed my forearm. "It's best we let this old guy finish so we don't get charged overtime. The rate he's moving, we probably will anyway." She forced a smile. "Don't worry. He'll take good care of Thomas."

"He's dead, May." I stared into the eyes of my longtime friend, remembering when our stuffed animals were real, and we thought Barbie's hair would grow back after we gave her a bob.

May cast her eyes down, the same way she had years ago when her mother slurred her words and told her she was rotten.

"I'm sorry. I didn't mean to . . ." I reached for her hand, but she slipped it into her overcoat pocket.

"It's okay. I know you're hurting." When she squinted, a deep crease I'd never noticed ran from her widow's peak hairline to the bridge of her nose. "We both are."

I wrapped my arms around my friend, the person who faithfully cared for my father while I went away to college to study business while she took art classes at the community college. It was never my intent to have May assume what should have been my role as daughter. It's just that she made it easy for things to go that way as I spun off toward my destiny.

May's shoulders heaved, followed by a muffled sob. "I didn't think I would miss him so much. Especially since he could be such a pain in the—"

"Ass." I smiled. "And for that, you deserve a medal."

"Ha." She fumbled in her pocket. "I've been wanting to quit, but what I really need is a smoke."

"Fair enough . . . and give me a moment." I kneeled at the side of the grave and stared at the simple bouquet of yellow tulips I'd bought at the grocery store before meeting May at the cemetery. For the life of me, I couldn't recall my father's favorite flower. But Mother's I knew . . . yellow tulips bursting each spring from the garden my father planted outside her cottage window, cut and displayed in cobalt vases strategically set on the kitchen table, next to her writing desk, and on my bedroom dresser. *Darlings, there's never a shortage of sunshine in life.*

Surprise attack! I hunched my back and sobbed until I felt May's hand rub my neck. "Liv, it's time to go." I laid the tulips on my father's grave, blew him a final kiss, and walked across the lawn, arm in arm with my childhood friend.

I was indebted to May. And now that my father was laid to rest, I would return to Washington, D.C. and an overflowing schedule of work at Axiom. My art forgery research and forensics company, strategically based in the heart of Georgetown, was my baby. I'd worked diligently to cultivate a unique, niche career—so much that I had to often pinch myself to realize its tremendous success. Sure, other things in life had been waylaid—pursuing a serious relationship, marriage, a family—tucked away for later, perhaps never. I was busy living my high-definition, surround-sound, Technicolor dream. But May Meriwether—she was still chasing hers.

CHAPTER TWO

Olivia ~ Cluttered Mind

As I pulled onto the rutted gravel drive leading to my father's house in picturesque Kennett Square, memories rushed back of our old dog, Leo, bounding through the front screen door. Short for Leonardo da Vinci, my father swore the gangly mutt was the smartest dog living on the East Coast. Whenever a visitor arrived, Leo was the first greeter, able to size up a person's worth with one sniff that was either followed by a ferocious bark or a sloppy face licking. I turned off the ignition and stared at myself in the rearview mirror. If Leo were still around to rule the roost of my childhood home, how would he greet me now?

May beat me through the few stoplights in town and her faded blue pickup truck was already parked under the carport as though it was home. Parking in the garage hadn't been an option for as long as I could remember . . . at least since *she* was gone.

Over the years, the majority of the garage became packed with all sorts of junk my father had dragged home from flea markets, garage sales, and even pulled from dumpsters. Broken chairs, rickety tables, metal signs, discarded flowerpots, rusted bicycle and car parts, cheap picture frames with *art treasures*, or so he said, steadily accumulated in the garage and around the house. He insisted things so beautiful should not end up in landfills but instead be given a home. "We don't live in a disposable world," was his mantra. If he was really on a roll, that declaration was followed with the sentiment, "When one finds things that were lost . . . it helps one become found." I never knew what he meant, but I remembered the words clearly.

Nestled in the remaining portion of the garage was a car. My father, who insisted we call him Thomas once we were old enough to drive, drove an old VW Bug. He'd bought it on his ten-year anniversary working as a chemist at the DuPont manufacturing facility in the neighboring town. He loved that car, and on occasion, he'd convince Mother to join him for a ride in the country. When they returned, he spent hours polishing the exterior and wiping down the inside. With Mother gone, and his job at the facility ended after the final round of layoffs, the car eventually lost its appeal. It remained in the garage, wrapped in a canvas tarp—a chrysalis that failed to turn into a butterfly.

May opened the front door and greeted me with a slight wave. I slipped my unused key into my Burberry and entered a house that had not been home for a long time.

"Sorry about the mess." May pushed a box aside with her shoe. "Watch your step."

I followed her into the living room, or more accurately, what once was the living room. Since my exodus to college, graduation, and the early years of establishing a career, and thus infrequent visits home, the space had transformed from the original family gathering room into a conglomeration of fixtures and supplies, all in the name of creating art.

Like moths around a porchlight, memories flitted in my mind despite the obvious passage of time. I pictured the annual Christmas tree, freshly cut and proudly dragged through the snow by my father from our surrounding forest and propped in the corner near the window. The floral sofa, once bright and cheerful, bought for Mother in hopes of brightening her mood, remained in the same spot in front of the bay window. Now it was sad. The fuchsia roses had turned a pale and sickly Pepto Bismol pink, and layers of once vibrant green fauna were putrid and lifeless. Any life remaining in its pattern was gone, bleached by the sun.

Precarious stacks of random art books and ancient issues of *Nature Magazine* dotted the wooden floor. The aroma of stale cigarette smoke and burned remnants from the ash-filled fireplace crept into the entirety of the room, leaving a stagnant smell and its yellowed fingerprint on walls, switch plates, and more. Piles of outdated newspapers, haphazard cardboard boxes filled with crumpled paint tubes, and Mason jars of linseed cluttered the floor around the focal point—my father's easel. Dutifully positioned next to it, a paint-splattered three-legged stool held his signature red Craftsman toolbox, crammed with paintbrushes, palette knives, drawing pencils, and blackened, balled-up erasers. Propped against one of the stool legs was Thomas's palette—like a faithful dog, waiting patiently for its owner to return and the next adventure that would play out on canvas.

"He was starting another landscape . . . said this one was really special." May stood next to me, looking at the canvas that displayed only a preliminary sketch of a country road leading to a covered bridge. "He'd seen that bridge when your mom and he went for a drive up north. Apparently, she really liked that one because you drove into the dark and came out into the light."

"I don't remember her ever talking about it." I ran my finger along a thin charcoal line. "I don't remember her talking about much at all, really."

Neither of us spoke. Most likely each of us was visiting some long-ago memory of my beautiful, dark-haired, blue-eyed mother. Surely, I was thinking of the woman who seemed to float in and out of my life—dictated by the ebb and tide of her mental health. And as hard as I tried, at that moment I couldn't remember her voice.

I don't know if it was delayed emotion from burying my father only hours ago or stepping into the house and into my past, but a surge of desperation overtook me like a momentous wave. I squared up to May and grabbed her shoulders. "What if even the good memories disappear? Do you ever feel that way?"

"What way?" The deep crease reappeared on her forehead. "Geez, Liv. You kinda have a death grip on me. What's gotten into you?"

I relaxed my hands, though they shook. There was no answer for May. I wasn't sure what suddenly gotten me so riled. But I knew this . . . I needed an answer from her, some sort of reassurance from the only person left in the world who understood, and sadly, shared a part of my nightmare.

For as long as I'd known May, if she was anxious, afraid, or worried, on cue she'd twirl a strand of hair around her forefinger— not only once or twice, but incessantly and compulsively. Now, as she sidestepped my embrace, her finger began its familiar whirling motion, mixing strands of store-bought, highlighted blond into ash brown hair.

As I watched my friend, my heart ached, just as it did when she would show up at our back door in the dark, breathing hard from running through the grove of trees that joined our properties. Often, her face was tear-stained and her eyes wild as my father ushered her in, kissed the top of her head, and whispered, "It's going to be all right. Now the two of you get some sleep." Hand in hand, we'd scurry down the hallway to my bedroom—May's free hand twisting in her hair.

I reached for her hand and felt my own cease shaking. "Our childhoods were pretty messed up, but despite it all, we took good care of each other. Didn't we?"

She nodded. "We did."

"We laughed, we played—"

"We dreamed, Liv. That's what I remember most. We dreamed really big."

"And I never want to lose that." My voice quivered. "I don't want to forget the good parts, May."

"We won't, Olivia. I promise." She squeezed her eyes shut and I wondered where her thoughts were taking her—dark places where her mother's hand struck out unexpectedly or the safe retreat in my bedroom where Thomas read aloud my mother's beautiful picture books until we'd fallen asleep. "Your dad gave me a childhood I never would have had. It wasn't perfect—no one's is—but for all he did for me, it was an honor to take care of him when he couldn't do it himself."

"Oh, May. You're a better person than me." I released her hand and felt the weight of guilt on my shoulders. I turned and stared at the sketched road leading to the bridge. Up to that point in the drawing, the road had a clear destination. But beyond the bridge, the path was unspecified and void of a direction or destination. "What if all you and I have of the past are each other?"

"Would it be that awful?" May half-smiled.

"No, it wouldn't." I returned a slight smile—completing hers— just as we did for each other when we were fragile little girls, awkward teenagers, and even now as grown women. But to be honest, our time together was limited to brief phone calls between my other commitments—mountains of appointments, meetings, research, travel—things that consumed my time.

I diverted my eyes and glanced at the piles of canvases strewn across the worn hardwood floors. As if she'd done it hundreds of times—a slow dance of sorts with my father's cluttered life—May stepped over the obstacles without even looking down.

"But I don't plan to live in the past any longer." This time, her tone was cutting yet awkward, like the dull edge of a blade.

Her sudden change of demeanor caught me off guard and I started after her into the kitchen. Instead, I stopped and stared at the pile of art resembling the aftermath of a row of dominoes toppled and scattered. So many pieces, beautiful and skillfully painted even as drink and early dementia blurred my father's mind.

Dutifully, I righted the paintings, leaning some against the walls and sofa, and stacking others into neat piles. I paused and took in the scenes. Some were familiar surrounding areas, but others most likely concoctions of his imagination and mixed memories of places visited—ponds, rivers, and lakes, trees bathed in sunlight and snowfall, and pathways leading over hills and through fields of grass . . . going somewhere . . . someplace wonderful and hopeful.

When I joined May in the kitchen, she was tossing food from the refrigerator into an already full, and obviously unchanged garbage can. A half glass of whiskey sat on the counter next to an empty bottle. How could my seventy-two-year-old father in failing health live like this?

"What's wrong?" She handed me an eerily murky pitcher of milk and motioned to the sink.

"Nothing at all. Something wrong with you?" I nodded toward the drinking glass and wondered how often she and Thomas shared a bottle or two.

"No." Her response was definitive and curt. "And sorry there's no more for you." She lifted the glass and downed a gulp.

I shrugged. I wasn't much of a hard alcohol drinker, but a nice glass of pinot noir sounded pretty good. Instead, I held my breath as rancid milk seeped into the drain. "You've been twisting your hair."

"What's that supposed to mean?" She slammed a head of wilted lettuce into the garbage can.

"You tell me."

Except for her glare that may have well screamed unspoken thoughts, she was silent.

There was no point making a fuss over the living conditions. It was what it was and there was no reason to complain at this point. Obviously, I had been negligent in attending to my father's daily existence. Better to change the subject to something more pleasing. But May knew me too well. Even though I tried to hide the disgust on my face over the state of the kitchen, let alone the entire house, childhood best friends know how to read each other like the ABCs.

Before speaking, I chose a light-hearted pitch. "I looked through the stack of paintings. It's sad that his talent went mostly unnoticed all these years. He was really good."

"He wouldn't let me clean the house." May's voice was matter-of-fact. "I tried, but he got upset. I gave up. Figured he was entitled to his own decisions."

If she isn't going to play nicely, neither will I. My hands went to my hips. "Clearly, he wasn't capable of making good ones." I stared at May in front of the kitchen window, her silhouette appearing as an apparition—a ghost paying a visit. "You were the one who said his mind was slipping."

"And you were the one who didn't do anything about it," she snapped back.

"What was I supposed to do?" I shoved a stack of papers off a chair and sat. The reality of the day's events and the dank house engulfed me. My head drooped into my hands in defeat. "Called more often? Visited every other week?"

"That might have been a good start."

My friend's words were the noose I'd avoided for years. *Convicted. Condemned.* Guilty of loving my father, but not acting on it out of selfish ambition and protecting my own heart. Was that so wrong?

May pulled out the other chair with her foot and plopped down next to me "Sorry, Liv. That was cruel." She picked at a hardened blob of grape jelly on the table until it popped off and stuck to the tip of her finger. "I think we're both a little on edge. Funerals do that." She leaned her head onto my shoulder, just like she did when we were young, stretched out on our bellies on the carpet, heads propped on pillows, watching *The Wonderful World of Disney* on Sunday evenings.

"But you're right." I twisted a stained dishtowel around my hands "Even though he made it so hard to keep a conversation . . . he seemed distracted and tired—"

"He was confused. Not all the time, but more and more often." She stood. "Don't beat yourself up. He wouldn't have wanted that." She opened the pantry and stepped inside. "Besides . . . " She poked her head out. "He loved you."

"I loved him too." I sat back and breathed out like a deflated balloon. "We'll get this done. He lived here a long time and nothing says it has to be cleaned out right away . . . except the rotten food in the trash."

"Fair, and if you want, stay at my apartment tonight and we'll make a plan and tackle more of this in the morning."

There was no sense in lying. "I need to get back to the office . . . sometime tomorrow. It's crazy, I know."

May leaned around the pantry door, her eyebrows lifted. "Already?"

"It's out of my control."

"But you own the company."

"That makes it even harder. My assistant, Joel, is as capable as anyone I've hired, but I can't stay out of pocket much longer. He's already sent me a few texts. And in all fairness to him, there's a fascinating case I can't wait to start. I have work in Italy for a good part of the month that's going to set me even more behind."

"But what about the necessary paperwork? Executing the will?"

"You said all of that was in order several years ago. Remember? When Thomas appointed you as the executor." I raised my eyebrows. A familiar sting resurfaced, a reminder that my father decided it was best to have May, "the consistent, reliable, and present person in his life be in charge of his affairs if and when anything should happen to him." Of course, as the only child of Thomas and Anna Danford, I would be the sole beneficiary—or at least, that's what he had said.

I took a deep breath, determined to keep a calm demeanor. "It is in order, isn't it? I mean, it must be fairly simplistic. He didn't have much besides the house and some money from his DuPont pension he'd been living off for years. Maybe a small amount in a checking account."

"I'm sure it's all fine." She puffed out a loud breath, again completing what I had started—another reminder that my best friend and I once even breathed in unison. But that was then. Now, we seemed to be separately gasping for air—May, to make something of her life, perhaps marry, or possibly break free of the town she'd never left. Me . . . despite being wired to get up and go, constantly on the move toward bigger and better . . . there were private moments I wished to let well enough alone and just breathe.

"Getting the house ready to sell will be a job in itself." She closed the pantry door, a little too hard. "I assume you have no plans to move back here, right? You're a city girl now."

"Wow, May. You're sounding a little judgmental." I shoved my chair into the table. "And no, I'm not returning here. My job, my friends . . . my life are in D.C. I've worked my butt off to make a new life and career, and quite frankly, I've done a good job." I'm sure my face had turned red. I tugged the overstuffed garbage bag from the basket and yanked the tie. "As for the house cleanup, it will get done. But for now, most of it will have to wait."

"If only my life was half as exciting and glamorous as yours." She rolled her eyes, and I wasn't sure if it was in jest or jealously.

As I held up the bag like a prized turkey, old coffee grounds escaped through a hole in the bag and sprinkled my shoes. "And you call this glamorous?"

May cracked a smile and I couldn't help but join her. We giggled for the first time in many hours, and it felt good.

*****

May gathered her purse and turned off the kitchen light. "Ready to go?"

I'm not sure why I wanted to stay. Rain was beginning to pelt the west-facing windows, dulling what little light filled the house. "I think I'll stay here tonight."

May pursed her lips, clearly put out I declined her offer.

"Maybe look at more of his paintings and do some cleaning." My hands were on my hips, and I wondered why I was justifying my decision to be in my family home.

"Are you sure? It's kind of depressing in here." May flipped on the kitchen light. "There's nothing to eat."

"That's okay. I'm not hungry, just tired. I think I'll try to get to sleep early."

"Are you sure? We could call it a sleepover, watch a cheesy movie, and eat ice cream out of the bucket like we used to do."

"I'll be fine. Really."

"Your choice." She fumbled for her keys. "At least leave the cleaning for tomorrow."

Before I closed the front door, I hugged May and thanked her again for all she'd done for Thomas and me. As I grabbed a blanket and settled on the worn sofa in the living room, I thought about the statement May had called out as she walked across the driveway to her truck. *Olivia, some people live life little and some live life big. You, no doubt, live big.*

As the words replayed in my mind, I wondered what they really meant—a backhanded compliment? Had my life become so big, living in sophisticated Georgetown, traveling the country and world while associating with fascinating and influential people, that I missed the smaller, important aspects of life? I actually liked my life—living *big*—if that's what it really was.

Piles of coffee-stained, scribbled to-do lists and incomplete crossword puzzles torn from last winter's newspapers covered the small end table. Did I really know my father, especially the man he had become? And May, was she the same, provincial, small-town girl who the local boys loved for her cute figure and sassy mouth? And why did they always dump her when they eventually ventured beyond the familiar and predictable side of the fence?

I closed my eyes and allowed my thoughts to drift back to when I was little—my mother laughing as she and my father came through the front door after walking around the lake. Now I could hear her melodic voice, rising above my father's deep tone as he kissed her neck and whispered loud enough that I could hear, "I love my girls."

I propped a pillow under my head and pulled the afghan blanket higher. Maybe I'd sleep here in the living room instead of my old, pale pink room down the hall. Yes, tonight I'd sleep on the sofa and hope for sweeter memories to arrive.

CHAPTER THREE

Olivia ~ The Letter

"You slept on the sofa?" A familiar voice stepped into my dream.

I blinked a few times, slowly returning to my father's living room turned art studio.

"Why didn't you sleep in your bedroom?"

I sat up and stretched to the protest of a cramped neck muscle. "Exhaustion, I suppose."

"Here." May set a coffee carrier and brown bag on the table. "Latte. Just how you like it. I think."

"It's perfect." I peeked in the bag. "And cinnamon crusted bagels. My favorite." I wrangled my thick hair into a ponytail. "You're sweet for bringing this."

"And hungry, too." She settled on the sofa next to me.

"You look great, May. Are you still seeing that guy from the bank?"

"A little here and there. He's nice enough but kind of boring."

"He's probably in love."

"Maybe, but it takes two for that to work."

I clambered from the sofa and pushed aside the curtains. "What time is it anyway? I never sleep in."

"Just past nine."

"Oh my gosh. I need to get back to D.C. this afternoon. Joel called last night when I was almost asleep. He said my new client left several messages and didn't sound accommodating to being put off any longer." I widened my stance and surveyed the room. "Let's put in some solid hours this morning. Where do we start?"

"I'll finish up in the kitchen and at least get anything out that could spoil." May lifted a crusted cereal bowl and spoon from the other end table. "And run a load of dishes."

"Dad wasn't too concerned with housekeeping, was he?"

"Or paying bills." May gestured to a teetering stack of envelopes on a small desk in the corner of the room. "I tried to intercept them before he could get to the mailbox but he insisted he could still take care of the finances. Problem was he'd set the mail all over the place and forget where things were. I always felt a little guilty reminding him to pay me every couple of weeks for helping him out."

"I suppose it was worth it to him."

May shot me a look, a quick conviction my semantics were poorly chosen.

Try again. "It was worth it to me . . . can't put a price on companionship." A lump formed in my throat, a bile mixture of my own guilt and frustration that I wasn't exactly sure what May did to help Thomas. Clearly, the house wasn't cleaned, paperwork was neglected, and there was no mention of taking him to necessary doctor and dentist appointments. Yes, there was food in the kitchen, albeit nothing too healthy or particularly fresh. She did take his artwork to the gallery to sell to the myriad of tourists flocking to the area, especially in the late summer months and autumn. Was it that May was simply an occasional, living, breathing person in his house? Someone Thomas could at least show his recent work and receive affirmation that what he did, who he had become, was valued?

My eyes drifted around the room, pausing at miscellaneous piles of junk, a disarray of boots and slippers, stacks of paintings, unused canvases, and a few new tubes of paint. "How was he buying his art supplies?"

"Mostly from selling his paintings at the shop. He was prolific. I took a new batch to the store every few weeks. The tourists especially like the smaller pieces. You know, the ones they can fit in their car or suitcase as a memento. They don't sell for much—maybe a couple hundred for the larger pieces, but people love getting an original piece of art."

May lifted a small canvas from the floor and turned it toward me. It was lovely and simple—a maple tree in its red, autumn splendor. "Don't you remember, Liv, the streams of cars passing through each fall so people could gawk at the leaves turning color?"

"I remember." And in my mind, I wondered when I last took a leisurely drive into the countryside to bask in the array of colors blanketing the rolling hills and forests.

"Well, your dad was a genius at capturing the colors on canvas." May paused and cocked her head as if arriving at a grand conclusion. "You probably didn't know Thomas Danford was something of a folk hero to the people around here, and even beyond."

"Well, I of course . . . I suppose . . . no. No, I didn't know." My face felt flushed at the admission.

Needing a moment to regroup my thoughts, I sipped my latte and pulled two bagels from the brown bag. I handed one to May and bit off a substantial chunk of the other. Finally, as if an enormous elephant filled the room, I asked, "How did I miss all of this, May?"

"What do you mean?"

"That he was painting up to the day he died, doing what he loved." I lifted a hardened paintbrush, unable to run my fingers through the soft bristles like I used to do when I was a child. "Yet he lived so frugally and in such disarray."

I turned and spoke to her directly, "Don't misunderstand me. You know I'm grateful for all you've done. I'm upset with myself that I didn't move him to assisted living closer to me in the city or someplace where he—"

"He didn't want that. This was his home and despite the appearance, he *was* happy here." She turned and walked to the window.

I knew where and at what she was looking, across the backyard toward the small cottage. "Plus, Liv, you know he never would have been able to leave your mother's studio."

I joined her at the window and looked at the clapboard structure, painted cream with a blue door—cerulean blue—the color of a clear summer sky. It looked the same over the years, except for patches of peeling paint and faded and drawn yellow gingham curtains.

After Mother decided two bottles of sleeping pills would cure her dark episodes of depression and whatever other illnesses that tortured her mind and soul, Thomas locked her studio. Twenty-five years ago. I never understood his reasoning—I suppose when a heart is broken, decisions don't have to make sense.

"His checkbook is in the desk drawer." May looked at me with sad eyes. "Why don't you go through the stacks and see what needs to be paid. You can take those with you and do that from home." She blinked a few times as if collecting her thoughts. "Although we'll need to get permission from the bank for you to sign. You know . . . prove that you really are his daughter."

Prove that I'm his daughter. The concept was odd. One I'd never considered. But it was true. I undoubtedly resembled my mother— deep chestnut-colored hair. Thick and unruly when the humidity was high. And the eyes . . . we shared robin's egg blue eyes. From Thomas

I'd received my height and slender build, but we were painted from different palettes—his eyes hazel, mostly brown, and light sandy-colored hair until it eventually turned gray.

"As soon as I'm back from Venice, I'll begin dealing with the rest of this. Promise." I settled at the desk and situated a trash bin nearby.

"That would be helpful because . . . " May crossed her arms. "I might be moving."

I spun in the chair and faced my friend. May hadn't left Kennett Square since she and her mother pulled into the next-door driveway in their tan, beat-up minivan over thirty years ago. "Really?"

"Is that so odd?"

"No . . . well, sort of." Now I crossed my arms. "I'm just surprised. You've never mentioned this before."

"I've wanted my own art gallery for years, Olivia. You've known that." She turned her back to me and busied herself flipping through pages of Thomas's sketchbook. "This town could never support a real gallery."

"Where would you go?"

"Maybe out west. Santa Fe . . . Taos."

"Wow. That's really moving away." I leaned back in the chair and sighed. "It's pricey out there. I can't imagine what a lease would be."

"I've done my research." She rolled her eyes. "I'm a big girl now, Liv."

I shifted uncomfortably as I tried to settle into my bumpy words. "I'm happy for you, May. You know that. I'd miss you though."

"Olivia, it's not like we spend time together. We haven't since you left for college."

The uncomfortable truth hung in the air. Our lives had taken different paths.

*****

While May worked in the kitchen, I sorted through several mounds of paperwork, tossing most of it.

I nearly pitched the note scribbled on a loose-leaf piece of paper in dull pencil. *To Olivia, my dear daughter.* I walked to the window and read the words bathed in sunshine: *Despite my shortcomings and the passage of too much time, there is no greater gift I can leave you— nothing else that will tell the entire story and show you how much your mother and I loved you.*

I reread the short passage. There was nothing more—no further explanation or even a closing signature. It was as if the letter was started and never finished.

"May, you've got to see this," I called into the kitchen.

"Don't tell me you've found something living under the sofa." Her voice sounded strained, and I wondered what mess she was attacking.

I walked into the kitchen and held up the letter. "Listen to this." After I read the note, the blank look on May's face confirmed she was as mystified as me.

"I have no idea what this means." I leaned against the counter and stared at the ceiling. "My father had something special to give to me, and I have no clue what it is."

May shrugged and returned to scrubbing the counter with a discolored dishtowel that clearly needed to be tossed in the trash.

"Something of my mother's? A wedding ring or a necklace that he would want me to have? This is so strange. I almost threw this paper away."

"Maybe you'll come across some more information as you dig in the piles." She hesitated and flung the rag over her shoulder. "Odd though, he talked with me about a lot of things but never about leaving his possessions to anyone, or for that matter, dying." She gestured to a pile of Tupperware, odd-sized, lidless, and tipping. "He probably figured most of this stuff would end up back at the flea markets or dumpsters he found it in. But, if it's okay with you, I'll take any of the paintings you don't want to the gallery and try to sell them... and of course, send you any money they earn."

My eyes stung and tears welled. "I don't care about the money . . . or if what he wanted to give to me was something valuable." The next words caught in my throat. "I want to know . . . the full story . . . what he had to say to me."

"I'm sorry, Liv. I wish I knew what to tell you."

I wandered around the house, flicking on and off lights as I glanced into rooms and loosely assessed the task ahead of me—to clean out what was left of my childhood home, put it up for sale, and close that chapter for good. As the mysterious sentiment from the letter replayed in my mind, I decided I'd let May take what she wanted from the house—sell Thomas's remaining paintings locally or use some of the better ones for her initial inventory if she were to ever open her own dream gallery.

I stood in the living room, holding the box of old mail and feeling out of place.

"You don't look too well. Are you sure you should drive?" May tilted her head to one side.

I nodded. More than anything, I needed fresh air and a fast drive down I-95 to the city to clear my head.

May took the box out of my arms. "Then let me help you put this in the car." She opened the front door. "Anything else you want to take with you?"

I was about to say no, but my father's palette resting against the stool caught my eye. Carefully, I lifted the wooden palette covered in an array of colors, in its own way a beautiful piece of art. The dollops of paint—placed like rainbow steppingstones across a sunset-colored pond—led me back again to my childhood. A sweet memory surfaced of my father letting me dab my fingers in the squishy paint and then walk my fingertips across an unfinished canvas. I loved the texture of the cool paint, how it oozed between my fingers and smeared across my palm as I mixed the colors into something new.

Gingerly, I touched a dollop of ultramarine blue, then cadmium red, yellow ochre, light green, and titanium white. With each hue, I pressed a little harder, running my fingers along the assortment of pigments as though playing a child's piano and wishing my father were here, alive and astute at his easel. When I reached the palette's edge, my fingers were bare. There were no paint-smudged fingertips to dance on his canvas. Instead, the paints were hardened and some even cracked—a harsh reminder my father was dead.

CHAPTER FOUR

Grant Richard ~ Pressing Matters

"**Y**ou might want to put on a tie before you go in there. The director of the Richard Museum should always be presentable." As my secretary fixated on her computer screen, I wondered where she hid her other set of eyes. "And maybe run a comb through your hair."

"My God, Shirley, you treat me like I'm a child." I grabbed a red-striped tie off the hook on my office door and worked the obligatory knot.

"Well, you look like one—running in here like you're late for the first day of school."

"First official board meeting. There's a difference."

"Not really." She peered around the side of her console, her speckled, horn-rimmed glasses perched at the tip of a pug nose. "And might I suggest . . . "

"Do I have another choice?" I pressed my hands on the edge of her desk. As I leaned in closer, a waft of her cheap, rose-scented perfume reminded me she was up for a pay raise.

She smiled a Cheshire cat grin—the same one I had been warned about by my uncle, the prior director for the last twenty years of the Richard Museum of Modern Art Museum.

Since its inception in 1921, my family-owned enterprise had been overseen by a Richard (pronounced ree-CHARD) heir. The founder was my great-grandfather, Garland Richard. Next, my grandfather, Gabriel Richard, took over and grew the twentieth and twenty-first century's modern and contemporary art collections to earn the museum prominent, international status.

My father, Gatsby, didn't fit the proverbial mold, or bronze cast, so to speak. I suppose having the same moniker as F. Scott Fitzgerald's obsessive millionaire character didn't help his outcast status. Instead, my father was happy to pass the responsibility to his younger brother, Glen Richard, while he instead opened a string of successful computer software companies in Southern California. Glen, so I am told, did a fine job. But finally, his second wife, twenty years his junior, convinced him he had served his family duty and it was time for them to move to the South of France.

And so, this is where I, Grant Richard, come in. Pretty much the only thing I have in common with the family lineage of art connoisseurs is my name begins with the same consonant—not that I'm letting anyone in on that little secret.

"The ladies and gentlemen can cajole each other a little longer." I winked at Shirley. "What is it, my dear, I desperately need to know?"

As she lowered her chin, her glasses slid precariously to the edge of her nose. "Don't bring up the Modigliani."

I lowered my voice to a whisper, "And why not? Wasn't that the main reason I called the board members in? To discuss the acquisition of a genuine Amedeo Modigliani portrait?"

"My point exactly." She leaned into the desk as far as her rotund stature would allow. "It's not acquired, or verified, and it could be a forgery." With oddly white, pearlescent front teeth perched on her lower lip, she silently mouthed the next word. "Fake."

I knew the possibility existed—art forgery was going around like a flu bug. But I had a good feeling about this one and maybe there was something to be said about beginner's luck. The recently surfaced portrait of a young girl, quaintly titled, *The Girl in White*, was brought to my attention after I'd been quoted in several industry publications as "the new director, actively seeking acquisitions." Perhaps this unknown piece by the Italian Modern painter with a short and tragic life would provide me a long and fruitful art career. With this addition to the museum, I'd earn the deserved and prestigious placement on the branches of my family tree.

"Well, what am I supposed to tell them? What do I do with a roomful of grumpy old people with nothing better to do than look at art all day?"

"Talk about plans for the upcoming donor gala. Tell them you want their input. Make them feel important. They love to dress up and invite their friends to throw money around the room." She stood and smoothed her pleated skirt. "Regardless, Ms. Danford called earlier. She said she can meet you tomorrow at nine."

"It's about time." I puffed out my breath. "She hasn't been easy to reach. She'd better be as good as they say."

"She's one of the best. Worth the wait to get her in here to take a look."

"Well, I'm relieved. We wouldn't want the owner taking the painting to another museum."

"Ms. Danford's assistant said she had a death in the family."

"Well, they must have been busy digging more than a six-foot-deep grave."

Shirley's signature grunt confirmed she'd had enough of me. I threw on my suit jacket and aligned myself in front of the gilded framed mirror next to her desk that assuredly had seen the lineage of finely groomed Richard men for decades. "At least I haven't lost any of my hair with the stress of this new job." I smoothed light brown tresses away from my forehead. "The California flow is still looking good."

"Grant Richard, really?" She propped her hands on her hips and pursed her lips. "Sometimes I feel like your mother."

"Thanks, Mom. I'll be home before dinnertime." I waved a hand at my secretary as I headed down the hallway to meet a most likely irritated, coffee-infused group of board members. Before I opened the heavy oak door, I called back to Shirley, "But really, how deep do you think they dug?" With my best schoolboy grin, I disappeared into the lion's den.

CHAPTER FIVE

Olivia ~ Joel

Nothing awakens my senses better than a brisk, early morning walk along the cobblestone sidewalks in Georgetown. It felt good to be home—not the densely wooded home of my childhood, but the tree-lined neighborhood, dotted with familiar quaint shops, favorite restaurants, and historic architectural homes.

As I did each morning at seven-thirty sharp, I headed from my federal row home on Book Hill, down Thirty-third Street and over the canal toward the renovated business area along the Potomac River. The short walk to my office, situated on the top floor of the 1790s brown and red brick Flour Mill, confirmed this charming place on the planet was where I was meant to make my own mark in history—however great or small it would prove to be.

As expected, Joel beat me to the office, brewed the coffee, and greeted me in his customary stance—hands clasped together and bent slightly forward at the waist as if he could hardly wait for the day to begin. This particular morning, I welcomed his added gesture of a big bear hug after the familiar, "All right?" in his precise Londoner's accent.

I only nodded in reply. There was no sense trying to hide that I'd been through an emotional wringer, and my assistant/researcher/ friend, would see through any pretense if I tried to fake that I had my act together so soon after my father's death.

"It's good to have you back, Olivia, but really, you look like you could use a couple shots of espresso or a better night's rest."

"Probably both, but not in that order." I ran my hand through my hair. "I thought I was looking pretty good this morning. Even made the jaunt in record time and took the stairs."

"Overachiever." He smiled. "The lift is my best friend in an old building like this. Especially since we're in the eagle's nest."

"With the best views of the river." I looked out the window and watched a shell filled with oarsmen, the signature crew from Georgetown University, glide along the river, seamless and synchronized. "And it's an elevator, not a lift."

"I may be on American soil, but a Brit I'll always be."

"Good thing our paths crossed in the twenty-first century. You would've been run out of the country by now." Now it was my turn to smile, and it felt good. "I'm glad I snatched you away from the Tate."

"Agreed." He nodded. "Although my parents will never accept me leaving that institution to work for a Yankee, especially one who adores the Impressionists and Moderns."

"You keep your love affair with the Dutch Masters, and I'll partner with Matisse."

Most single, twenty-eight-year-old sharp-looking males would buy fancy cars, live in hip apartments, and partner with long-legged and thick-eyelashed girls. Joel was oblivious. However, put a Vermeer painting in front of his eyes, and he was smitten—entranced by the beauty of the blending of brushwork, depth of color, and the exquisite light emanating from the composition.

After graduating with honors from the prestigious Courtauld Institute of Art, Joel was immediately hired by the Tate Britain Museum in London and catapulted under the mentorship of acclaimed art historians. It would have made perfect sense for him to remain in the centuries-old institution—continue his studies and research, lecture about famous British artists and paintings, watch his hair gray and perpetually grow old alongside his art-loving cohorts.

But when he approached me after I'd lectured at the Whitechapel Art Gallery about the prolific art market for fakes and forgeries, he claimed a personal epiphany had thumped him over the head. After more discussion, exchanged emails, and phone conversations, Joel hopped a plane across the Atlantic. With the exception of visiting his parents on the outskirts of London a couple times a year, he has remained in loyal service as a crucial member of my company, Axiom, for the past five years.

I pointed at the wall behind my desk and the prime location of a vibrant painting of a dark-haired woman wearing a purple jacket reclining on a green-striped chaise. "I never tire of looking at Matisse's work . . . even though this one's a fake."

"But by one of the best. Good old Elmyr de Hory knew how to fool even the experts." Joel ran his fingers over his tightly trimmed beard. "Speaking of which, what do you think about the sudden appearance of the purported Modigliani?"

I plopped into my chair and then swiveled to face Joel. "I guess I'll find out this morning." I glanced at my cell phone. "Need to grab an Uber instead of walking to Dupont Circle. You know me, early is on time and on time is late."

"I know you well. You certainly keep a clip in your step and everyone else marching." Joel high-stepped in place. "And I'm anxious for you to get to know the new museum director. Word on the street is Grant Richard is quite different from the old guard." Joel crossed his arms. "But the article in *ARTNews* said he's a Courtauld man so he must be well-versed about art . . . green when it comes to running a museum, but he has a big head for business and appears to be aggressive about making new acquisitions for the collections."

Whether from lack of sleep or too much to think about, I caught my mind wandering as Joel spoke. Thoughts of my father slipped into my consciousness—a man with little business sense, but a heart filled with a passion for painting and an urgent and untamed need to outwardly express.

"Olivia?" Joel's voice called me back. "Are those tears?"

I blinked a few times, realizing my emotions had once again played a sneak attack. "I miss him," I whispered.

For the second time that morning, my employee and friend, who saw me at my best and knew me at my worst, wrapped his arms around me in a big-brotherly sort of way.

"Just don't blow your nose on my shirt." He gave me a quick squeeze and then held me at arm's length. "Marc and Spencer's new spring line. Smart, isn't it?"

"Perfect. Just like you." I pulled a tissue and blotted under my eyes. Joel's levity along with a good dose of focus was what I needed now. Later tonight, when I slipped under the covers and turned off the nightstand light, crying would be allowed—tears of sadness, loss, remorse, resentment, and guilt—a confusing and exhausting mix of my reality.

I had an hour until my scheduled meeting with Grant Richard. Until the car arrived, I had work to do and the stack of paperwork and neatly written to-do list on my desk awaited my attention.

But for a moment, I smiled. "Truly Joel, I don't know what I'd do without you keeping it together around here. You even transferred all my sticky notes and scribbles on to one list." I lifted the paper. "And a fresh notepad personalized with my name. Nice touch."

"If I were true to my English roots, I'd have printed your monogram instead, but I realized I've never known your middle name."

"Fiori." I scanned the list, making a mental note of several other items to add. "It means *flower* in Italian." I shrugged. "Funny though . . . I've never been attached to the name—doesn't seem to fit with Danford. If I were ever to marry, I'd ditch the middle name and use my last name in its place. Or, more likely, I'd just keep my name as it is."

"Ah, the million-dollar question . . . who would be the lucky man?"

I rolled my eyes. "I am perfectly content with me, myself, and I." I fanned through the pad. "Besides, this supply will last me a lifetime at the rate I *don't* make lists. No offense. I appreciate the gift, but I do fine keeping it all in my head." My forefinger tapped my temple.

"I'll convert you sooner or later to membership in the International List Writers Association." He winked.

"Is that for real?"

"Not sure, but if a group of like-minded tidies doesn't exist, I may start one up and name myself president. It would look good on a résumé." He smiled. "Don't you agree?"

My raised eyebrows begged the question.

"No, no, no. I'm not going anywhere. Call me loony, but I enjoy working for you . . . and *you* need to get to work."

The door shut behind him and I was left with my own thoughts. *Work, Olivia . . . that's what you do best.*

CHAPTER SIX

Grant ~ A Pleasant View

Note to self. Tell my realtor to jump in the Potomac next time she passes this way. Residing in Old Town Alexandria had its perks, but I could have made it quicker to my office in D.C. had I traveled on horseback like the colonists once did. My foot wanted to press the accelerator to the floor, but the blur of red taillights ahead on the GW Parkway chastised me. Once again, I hadn't allowed enough leeway to get to work on time. The supposed half hour drive from my home to the museum typically turned into a turtle's marathon, especially if I squeezed in my morning workout and stopped at the local coffee shop.

"Not even time for a second." I lifted my coffee cup from the console and downed the last drops. "Ms. Danford will have to wait until I grab a cup in the café. Besides, I'll be the better for it and she'll appreciate my caffeinated demeanor."

Talking to myself again. Maybe I would benefit from some companionship. "Too much work to do." My declaration boomed above the drone of Elvis Costello's "Allison" before I joined him in the chorus, singing, "My aim is true."

The traffic slowed to a stop just before the Arlington Memorial Bridge. I punched in my secretary's number.

"Good morning. You've reached the office of Grant Richard, director of the Richard Museum of Modern Art. How may I help you?" Shirley had repeated the same line thousands of times, albeit with a different director's name depending on how the moon, sun, and stars were aligned at the time and which Richard family member was in charge. I'm sure she could repeat the greeting in her sleep and perhaps she was slumped over, head on her mahogany desk, face imprinted with keyboard squares. No, not my Shirley.

"I'd like a coffee." I spoke in my most chipper voice even though the effects of low caffeine were beginning to play out as a dull headache.

"I can transfer you to the museum café. Hold on one—"

"It's me for God's sake."

"This is God?"

"No, it's Grant." Was she playing me for the fool or was my secretary loony?

A chuckle followed. "I know it's you. Even in our brief time working together, I can detect a Richard's voice in one word. Plus, your name came up on my phone. You're in my contacts since I need to be able to reach you at all times."

"Please, not in the middle of the night."

She cleared her throat, and I knew the question to follow. "Where are you?"

"Crawling over the bridge. It would have been faster to walk."

"Or leave earlier before the rush. I told you D.C. traffic is horrendous."

"Touché."

"How soon will you be here? Ms. Danford is already waiting."

"Don't tell me you let her see the painting."

"Of course not. The art handlers will wait to bring it in once you give the go ahead. Good thing two of our best are on duty today… especially if it is a *real* Modigliani."

"I feel good about this one, Shirley. Trust me." I tapped the lid of my empty coffee cup. "And I'll feel much better if you have a steaming cup of coffee, black please, ready when I walk in the door."

"Shall I put your call through to the café so you can pick up your own?"

"My dear, don't you dare." I ended the call and shook my head. *How in the world did I end up leaving the beaches in L.A. and vineyards of Northern Cal for the rat race of our nation's capital?*

*****

After peeling into my parking space, I dashed up the limestone stairs, skipping two at a time, and waved a cursory good morning to the greeter near the propped door. I wondered if Shirley put out the red alert that I would be coming in harried and prepared the staff for a crash landing.

My quickened pace was from anticipation that had been growing for nearly two weeks. Ever since I received a call from the anonymous collector who claimed to own an authentic Modigliani painting and was interested in selling, I was fixated on the possibility. Finally meeting with Olivia Danford, one of the world's foremost authorities in authenticating fine art and detecting forged pieces, was the icing on top—especially if the comments shared in the artsy circles about her good looks equaled her intelligence.

"Good morning." I nodded to Shirley as she handed off a steaming cup of coffee like a relay baton. "I owe you lunch for this."

"Or an extra week's paid vacation."

"You drive a hard bargain." I glanced at the glass door leading into the conference room. "Are the handlers on deck?"

"Just give the word." Shirley lifted the phone. "You do know this is highly unusual to have a piece of art marched in like this? You could have already had the painting in the room . . . perhaps draped to heighten the drama."

"Of course, but why would I want to do that the predictable way?" I ran my hand through my thick hair—a family trait that served me well. The touches of early gray at my temples only added a distinctive air to my forty-two years of age. "Besides, this gives me a minute to introduce myself."

"You're on, ol' boy. Make a good first impression" I spoke to myself as I leaned into the door and entered the same room where my predecessors had negotiated and secured valuable and notable art to build a prestigious collection. Now it was my turn.

*****

She was looking out the window facing the courtyard and garden. Her arms were relaxed at her sides and her head tilted with eyes cast downward—contemplating, maybe dreaming. I almost spoke but then paused. Like watching a California sunset, it was an opportune moment to take in her beauty. But now, my world had shifted and I viewed her in a different way—like Falconet's *Bather,* a sculpture I'd admired in the Louvre—slender and curved, sensual, yet modest. She wore a beige linen dress, ending just above her knees. My gaze followed shapely calves downward to smart, short-heeled pumps.

"Mr. Richard." Her voice broke my silent appraisal. "I didn't realize you were here. I was—

"Admiring the cherry blossoms and tulips?"

"Yes. They're beautiful."

As are you. Even though she was partially silhouetted by the cascading morning light, her eyes were captivating—robin's egg blue.

"Please, call me Grant." I shifted my coffee cup into my left hand and extended the other. "And forgive my tardiness. Once again, the traffic proved to be horrendous."

"I walk as often as possible." She returned the handshake, firm and confident. "Olivia Danford."

"It's a pleasure." I smiled, but strangely felt a bit off-keel—reminiscent of asking the high school belle to the prom.

She approached the oval conference table and pulled a notepad and pen from her purse.

"Kate Spade." I gestured toward the black bag. "Bought the same one last fall."

"You carry a Kate Spade bag?" She raised a brow.

I felt my face redden. "No, it was for my girlfriend . . . actually, my ex-girlfriend." *Shut up, you bumbling idiot.* "We broke up when I left California to take the director's position. Decided the distance would be too much."

"Lucky woman."

"For breaking up or the purse?" I forced a chuckle.

"The purse, of course." She grinned. "Although you and I just met and I don't really know anything about you . . . so I guess it could be the other." She continued to rummage in her handbag. "Here they are. I thought I'd forgotten my gloves. Usually I have the preliminary inspection items in another bag." She paused and looked at me. "Life's been a little hectic lately."

"I'm sorry to hear about your father. My secretary told me he passed recently." I folded my hands. "That must be very difficult."

She nodded and turned toward the window again, where I suspected she had been thinking of him before I arrived. She was silent for several moments until she whispered, "He was an artist . . . a very good one, too. I believe painting was what kept him alive longer than what his failing health warranted."

I joined her at the window, gazing over the manicured garden that was designed and implemented long ago by Garland Richard as an anniversary gift to his beloved wife, Katherine.

"The story goes that when my great-grandfather lost his father, he was heartbroken. His journal is in the library archives . . . it's one of the first things I read when I moved here to lead the museum. He had a discerning eye not only for beauty in art but was also an eloquent writer."

As I watched the springtime breeze dance with the cherry trees and send pale pink blossoms into flight, I realized there had been rare times lately when I stopped to notice things beautiful. In a moment of reverence, I whispered, "He had written, 'Sorrow all but overwhelmed me. Then I turned to my love of painting for the will to live.'"

Olivia cocked her head, as if listening to my ancestor's words trickle into the present. "I understand."

Like a shattered spell, she tucked her hair behind her right ear, and then the other, and walked to the empty viewing table. "Unless it's invisible, I'm ready to see the Modigliani." She slipped on her white cotton gloves. "Or at least a really good forgery."

"You know how to break a guy's heart." I lifted the intercom to give Shirley the go-ahead to have the painting brought from the secured storage room. "I'm banking on the former, Ms. Danford, and in a few moments, you and I will be in the presence of a masterpiece."

CHAPTER SEVEN

Olivia ~ The Girl in White

Two men flanked *The Girl in White*, one tall and bony, the other stout with thick biceps. In their matching black aprons, white long-sleeved shirts, and white gloves, the handlers looked like penguins, balancing the dark patina stained frame as if it were a rare and fragile Limoges . . . or perhaps a penguin egg. The room was silent as though we were in the presence of royalty, and the young girl portrayed in the painting was clearly the princess.

The painting was smaller than I expected, about twenty-two by eighteen inches. In syncopated movement, the men laid the artwork flat on the viewing table, carefully unwrapped the Tyvek soft wrap, and reverently stepped away. Did they have a sixth sense? An instinct? It would be a staggering discovery, not only for the museum and my career, but the entire artworld if they actually carried an inimitable, one-hundred-year-old painting by one of the twentieth century's greatest painters.

Ugh! Had Grant caught my quick intake of breath when I first laid eyes on her—*The Girl in White*? His slight smirk followed by a coy wink made me wish for a grand entrance do-over. I knew better than to be deceived by appearances.

I slipped on my readers and approached the table. It was a lovely portrait. The sitter was two years old at most, probably younger. She was really just a baby. Innocent and at the same time complex. Two-dimensional though layered in a myriad of colors and textures—what the master Modigliani did best. My eyes met hers, and for a moment I was drawn in . . . into a strange meeting of the unknown yet known.

Oval eyes perched above rosy cheeks and cradled along the sides of the bridge of a petite nose. Framed with slight lashes below delicate brows. Innocent, open, and welcoming. But as if newly awakened from an afternoon nap, the delicate lids draped ever so slightly . . . softly. However, it was the color of her eyes that captured me—blue, undulating between light and dark with hints of green, like the sea.

Pulled away. Drawn toward. Drowning. A puff of air escaped my lungs as I realized I'd been holding my breath. Willing myself away from the Siren's call, my eyes left hers as I studied the cherubic pink lips, another Modigliani element. Like following landmarks on a treasure map, my eyes swept upward, toward the hair— short, cropped at the earlobes, and held back with a pale yellow ribbon that contrasted against chocolate brown tendrils and wispy bangs. The tilted head propped on an oddly long neck—again, one of the master painter's stylistic hallmarks.

The little girl's dress . . . at first glance appeared white. But on closer inspection it was created from a spectrum of colors—subtle hints of grays, blues, violet, periwinkle, and even soft yellow that gave the illusion of folds and creases in the soft linen fabric. Like an angel contemplating prayer, the girl's hands were poised with palm nested in palm, waiting for generation after generation to greet her.

"She's beautiful," Grant whispered as if in the presence of something holy. I wondered if he sensed the same angelic apparition. "I could stare at her all day." He stepped closer to the viewing table.

"She won't be beautiful if you spill your coffee." I gestured to the cup in his hand. "Do you mind?"

The tall handler stepped forward, offered his open hand like a fine-dining waiter, and retrieved the mug.

Grant walked to the other side of the table and stopped across from me. "What do you think?"

"Mr. Richard. My professional reputation would be at risk if I were so quick to make a verdict. A series of analyses will need to be conducted and it will take time to do them accurately. The purpose of this meeting is merely an introduction to the portrait and determining whether further tests are warranted."

"Well, are they?" His voice was stern and direct, commonplace for a director's role.

Early on, I had learned not to be pressured by a high-rolling collector, an overzealous buyer, or even a highly respected scholar to make a quick call as to the authenticity of a piece of art. The backlash of an incorrect conclusion wasn't worth the reputational repercussions. Instead, it was better to inflict the pain of patience on the client while the materials analysis and due diligence regarding provenance were completed.

I flicked on another tool of my trade, the illuminated magnifying glass, and slowly scanned across areas of the painting. Like scattered spider webs, a fine network of cracks covered the surface area—the craquelure indicative of the natural process of aging paint and varnish. At least on the surface, nothing suspect of an obvious fake was evident.

"She's real?" Again, his words were pointed and his question sounded more like a command.

I continued peering through the glass until I hovered over the signature. *Modigliani*—Amedeo's scrawled cursive letters with the *d*, *g*, and *l* looped. The name was prominently placed in the upper right corner of the painting—a favorite nesting place for his final brushstrokes at the completion of each work of art.

I paused, looking through the glass longer than usual. My pulse quickened as I reread the name spelled out with the same raw sienna pigment that was woven in the girl's hair and speckled in the worn floorboards beneath her black shoes.

I stood upright and faced the director. "It's worth looking at more closely. I'll be back from a conference in Venice in a week and then I'll get to work with the sampling and testing." I took off my gloves. "Until then, gather whatever information—collection records, exhibition documentation, sales receipts—anything from the owner that will help establish the provenance."

Grant nodded.

"The history of the painting is essential to know the truth." I folded my readers and blinked a few times. "My advice is not to get your hopes too high."

"She caught even *you* a little off guard."

I settled the strap of my bag on my shoulder. "It's human nature to be drawn to that which is beautiful . . . but no one wants to be lured by deceit."

"Ah, 'beauty is bought by judgment of the eye.'" He flashed a stunning set of straight, white teeth that complemented a natural tan.

"Shakespeare." I extended my hand. "It was a pleasure."

CHAPTER EIGHT

Olivia ~ Venice, Italy

As though I'd stepped, or more exactly, floated into a postcard, the dark-haired gondolier navigated the boat along the Grand Canal. He seemed oblivious that his red and white shirt was soaked through by the warm, late afternoon rain that came in torrents, swirling and flapping around the sleek gondola like bed sheets blowing on a clothesline.

In alto, he sang an unfamiliar and melancholy song as he and I glided past motorized vaporetti carrying loads of tourists and working-class Venetians. A private water taxi zipped by—perhaps transporting a banker, or one of the well-known exhibitors, or a deep-pocketed collector attending La Biennale di Venezia, or more simply called, the Biennale. And even though the renowned art exhibition, bustling with hundreds of eclectic artists and thousands of attendees, was my purpose for traveling to Italy, I chose the slower mode this afternoon. Venice hadn't been part of my travel agenda for several years and I wanted to reacquaint myself with her, like an old friend—her sights, sounds, touch—even the scent of the City of Canals.

The surroundings were surreal. Even if I was returning for the hundredth time, the city built on water would forever awe and mystify. After a full night of travel, then to be whisked away in a taxi from the Marco Polo Airport, the other civilized world was now far behind.

Now, as I took in the panorama before me, the roads and byways had disappeared as travel gave way to ancient waterways bordered by tall leaning buildings, pressed side by side as if to keep each other from tumbling into the ever-changing tide. Window boxes overflowed with red and fuchsia bougainvillea and trailing ivy. Colorful flags draped across building facades and crowned ornate poles. Brick and stone, washed for centuries in layers of ochre, crimson, cadmium yellow, burnt sienna tile roofs, and rich green shutters, were oddly vivid despite the rain casting a sheer veil across the scenery. It was as though the city was on stage—the prima donna of the Adriatic Sea—reveling in her beauty as the audience demanded an eternal encore since her inception back in time.

The gondolier offered a dry blanket. The first one he had tucked around my shoulders when the rain started was now damp and heavy. Instead, I politely declined, pushed the limp blanket aside, and leaned my head back. With my face toward the sky and the centuries-old Rialto Bridge passing overhead, the moisture ran along my temples and into my hair. Despite the warm weather, the water was cool and awakened my senses. It felt good to be alive. Venice beckoned me, promising renewal.

*****

The gondola coasted to a silent stop at the end of the private pier. I laughed despite my matted hair and damp sundress that stuck awkwardly to my legs. I took the gondolier's hand and stepped from the boat and on to a red carpet leading the short distance to the ornate doors of the Sina Palazzo Sant'Angelo Hotel. Joel, with his impeccable taste, booked my week's stay. He had asked if I preferred the legendary Danieli, situated on the Grand Canal with its elegant sienna facade soaking up the late afternoon sun, its name emblazoned in gold lettering above white Venetian colonnades.

This visit called for some place different. It had been nearly ten years since I lived in Italy. After completing rigorous postgraduate studies in International Art Crime, a charming, wealthy, and excessively handsome colleague and I decided a weekend getaway from Florence to Venice would be a well-deserved adventure.

On the patio at Terrazza Danieli, we had sipped the Venetian's famous Spritz drink and watched the daylight dim. The dayshift gondoliers tethered black lacquer boats to Dr. Seuss-like, brightly colored poles—retiring for the night so they could weave their way home through the maze of cobbled streets and make love to their wives. And as we held hands across the candlelit table, in the distance, the white Gritti Palace seemed to float on the water's reflection like a dollop of whipped cream on an orange and pink sherbet sunset.

However, even though we *oohed* and *ahed* at the magical scene, there really wasn't a fanciful or meaningful attraction between us, at least on my part. After a customary kiss or two we must have both sensed the impending dead end. We retired to separate rooms in the shared suite and the next morning our paths diverged. His direction included traveling the Far East. My compass pointed northwest, back across the Atlantic to Georgetown. From time to time, I'd wondered if my heart would ever yearn for a husband—that after a hard day's work, we would greet each other at home with ready and open arms.

*****

Once the bellman pulled my room door shut, I kicked off my shoes and flopped on to the bed. *Only twenty minutes and then I'll go exploring.*

When I awoke, the room was nearly dark except for the lampposts glittering outside my window. I pushed myself upright, waiting for a light dizziness to subside. My stomach gurgled a reminder that I hadn't eaten since the tiny, compartmentalized food portions on the airplane.

"Shoot, I told him I'd call when I got to my hotel." I rummaged in my purse for my cell phone. Luckily, it had enough battery power to make a quick call.

The call went straight to voicemail. "Marcus Elliot here. Leave a message and I may or may not call you back."

Through my jet lag fog, I had to grin. Mr. Elliot—a fine art appraiser specializing in works of the Fauvists—shared the same passion with me for Matisse. Originally from New York City, and now tucked away in the Blue Ridge Mountains of North Carolina, he was no-nonsense. Despite his tough-as-nails demeanor, I appreciated his direct and honest approach. He had a reputation of being hard-nosed in the business of valuing fine art. Ethical? Certainly, and not one to be swayed or taken advantage of in any way.

I often wondered what the local "creatives" in the Asheville art district thought of the elderly man, dressed in his customary navy suit, paisley bow tie, and round glasses as he regularly strolled eclectic, throw-back art studios along the gentrified railyard. The painters, sculptors, jewelers, ceramists, and even basket-weavers most likely didn't know who was in their midst—a person who, on a regular basis, spent time with creations by the great masters.

"Marcus, it's me, Olivia. Wanted to let you know I've arrived and staying near Piazza San Marco. I'm heading out in a minute to grab a bite to eat but still planning on meeting you tomorrow. I think you said Liam would be here, too. Can't believe I've never met your son after all these years. If he's up for it, I'd love to pick his brain about Modigliani. Interesting case when I return home. Let me know where and when to meet." I was about to end the call, but added, "And I know you'll call me back."

There would be plenty of occasions during my week-long stay to fix my makeup and make good impressions. Tonight, jag lag had won. Besides, I'd only go for a short stroll—get a little exercise before falling into bed.

I pulled on a pair of slacks, a light sweater, and loafers. My phone had already retired for the night—its screen saver of the last photo I'd snapped of my father and me after I'd made a fly-by appearance on Christmas morning—disappeared as the phone battery died.

Was that really the last time I'd visited? Over four months ago? *What is wrong with you, Olivia? Why did you ignore he wasn't doing well?* I slapped my palms on the marble bathroom counter and sneered at myself in the gilded mirror. *Did you expect nothing . . . nobody . . . to ever change?*

After scrounging in my carry-on bag for an international adapter, I jammed the charging cord into the wall outlet, grabbed a small purse, and set out to find some food. *Tomorrow I'll be back on track.*

CHAPTER NINE

Grant ~ In Pursuit, Venice

My legs stretched out only as far as they could in the cramped taxi. *Who uses a Fiat to haul people and luggage around? I may have to squeeze in a workout in the morning before going in search of her.*

My phone vibrated and I was relieved to see Shirley's number on the display. "Sweet Shirley, what were you able to arrange?"

"Well, good morning to you too. Or I think it's morning."

"It's early by good old Yankee standards." I glanced at my phone. "But over here it's evening. This time travel really messes me up. My body tells me it's time for coffee, but my brain says have dinner once I get to the hotel."

"I'd say listen to your brain . . . usually a better choice. Your body will adjust."

"Well, since you made me take the redeye flight and I had to try to sleep like a sloth holed up in a tree."

Shirley half giggled, half cackled, and I could only imagine the wide-mouth smile spreading across her wrinkled face like curtains opening at the beginning of a show.

"You're laughing at my expense?"

"No . . . well, yes. It's just a great visual. But for Pete's sake, I booked you in first class, so you have nothing to complain about."

"True." *Got me again.* "So, what about the hotel? My taxi just arrived at the Piazzale Roma, and if I can fight my way through all these tourists, I'll be embarking into Neverland in a few minutes."

"Well, with the Biennale in full swing, the nicer hotels are full."

"Please don't say you stuck me in some hellhole, nose-level with stagnant water." I paid the driver and stepped onto the platform into a surge of humanity spilling from a tour bus.

From my memories of Venice—after my high school graduation when my father sent me on what he tagged "Grant's Italian Cultural Coming of Age Tour"—neither the backpack-laden students, or the Louis Vuitton matching-luggage-set travelers were remotely aware of the mystique they would soon discover in this otherworldly place.

In all fairness, I hadn't been prepared for what awaited when I first met Venice. All I knew was my father had sabotaged my summer plans to hang out all day and into the night at the beach with my friends, chugging cheap beer and hooking up with the local bikini babes. But Dad was a master schemer. My absence gave him free rein to drink expensive scotch with his friends and spend what he referred to as "quality time" with Monica, or as I dubbed her, Monica the Mom Replacer.

The day after my mom's fiftieth birthday, just like an odometer hitting two hundred thousand miles, Dad traded her in. It was as if he woke up that day and decided after twenty-five years of marriage, he was ready for a new model—faster and definitely sleeker. Shortly after, Mom checked herself into a spa somewhere in the Arizona desert and a month later came out twenty pounds lighter, lips like Mick Jagger, and her beautiful brown hair was bleached like Malibu

Barbie. That was over twenty years ago. The last time she called, she was headed to Kauai to attend a goat yoga retreat.

"I got you the last room at the Danieli."

"Shirley." My stress dissipated like the steam rising from the puddles scattered across the pavement. "You are a dream."

"That's what my husband tells me."

"Well, he's a lucky man."

"And I hope you have luck finding Ms. Danford among the thousands of attendees. I suppose it makes some sense to get to know her better . . . like you said, encourage her make this case a top priority and move things along faster than usual. Maybe she'll even take a personal interest in the painting—"

"I have the nose of a bloodhound. Might take a few days to spot her, but I believe I'll be able to discern which of the galleries and exhibits would grab her attention."

"She could be a needle in a haystack, but if you're right about the portrait being the real deal, and you can get her to confirm that well before the Donor Gala, you just might have a shot at taking the museum to a whole new level."

"Thanks, Shirley. I work best under pressure." I grabbed my suitcase, strategically packed with my smartest clothes to schmooze with the best of the art world's elite . . . and perhaps even garner a second look, or more, from Olivia Danford.

CHAPTER TEN

Olivia ~ Wishes

The time change had my mind and body doing flipflops, but I was invigorated as I breathed deeply and strolled over bridges and wandered along narrow passageways. A few hotel and restaurant names were familiar—illuminated by downcast lanterns perched like gargoyles on precipices of the Renaissance and Gothic structures.

The majority of my recent work in Italy had taken me to Rome and Florence, ancient cities in their own right. But Venice, she was different—a unique thumbprint in the span of history. It was as though time stood still beneath the fog that crept in from the outlying Adriatic Sea where long ago, mercantile ships from the east and west converged in the wealthy and prominent seaport.

Tonight, with crowds of tourists migrating back to hotel rooms and locals finishing meals in candlelit rooms, the city built on more than 100 small islands in a lagoon was being gently rocked into another night's sleep.

Even though I was determined to enjoy several authentic Venetian meals during my stay, I craved familiar fare. *Pizza. Hamburger. No fancy meal at Harry's Bar tonight . . . maybe that's tomorrow while sipping a famous Bellini with Marcus.*

After what was surely another bustling day, many of the small cafés had already closed their shutters, and awnings were collapsed like silent accordions. I decided to walk a bit farther, perhaps find another eatery that would be open closer to Piazza San Marco.

Lured by the sound of a gurgling fountain and the aroma of window boxes pregnant with flowers and vines, I entered a courtyard, dipped my fingers in the cool water, and walked in a slow circle around the centerpiece emblazoned with a stone roaring lion. It was cliché, but I took a coin from my purse and held my hand above the basin. Like the water spilling from the sculptured feline's mouth, a memory poured over me.

*****

I was a little girl—young by the world's standards but beginning to understand that there was more to my existence than the perimeters of our home tucked in a forest someplace in Pennsylvania. It was my fifth birthday when my father took me on a day outing, away from my tiny nook and to the big city.

We had spent the morning climbing snowy white marble steps to visit the monuments and enter the doors of Smithsonian museums. I remember my legs were shaky and my stomach growled. After eating a street vendor hotdog, and my feet aching, Father carried me piggyback for several blocks until we arrived at his favorite spot of all—the mountainous Dupont Circle Fountain.

"Here, Liv. Put out your hand. I've got something special for you." A shiny penny reflected the sun as it rested in my palm. "Now, close your eyes and reach your hand over the water."

Squeezing my eyes shut, I tried to hold my hand steady as I extended my arm.

"Now . . . make a wish . . . a really important one." Father kneeled next to me as I leaned into the cool stone of the fountain basin. He whispered into my long, curly hair. "Think hard, doll. Think really hard and then toss the coin into the pool."

But instead of releasing the penny, my fingers curled around the coin and held it in my grasp.

Olivia, wishes only come true if you are willing to set something free. His calm voice played over in my mind as I remembered staring at thousands of silver and copper circles scattered and sparkling under the water on the bottom of the basin. As though on a grand stage, the coins danced like ballerinas in the rippling water.

"You like presents, don't you?" His smile was wide.

My head bobbed as I continued to clutch the coin.

"The fountain does too." With his forefinger, he lifted my chin and redirected my face toward the top of the fountain. "See?"

My eyes met the stoic gaze of a giant statue staring down at me—a woman with long, twisting hair falling around her shoulders as she cradled a ball in the crook of her arm.

"She is called Stars." My father pointed at the sculpture positioned beneath a circular tier overflowing with three cascading waterspouts. "She's holding the earth. The other statue, the one holding the boat, she's Sea. And the man on the other side with the sail wrapped around his legs . . . he's Wind."

The women were beautiful and mysterious and the man muscular and strong. Sea stood with one foot upon a dolphin and Wind towered above a small boat.

"I only have one penny." I held up my forefinger and then uncurled two more fingers to join. "And there are three of them."

"But when you give all you have a gift has a way of becoming more than you ever imagined." My father wrapped his arms around me and kissed the top of my head.

Slowly, I reached my arm over the water.

"Don't forget to make a wish."

I closed my eyes and silently wished. My grip loosened and the penny plopped into the water. I opened my eyes and watched it sashay toward the bottom. As the rippling water distorted the view, I could no longer discern what I thought was once mine.

I raised my hand to my forehead to block the bright sun. "Do you want to know what I wished for, Daddy?"

"Well, that's up to you." He cocked his head like a sea captain sensing a change in the weather. "Wishes are often secrets."

"I'll tell you mine if you can keep my secret."

He nodded. "All right then, what did you wish?"

"I wished Mother wasn't sick so much. I wished she could have come with us on my birthday to see the fountain." I took a quick intake of breath. "Oh, no. I made two wishes. What if I ruined it?"

My father's smile drooped. He was silent as he stared into the water. Finally, he pulled another penny from his pant pocket, held out his hand, closed his eyes for what seemed a long time, and then dropped the coin.

He turned and looked at me with sad eyes. No words were spoken, but I knew he had echoed my second wish with his own offering.

*****

The temperature dropped enough that I was ready to return to the hotel and take a warm shower. Squinting, I tried to focus on my surroundings. Three pathways, not including the one from which I had come, exited the cobblestone courtyard.

Before I had a chance to choose a path, a white-haired couple ambled into the courtyard. They held hands and spoke in French, softly and endearing, as though they had discovered one of the most romantic places in the world. Even when I stepped aside to let them pass, they seemed not to notice me—lost in their own world and lost in each other. And when they exited the courtyard, effortlessly and predictably like sand slipping through an hourglass, I was once again alone.

Except for the lingering sound of the fountain and a shutter latching overhead, the courtyard was quiet. I surveyed my choices from left to right. Each narrow walkway disappeared into darkness, and I reminded myself that one of the most special things about Venice was allowing oneself to get lost in her—consumed by the past, confused by the present, and confident in finding oneself. After all, eventually all paths led to another open space, and signs, some hanging and others etched into stucco walls, would point me toward a known landmark in the city from which I could find my way back home—back to the hotel.

Go right. No, too logical. Middle. Too indecisive. The breeze curled its way between the buildings as the words of Robert Frost arose from a long-forgotten high school class . . . *and I took the one less traveled by, and that has made all the difference.* I stretched my sweater sleeves over my hands and stepped to the left, into the dimly lit passageway.

CHAPTER ELEVEN

Grant ~ Jet Lag

The hotel bar's double shot of espresso was surging through me like an electrical current—so much that if I dipped my hand in the waterway at the end of the pier, I'd most likely electrocute myself. What a headline—*Highly Caffeinated, Stupid American Electrocuted in the Grand Canal.*

I should have listened to Shirley and stuck with Plan A: getting a decent meal and a good night's rest before attending the oodles of exhibits at the Biennale would have been the smart thing to do. It was especially important to be on my game when initiating my double-secret mission . . . Find Stunningly Beautiful and Imperatively Important for My Success Ms. Danford. However, since my amped-up state made sleep elusive for a while, I had to go to Plan B. The only thing I could come up with was a power walk along the canal and around Piazza San Marco. Hopefully, that would take the edge off. I grabbed my room key and closed the door.

*****

The plaza was quiet. A white-aproned waiter wiped the last drops of spilled drinks at the Quadri and tucked café chairs beneath tables. Tomorrow, the tables would host hundreds of patrons, but tonight they slept. Even the hordes of pigeons that gathered in the center of the square, in constant take-off and landing pattern wherever bread crumb handouts from camera-wielding tourists were near, had retired. Now they were tucked in the alcoves of the Basilica di San Marco and nestled in the upper tier of the Campanile Tower that was once used by approaching ships as a beacon to guide them home.

I turned a half circle, looked across the plaza at the illuminated clock face on the Torre Dell'Orologio. During my prior time in Venice, the mosaic of gold stars against the cobalt blue background had captivated me as I sat for hours on the marble steps, watching the pigeons, people, and the passing of time. The face of the clock was encircled with the zodiac, displaying the phases of the ever-changing moon, and the current hour—as if time even mattered in a magical place like this. Perhaps it did, because on cue, two bronze statues, Moors, struck a giant bell, announcing the hour. Eleven o'clock. *An hour to spare before I turn into a pumpkin . . . or something like that.*

Across the plaza, a lively commotion pulled me away from my reminiscence. A mixture of testosterone-infused bravado and giggly screeches echoed off the marble pavers and colonnades as a small group stumbled into view. Probably college kids on study abroad, and despite their parents' naivety, I'd bet big money they weren't learning much about Renaissance architecture and art.

Even though the traditional Masquerade de Venice had come and gone in the latter half of February and into early March, tonight's revelers wore gaudy masks. Most likely they'd bought the garb at one of the many tourist shops along the Grand Canal that offered the "made in China" version. This group probably didn't care theirs weren't the expensive and ornate works of art sold in tiny shops tucked away on offshoot canals. And based on the laissez-faire attitude that accompanied my own youth, the disguises would eventually be abandoned as the night progressed. Tomorrow, on an early morning stroll, another foreigner would discover the treasure on a vacant table or atop a stone bridge archway. Disposable. Even the masks we wear.

As the group of kids passed, a rainbow of sequins outlined dramatic eyeholes and gold and silver metallic harlequin diamonds glittered under the moonlight. One lanky and noticeably loud boy wore a dark mask covering his entire face with a long, curved, beak-like nose. I smiled to myself. Of course, he thought he was witty in his choice of mask that actually made him appear like an overgrown crow. One short-skirted girl lifted her glittery half-mask, offered me a parade wave, and then quickly rejoined the oblivious mass as they floated on to more late-night Venetian adventures. Then, as quickly as they appeared, their laughter and jesting faded away into one of the many walkways exiting the plaza. Again, I was alone.

I ran my fingers over the prickly travel stubble on my cheeks and chin. I paused and listened to the silence. Oddly, I felt old—old as the heart of the ancient city in which I stood.

In the physical sense, forty-two years was merely a number. Impressive physique, full head of hair—not bad for a man bearing plenty of stress and responsibility. The California sun and saltwater would forever, or at least until my hair turned fully gray like my father's, linger in my blond highlights. No, my lament was more than that.

Could it be it the sound of the young people's carefree laughter? Their abandonment of the time of night, plunging themselves into a dark and forbidden alleyway without regard for danger or the unknown? Hadn't I once been like them? Spontaneous. Adventurous. Confident. The world was mine to be had.

I turned away from the tower and stared into the darkness. No, I'd lost that when our family splintered—Mom left and Dad veered after the youth he feared losing. He assured me we'd all be happier after the *adjustment period*. I never was very good at change.

CHAPTER TWELVE

Olivia ~ Mazed and Confused

Behind its beautiful facade, Venice is deviant and sneaky—
it steals one's sense of time as mazes of walkways, bridges,
and canals disorient and confuse. I'd been wandering for
well over an hour. Without my phone and the shops and restaurants
closed, I estimated it was near or after eleven o'clock. After a long day
of travel, my feet ached and my growling stomach gave up on being
satisfied. Exhaustion surpassed my need for adventure. Once I was
back in my room, I would skip the shower and go directly to bed.

Pausing on top of yet another bridge, I turned a full circle,
stopped, and then rotated in the opposite direction. Like a compass
pulled by opposing magnetic forces, I was without bearings—sensing
my true north was one way, only to discover I wasn't sure at all.
Without notice, and perhaps on instinct, my heart raced. I wasn't
simply disoriented. I was lost.

A panic I hadn't experienced since childhood danced around
me—sneering and jabbing—mocking me for thinking I was capable,
independent, and in control. Instead, echoing off aged building walls

with peeling paint and water-stained marks, voices shouted the truth. Afraid. Terrified. Scared. Alone. And worse . . . I was revealed.

Olivia! Where are you? Answer me right now, young lady! Your father is going to be as upset as me this time. He's not going to think this is one of your cute tricks. Little girls don't go running off into the forest and hide unless they want something awful to happen to them.

My mother's voice spiraled around me as words reverberated off confined walls. I hadn't thought of that fateful morning for years and now it seemed to emanate from the eerily dark water as though she was rising from the grave.

This is nonsense. I scolded myself for the surprise attack of adult hysteria. *Olivia, get a grip.* I clenched the stone railing, my legs shaking. Tears swelled. *Breathe, breathe . . . you've got this. You can find your way home.*

It was illogical, but it appeared the scattered illuminations across the water and hovering over doorways were dimming. Darkness was descending and I was trapped in its veil. From some primeval place, I had become prey and the dark was predator. Hide. Run. Hide . . . RUN! I committed to take the stairs two at a time and turned to run . . . something caught my sleeve.

I spun around and swiped at the object.

A dark hand recoiled. "Denaro?" An odd form, crouched near my feet, head covered with a shawl, gazed at me with dark eyes. In the dim light, I could make out the shadowed face of a woman. Like a snake, a long, black braid fell over her shoulder, a strip of fabric securing the end, waving and ready to strike. Without warning, her hand struck as she grabbed for my pant leg. Startled, I stumbled backward, everything happening so quickly.

My loafer, caught on a loose stone, slipped off my heel. I bent over to secure my shoe when three, maybe four urchins encircled me, touching my back and arms and reaching for my hair. One boy, taller than the others with messy bangs hiding half his face, lifted a rose—red, wilted, and thorny—shoving it toward me in a forceful offering. With his other hand, he held out a grimy palm, demanding an offering from me. Two petite girls, who couldn't have been older than five or six, chanted in eerie unison, hissing and jesting at my plight, "Bella signora . . . denaro, denaro, denaro."

I knew of the gypsies—I had seen them during my other travels. Old, young, alone, and in groups, they approached unsuspecting tourists in open plazas and in hidden subterranean subway stations. Often it was brown-eyed, innocent looking children who swarmed victims like bees on honey. Surprised sojourners would attempt to politely shoo them away only to discover wallets, purses, and jewelry gone.

Tonight, trapped on a bridge, I had a strange premonition this group of wanderers wanted more than my handbag . . . they were after my soul. Alone and confused, I was easy prey for a mother lion intent on feeding her hungry lot with whatever satisfied their deprived souls.

No! It was obvious what they wanted. Money. The universal word. But with my limited Italian phrases, there was no use in speaking and I feared opening my small handbag would be like opening a wound only to attract more to the hunt. No time for genteel conversation. Run!

With a blind shove, I broke free from the cluster and ran down the steps at the bottom of the bridge. My feet pounded on the cobblestones as I ran along a random corridor. Pain shot up my left leg—my abandoned loafer left behind. Despite my imbalance, I kept running . . . dead end.

The walkway led into another small courtyard surrounding a fountain. I stopped, catching my breath. The gurgling water reverberated like thunder as walls inched in and heavy air seemed to descend from above, sealing me into a box. The only way out was from where I had entered, and hopefully not into the pawing fingers of the gypsies out for a midnight game of hide and seek.

With a quick pivot, I spun around and ran. Relying on what little sense of direction remained that would point me toward the Grand Canal from which I would surely be able to find my hotel, I took a sharp right around the next corner.

"Whoa, there." Strong hands grabbed my shoulders.

An intake of breath left me speechless.

"Ma'am, I'm sorry, I didn't see—"

"No, it's completely my—"

"Olivia?"

I staggered back and tried to focus on the face . . . the voice.

"Are you all right?" A tall figure leaned toward me.

Daddy? No, it can't be. I pushed stray hair to the side and squinted at the shadowed face.

"It's me. Grant." The words were out of place. "Grant Richard. Are you okay?" Again, strong hands held my shoulders. "You're shaking."

As my legs began to give way, an arm wrapped around my waist and I leaned into the embrace.

Yes, I knew the voice . . . and the face. Kind eyes, dark lashes above defined cheekbones and a strong, set jaw. Reassuring . . . handsome.

Words surfaced. "A little startled." I straightened my legs and leaned away. "Just out for a jog and wasn't looking where I was going."

His eyes cast downward. "With only one shoe?"

Despite the dark, I'm sure my face reddened to an embarrassing shade, especially since his hand pressed against the small of my back. Unsuccessfully, I willed my legs to stop quivering. Instead, I slipped my hand around his waist. He was broad shouldered and muscular . . . steadfast.

My heart hastened its pace again, but not because of the darkness and fear that lurked in the alleyways. I knew it raced from a deep, instinctual place—never awoken or perhaps realized for a very long time.

I looked up. Genuine concern, even compassion, was written on his face between furrowed brows. *Say something, Olivia . . . anything that possibly holds an ounce of sanity.* "And what, may I ask, are you doing here?"

He was silent at first. Then, he pulled me closer and spoke softly. "Looking for you."

Our eyes held one another. My breathing found a new rhythm and I was safe.

CHAPTER THIRTEEN

Grant ~ Wild Hair

I didn't feel right leaving her alone. We had walked another fifteen minutes or so to the Rialto Bridge, our silence eventually ebbing and flowing into small talk about the exhibition and lecture series schedule, my late decision to attend on behalf of the Richard Museum, the good luck at getting a reservation at the Danielli, and the uncanny chance she and I would run into each other . . . literally. Strategically, I didn't mention *The Girl in White*—that would happen later when she and I had caught a similar stride and conversation could mix business and pleasure.

She had her own topic to avoid and gave no explanation as to why she was alone—going somewhere, running away—and why her styled hair was now wild and untamed. Something had unnerved her—cutting loose her composed demeanor, leaving a residue of fear as she glanced over her shoulder.

She stopped suddenly and I had to take a couple steps backward to realign with her.

"I'm fine the rest of the way. I'm staying at a lovely hotel on the next canal to the right." She spoke matter-of-factly.

Catchlights from the bridge lamps flickered in her eyes. She was beautiful. "Let me walk you to the door. It's the least a gentleman can do."

"If you're at the Danielli, it's the opposite direction and it's late. We both need rest before taking on an early morning." She nodded as if agreeing with the person whose opinion mattered . . . herself.

It was clear the night was over. Was the woman I held minutes ago only my imagination? Was she an apparition gliding through time and space, existing only in the minds of lonely travelers? No, we both sensed what had happened—even if the moment drifted away.

Before I could register her obvious hint and concede the evening's encounter was a misfortunate accident, I spoke. "Then let's meet for a coffee before the day begins. Meet in your lobby at eight?"

She paused, long enough that the stupid schoolboy persona took a good jab to my gut.

"That would be . . . nice." She smiled a bit awkwardly.

I wondered if she had always been so poised and perfect. Perhaps we all go through some form of metamorphosis—even a creature as beautiful as her.

"But seven-thirty. I'm sure we both have full agendas." She took a few steps away.

"Seven-thirty it is." I waved in a dorky sort of way, confirming I hadn't fully shaken my adolescent past. "I'm glad our paths crossed . . . collided."

"Me, too." She offered the same sort of wave.

I watched her walk along the canal, off-kilter with one shoe on, one shoe off, but clearly determined to make her own way.

"Olivia Danford, you are a mystery . . . and one I intend to solve."

*****

When I woke, I thought about calling Shirley to share the good news that I had located Ms. Danford. Considering the strange circumstance by which we met last night, I decided it best to let the day play out. No need for my secretary to think I'm a creep who surfaces at night in dark alleyways. With the Biennale schedule and map in hand, I nodded a good morning greeting to the stiff doorman and started for Olivia's hotel.

As I walked along the canal, the air smelled fresh. Not the stereotypical complaint by many visitors that Venice reeks of stagnant and murky water. Early on, during my stay as a teenager I learned one could despise the city and swear never to return. Or one could choose to embrace its intrigue and etch it into the soul. Even though my past visit was marred with the tugs and turmoil of youth, I had left the city smitten by her charm and good looks.

Now, more than twenty years later, I was still infatuated, romanced by its beauty. The city? Or . . . could it be . . . her? I paused at the edge of the water and gazed to where boats whisked toward the open ocean with purpose and direction in mind. At the same time, other boats, tethered to poles, bobbed up and down on the wake. Like highbred horses, the boats were anxious, ready to be loosened and set free to run.

Which was I? Focused and loyal or wild and independent? Was the answer waiting for me here, grounded by centuries of history, yet forever changing with the tide? Pursuing a gorgeous and talented woman across the ocean in the name of art authentication was a noble and professional excuse. I shook my head, attempting to knock the voice whispering in my ear. *You may fool others, Grant, but this time something is amiss with your previously hardened heart.*

Convicted, I pulled away from the magnificent view and quickened my steps toward the woman who, hopefully, was waiting for me in a hotel lobby.

*****

Her hair was pulled back in a ponytail, showcasing high cheek bones and forehead—*signs of royalty*—my mother used to say. Olivia looked like a princess. A white sundress accented tan, slender arms, and a strand of natural pearls encircled a delicate neck. Unlike most other women who caught my eye, she wore little makeup and needed no adornment to be stunning.

She was alone at a two-top café table on the patio. As I approached, the soft morning light brushed across the side of her downturned face. She was angelic.

"You look heavenly." I breathed out the words.

She looked up and smiled. She had been reading the same schedule I had brought. "Thank you, and good morning to you, too. Sorry, I already ordered since it's past our meeting time. I thought you decided to sleep in."

I glanced at my watch. "Seven thirty-eight." *Not too bad for how I roll.* "My apologies. Couldn't help but pause to take in the sights on the Grand Canal."

"Early is on time. On time is late." She motioned to the other bistro chair. "An old adage I've held for years, especially with clients."

"Ah, a business coffee?" *I can match her on the same playing field.* "I'm looking forward to more discussion and an update about our favorite Modigliani. We may be all the way across the ocean, but I can hear the Museum Board of Directors chomping at the bit for a notable acquisition."

"And of course, an authentic one." She lifted her cup and paused as if in mid-thought. "And I'm sorry about last night . . . that was awkward. Jet lag must have gotten the best of me."

As her cup hovered in front of soft, pink lips, a crazy urge to lean across the table and kiss her flashed across my mind. Thank God the waiter interrupted with "Ah, hem, signore?" His pen tapping on scribbled piece of white paper indicated he had more to do today than dawdle over a love-struck buffoon.

"A double shot espresso . . . grazie." Obviously, an essential survival tool if I was to be bold enough to ask to join her—to match the pace of this art lover, Type A, Myers-Briggs that most likely set her apart from me.

"Later today I have a meeting with another client. His son is joining us." She sipped her coffee. "He happens to be an expert regarding Modigliani's work, his life . . . pretty much an authority about all that's known about an artist who remains somewhat a mystery."

I folded my arms on the table. Not the most mannerly, but this woman had an uncanny way of knocking me off my own A-game. "Well, fancy that. What do you plan to ask him?"

Now with her elbows propped on the table, fingers folded together, and eyes directed at mine, she spoke intently. "If there's any history, any indication that Modigliani could have painted *The Girl in White* . . . and if so, where, but mostly why, has she been hiding all these years?"

Then, as quickly as she engaged, she set off in a new direction, pulling a map from her handbag and smoothing it open. Apparently, it was the end, or at least an abrupt pause, of further discussion about my little gem waiting back home to be discovered.

A red pen had already made its mark on her map—circles, stars, and exclamation points filled margins next to names of artists and exhibit titles.

"Ready for a big day? Not much time to spare though. I've been making a plan of the exhibits I want to be sure to see." She tucked a loose strand of hair behind an ear and beamed.

Was she inviting me to join her for more than a pre-game coffee?

Nothing to lose. "Since you've already concocted the perfect plan, mind if I join you? It would save me the hard work of figuring out where to even begin with this myriad of artwork."

"You don't care for hard work, Mr. Richard?" One perfectly shaped brow lifted.

I could lie. But sinking my tanned toes in the sand on the Santa Monica Beach, lounging in my poolside cabana, and ending the day with a plate of West Coast oysters and a bottle of fine wine at a favorite restaurant along Ocean Avenue was blissful. Only a fool would argue and I was definitely not that. Being a connoisseur of the finer things in life wasn't a vice. Besides, I was quickly joining Olivia in her appreciation of fine art—a noble addition to my repertoire.

"Life grants nothing to us mortals without hard work . . . Homer."

"Actually, Horace." She grinned and pushed her chair back. "If you wore running shoes, you're welcome to join me."

I lifted my tan Gucci loafer. "Fashion first, my dear." I flashed my best white-toothed smile. "After all, we are in Italy."

"Point taken." She extended a slender calf and pointed to a delicate, strappy white sandal accentuated with perfectly pedicured, coral toes.

"Versace?"

She nodded. "And I recall you like Kate Spade. I'm beginning to wonder if you're in the wrong profession."

She was witty, too. "So . . . " I tapped the middle of the map. "Which part of this do we tackle today?"

Her brows furrowed as if my question was absurd. But this must be her plan to spread out over the *entire* week.

"This is day one." Like a child on a treasure hunt, her forefinger traced the map, brushing against mine and pausing, as if two sojourners were deciding whether to journey together. "Are you up for it?"

I nodded, making a mental note to grab a baguette and cheese on the go before I passed out from exhaustion by the end of the day.

"I'll be touring the different venues and end with the Arsenal before I need to freshen up before my meeting my friends for dinner."

"I thought they were clients."

"True." Her head tilted to the side like a delicate bird. "But sharing a passion for discovering, preserving, and . . . I suppose you could say most importantly, weeding through what's true and false, real and unreal . . . has a way of forging friendships." She squared her shoulders. "Isn't that what makes relationships worth having?"

All I could do was offer a slight nod and simply be awed. A dull headache crept into my forehead. Either the caffeine hadn't kicked in or this woman was making me think too much. I signaled for the check.

As we waited for the server to return on his Italian time, her eyes remained focused on the map. "First the Giardini for the international exhibits, especially the Pavilion of Artists and Books and then the Pavilion of Joys and Fears. It's fascinating how Christine Marcel had the vision to organize the exhibits."

"And she would be . . . ?"

"The head curator." Eyes rolled. "Look." She flipped over the program paper and read aloud the introductory paragraph. "In a world full of conflicts and jolts, in which humanism is being seriously jeopardized, art is the most precious part of the human being. It is the ideal place for reflection, individual expression, freedom, and fundamental questions." She blinked several times as she folded the paper, and a single tear rolled down her cheek.

Despite her elaborate strategy to take in every possible moment of one of the world's most prestigious, abundant, and well-attended art events, and her passionate reading of a fellow art lover's proclamation, my concentration waned as I listened to her voice. It was soft and pleasing, confident and purposeful. Olivia's fiber was woven from art, its history, and the geniuses behind the creations. It was evident those pulsed through her heart.

I leaned back in my chair and watched her—like taking in a favorite movie, memorable, emotive, and one I desired to replay over and over again.

CHAPTER FOURTEEN

Olivia ~ Sidetracked

I couldn't suppress a groan as I slouched into one of the few vacant benches along the canal. The fourth call from May in less than two hours had ended worse than the previous three. The fact she was calling me from her Eastern time zone when she should have been asleep, not to mention slurred words and jumbled sentences, made it difficult to understand her ramblings. Clearly, she was upset, desperate to talk, and back to the cheap wine or whatever else she swore she had given up.

"I apologize." Before slipping my phone in my purse, I considered turning off the power and feigning poor service if she tried to call again. "There's a situation that can't seem to resolve itself . . . or at least wait until I get home."

"No worries. Make a little room for a weary traveler." He gestured toward the bench. "I don't know how the Europeans have walked these cobbled streets forever."

I slid to the side, relieved for a distraction from the long-distance conversation that was going nowhere.

"While you were on the phone, I've been staring at this guy's sculpture. No luck though." He extended his arms into the air, imitating the gigantic installment of plaster arms emerging from the canal and extending the height of two stories of the Ca' Sagredo Palace. "Has me stumped . . . even if I studied it for days . . . maybe years."

"Support." I sighed.

"Come again?"

"Lorenzo Quinn. The artist. That's what he titled the piece." I paused, considering my next words that perhaps should be guarded, especially with a client. Or, had Grant become more than that so quickly? A friend . . . or possibly . . . more? "Support. I'm thinking that's what I need right about now."

He leaned his head toward mine—cologne lingered with a manly scent, a delicious mixture even after hours in the sun. I breathed him in and tried to push May back to her place on the other side of the ocean, at least for a while longer.

"The world is a small place these days. Makes it more difficult to steal away and not be found." His voice was calm and genuine. "Although, I hope everything is okay."

Grant Richard was a unique character, somewhat of an anomaly in the world of museum directors—not stuffy and pompous as many I encountered. Instead, his laugh was lighthearted and warm, his comments witty and refreshing, especially with regards to many of the artists who took themselves, and the world of art, much too seriously. He was boyish in a fun, innocent, and admittedly, flirtatious manner. *Permission granted.* I leaned my head onto his shoulder, sighed, and closed my eyes.

The morning replayed in my mind like an old film projector movie—bits and pieces of images, erratic and choppy, but sacred in a hold-on-to-forever sort of way. Our time together, making rounds through cavernous exhibit halls and hidden and surreal courtyards, had been a visual feast, and admittedly, Grant's charming demeanor had whetted my appetite for long denied male companionship. But business was business . . . just not now.

Later, when the allure of Venice had dissipated like a lifting fog and I was back to reality, then business would once again trump pleasure. Like a priceless painting, untouchable and only to view, I'd have to admire him from afar.

"Do you want to talk about it? The calls?" Grant rested his fingertip under my chin and tilted my face toward his.

I squinted, partially because of the midday sun but mostly from tears stinging my eyes. "Everything happened so fast. One day my father was alive and now he's gone."

"I'm sorry, Olivia."

"His house. My childhood house . . . that's all that's left. And now my friend says there's a couple who apparently have been watching the area, caught wind of the situation, and now are anxious and offering cash if we don't take the house to market."

"Like a seashell . . . washed up on the beach." He nodded matter-of-factly.

I cocked my head, unsure of why our talk had turned to the ocean.

He continued, "I'm not making light of the situation. It's just that I learned not to be attached to a house. Serves a purpose for a time. Beautiful, sturdy and safe, but then . . . we leave and it's empty. Eventually takes on a new inhabitant."

"Interesting analogy. My home as a seashell. Beautiful? I suppose so in its own clapboard, painted-shutters, tucked-in-a-forest way. Safe? Not so much."

Now it was his turn to cock his head, seeming to have thoughts unspoken. "I understand. Homes have a way of becoming only houses. And if they slip too far away from what they were meant to be, they can become—"

"Nightmares." My throat went dry.

He nodded and a sadness washed across his face. "Living nightmares."

I slouched into the bench a little lower, fixing my eyes ahead as my mind wheeled into the past. He joined my posture, and I wondered if he was also tiptoeing into bygone years, careful not to disturb and awaken the sleeping giants of emotions and fears that had been put to bed years ago.

He took my hand in his, and at first it felt odd to sit on the bench together, hand in hand as if we were lovers. Finally, I allowed my hand to relax into his . . . *it's okay to just pretend.* This was a good place to rest for a while. Watch the water flow by and hope the new current would provide some clarity to the confusion stirred up by my conversations with May.

It was logical. The home would eventually be sold. I had no intention of moving away from Georgetown, especially to relocate to the area that was riddled with bullet holes of emotion. When college presented me a ticket to leave home, I sped off in my rusted yellow VW Rabbit and never looked back.

Now, as if the sunroof had been rolled open, a fresh breeze blew in. The once comfortable and safe cocoon I had built for myself in the name of busyness, success, competence, and independence was falling away. Like a GPS gone haywire, my long-held assumption that I would veer and lose control of my life if another person shared the ride was quickly becoming disoriented. Could it be this especially attractive and intriguing man was pointing me toward true north?

My phone's ringtone bumped me back to reality and I instinctively fumbled in my purse to answer the call.

Marcus's gravelly voice announced dinner would be earlier than expected as the grandeur of the Biennale wore him out and an earlier bedtime was in order for what he termed a well-seasoned gentleman.

"Not a problem. I'll hurry to freshen up and see you then." I grinned at the thought of seeing my old client who reminded me of the grandfather I'd never known. "And I'm sure you'll be as dapper as ever. See you soon."

I gathered my purse, stuffing the piece of paper with scribbled notes from my conversations with May into the side pocket. "I'm sorry I have to rush off. Acquiescing to Mr. Elliot is how I have to roll. He's been an excellent client for a long time, plus he's getting old and I'm not sure how much longer the art world will . . ." My words caught with the thought of losing another person with a unique passion and deep respect for art. Marcus understood the magic—the moment, repeated over the centuries, when paint and brush dutifully carried the fibers of human imagination and spilled onto canvas.

"Olivia." Grant brushed my hand with a kiss. "Enjoy a wonderful meal with Mr. Elliot and his son. And later tonight, if a stroll is appealing, give me a call."

I stood and smoothed my wrinkled dress. "Only if we stay on the beaten path."

"Deal." He leaned back and stretched his arms along the top of the bench. "Besides, before I call it a day, I'm going to spend more time with ol' Lorenzo's gargantuan sculpture right here in front of me . . . see if I can discern what that artist was thinking, how in the world he installed it in the water, and most importantly, what I must be missing." The boyish grin returned.

I smiled as I waved goodbye. Grant's charm had surely gotten him out of trouble more than once with numerous schoolteachers.

The memory of the day and the anticipation of seeing him soon, perhaps tonight, lightened my step as I effortlessly made my way through the late afternoon crowds. Silently, I scolded myself for even having the thoughts. But when in Rome, do as the Romans do. Surely, Venice was close enough.

CHAPTER FIFTEEN

Liam ~ Like Father, Like Son

Marcus and Liam Elliot. Father and son. We've been accused of sharing the same brain. Even though I scoff at the common remark for no good reason, except to assert my independence since I spend more time with my grown father than other adults, silently I take it as a tremendous compliment. After all, Marcus Elliot is the kind of person who comes along once in a lifetime—wise, compassionate, and fiercely loyal—the kind of guy you want on your team. Most importantly, he's my best friend.

Now, as the cartoonish accordionist teetered away from the main dining area, Dad and I rolled our eyes in unison. The rowdy patio patrons with their fat bottles of Chianti would be more receptive to the squeezebox melodies. Don't get me wrong. We love music, but Mozart's compositions or Miles Davis's jams better suit the cerebellum between our ears, especially when our talks involve art.

I'm the proverbial apple that didn't fall far from the tree. But at forty years old, a respected art historian, and basically happy guy, it seems I'm still tethered to the branch. Regardless, I love the man.

Grayed through a respectable head of hair, custom suits and pressed shirts (though not to the level of Mom's vicious ironing), and big, brown puppy dog eyes—kind, caring, and committed—the same DNA etched in me.

When Mother died after a long slow dance with dementia, I'm convinced she used her last coherent sentence to make Dad promise he'd find me a wife before it was too late . . . whatever that meant. Since then, Dad downed a double dose of meddling and took it upon himself to make sure I wouldn't be, heaven forbid, a perpetual bachelor. I didn't need to be a genius to realize his insistence that I accompany him to Venice had more to do to with introducing me to Olivia Danford than helping him with his suitcases and logging another father-son vacation.

"Buonasera, Mr. Elliot." The maître d' offered a bow as if he'd completed a grand performance. "It's a delight to have you dining with us again. La Biennale has brought you and your son back to my beautiful city."

"Grazie, Luca. Good to see you too. My son and I have been away too long and my stomach's longing for the carpaccio to get us started." He patted a noticeably reduced gut in light of cooking, or not, for himself. "And of course, the Biennale has been a part of our agenda for years. Hard to imagine, but I first attended when I was freshly out of graduate studies and ready to take on the art world. Who would have known it took on me . . . grabbed my heart and never let go."

"Speaking of love, is your lovely wife joining you tonight?" The waiter motioned to the empty chair.

Dad's momentary pause was enough for me to interject. "She's no longer with us . . . she passed nearly a year ago." Somewhere between watching my parents desperately hold on to each other until death pulled them apart, I'd become the gatekeeper to my father's heart. The pain he felt, I experienced as well.

The dark-suited man lowered his head and muttered something in Italian. "I am so sorry. My heart breaks for you." He cupped his hands together for a pensive moment. "Saying goodbye to one you love is so difficult." His downturned mustache confirmed the Italians really do know how to love.

A little lump caught in my throat. "Thank you. I . . . we miss her terribly." I motioned to the vacant chair. "We have a friend joining us tonight."

Even though the meal hadn't begun, Dad lifted his napkin, a recent habit for wiping away a stray tear.

Luca raised both arms in the air as if an epiphany had clunked him over the head. "While you wait for your guest, let me bring you a glass of my best cabernet." He smiled, the waxed tips now pointing skyward. "Fine wine has a way of soothing the heart."

"Oh, I'm sure it does, but I pass on the grapes. My son may order some when our guest arrives, but he'll wait for now." Dad looked at me and mouthed the words. "She's worth it."

I'd like to think my personal life is off limits to others. Most of my weeks are spent where I teach—Duke University—researching, lecturing, and propping my eyelids open while the head of the art history department drones on about the grad students' lagging work ethic and erroneous, semantic line items in six hundred-page dissertations.

But what keeps my blood pulsing is traveling to other schools and institutions to share my love—the Modernist artists. It's even better when I get some side work and a highbrow art collector or museum curator hires me to give my two cents if a painting is the real thing or not. For everyone involved, it's best on a monetary and ego level if the piece of art is authentic.

For me it goes deeper. It's like excavating an unknown and untouched part of the world—an Indiana Jones moment—staring an actual treasure in the face, holding it, touching it. Even through white cotton gloves, it's sensual and stirring. The painting becomes part of me. On the flip side, if the piece is a fake, even a good one (and I've seen my share of great forgeries), the attempt at deception is so real, it's disturbing. I hate lies.

If the job involves my all-time favorite, Modigliani, the gig couldn't get any sweeter. Amedeo Modigliani, or to me, Dedo. His Italian mother gave him the pet name, and crazy as it sounds, I feel I've earned the position to refer to him with the same endearment. Over the years, my studies and research about the eclectic artist have made the two of us tight, intimate in an odd sort of way . . . even though he's dead.

Weekends? Well, let's just say I'm happy I have Bella. Sunshine blond, prettiest eyes on the planet, content to take a long walk through the park or sit on the couch together and catch a movie. The perfect companion. Oh, she's a dog. Clarify that. She's a golden retriever. Maybe Dad has reason to worry.

Dad was saying something to me. I was distracted. Worried again that the dogsitter forgot to take my girl on a walk this morning, or worse, neglected to give her the new stuffed ducky I'd picked up at Pet World before I left for Italy.

He plucked my forearm, and like Bella's favorite green fuzzy tennis ball that occasionally takes an awkward bounce and sails over the fence into the unknown, my mind turned back to reality . . . game over.

"What'd you do that for?" I turned to him.

Ignoring my question, he pushed from the table, stood as quickly as his seventy-five-year-old body would unfold, and embraced a woman, an exceptionally beautiful woman.

"Olivia," he extended his arms, viewing her like a masterpiece. "You are as stunning as ever. Better on the eyes than the finest Rembrandt."

"Marcus, you are the eternal flatterer." She gave him a stern look. "And thinner. You promised to take care of yourself. I may have to come down from D.C. and fatten you up."

Though American, she pecked both of his cheeks in the customary Italian fashion and Dad blushed. *Not a bad custom.*

She held my father at arm's length. "But, my dear friend, it's wonderful to see you in person. Much better than those live video sessions you insist on, especially since you can't sit in one place, and half the time I'm talking to the shelving behind your desk." She playfully wagged her forefinger. "Which by the way looks like it's about to fall over and crush you beneath all those stacks of books."

"Tools of the trade, my dear." Dad chuckled. "I've yet to meet a short-winded, non-bibliophile art historian."

Taking in their exchange and late on cue, I shuffled from my chair, albeit awkwardly, as I considered being next in line for the double-cheek-kissing custom. Instead, she offered her hand.

We exchanged the customary American business-as-usual handshake. "Ms. Danford, it's a pleasure to meet you. I've heard and read so much about you."

"A researcher?" She eyed me with a sly grin. "I hope it's all true."

"If truth is golden, then yes." I chuckled at my own wit. *Where did that come from, you idiot?*

"Good. Then we should have a productive *and* enjoyable meeting." She slid into her chair as Dad and I followed with our best gentlemen's flair.

*****

Dad was spot on. Olivia Danford was bright and beautiful. It was obvious why she held a lofty status in professional art circles. She listened with a keen ear about Marcus's recent case, asked the right questions about provenance, and summarized an efficient and effective plan to perform the requisite scientific analysis on the painting Dad hoped was the real thing—an authentic Matisse, possibly painted during the French master's early career.

Most of the dinner conversation was about the Biennale, which exhibits and lectures to skip and which were a must-do. Industry gossip and updates were sprinkled in, but it was the tender moments about Mom's illness and inevitable passing, and Olivia's news of her father's death that reminded me that she and my father shared a friendship even deeper than their long-standing working bond.

Of course, when Olivia mentioned a recent case involving a purported Modigliani, my ears perked. She didn't offer many details and only said it would consume a good deal of her attention when she returned home.

My heart quickened when hearing the artist's name, and obviously Dad knew that was one of the few topics that would get me talking. But strangely, he quickly redirected the conversation. Like a door-to-door salesman anxious to dig into his sample bag, he unlatched the spring clip with the familiar pop, slipped his hand inside his worn attaché case, lifted a small, unframed canvas, and laid it gingerly on the white linen tablecloth.

A casual observer at a nearby table might not have taken a second glance at the painting. It was composed of playful broad strokes of brilliant yellows and oranges complementing hues of moody blues and earthy greens—a pretty piece—nice hanging in a kitchen or guest bathroom. Flowers in a crooked vase. Odd, whimsical—maybe the artist was drunk, one might say.

But when I watched Olivia slowly scan the surface of the floral still life, her eyes lit and her cheeks took on the same hue as the pale peonies. Like a bloodhound, she was on to something, and I was fascinated watching the hunt.

Dad was the same breed—on point and on her trail. He had put on his invisible cape and was now Marcus Elliot, the seasoned art appraiser, connoisseur of truism, and defeater of deceit. "It's possible, isn't it?" His bushy brows raised. "You're thinking the same."

She didn't answer, but instead slipped her half-readers from her purse and lowered them toward the tip of her nose.

For me, half-readers implied my old high school geometry teacher announcing to the entire class that mathematics and Liam Elliot were not meant for each other. Olivia was certainly not the aptly called Rotund Roberts, but she was definitely out of my league on the potential dating spectrum.

What was Dad thinking? Worse, why was I even going there as these two experts were much more interested in the validity of a piece of art that quite frankly, Dad hadn't made too big of a deal about it until tonight.

My work, Bella, and Dedo. That's the triad of my daily life. And, if I learned one thing from the plump teacher, the triangle is the sturdiest structure—strong and independent—no need for another dimension. So, despite my father's good intentions, and admittedly

Olivia's smarts and good looks, all was well with me, myself, and I. Clearly, I was destined to be a triangle.

*****

After we walked Olivia to her hotel and said our goodnights, Dad gave her a bear hug that was reminiscent of dropping a child off at summer camp. She laughed, squeezed him back and said she'd be in contact soon to follow up with the forensic work for the suspected Matisse.

"Marcus, whatever you do, don't take a wrong step and end up in the canal." Her hand covered her mouth in mock surprise. "You just may have something in that briefcase, and Liam would have to fish you out of the murky pond."

"I'll keep a close eye on him . . . and the case." I thought about following Dad and exchange a quick thank you, it-was-nice-to-finally-meet-you-I'm-sure-our-paths-will-cross-again hug. Instead, my arm jutted awkwardly, offering my hand like a nerdy first-time camper, afraid his underwear might end up the flagpole by week's end.

With the grace of a ballerina, she shook my hand, made a half pirouette, and walked toward the hotel entrance. But before she disappeared inside the arched doorway, she called back over her shoulder, "And Liam, I'm looking forward to your offer. I'll meet you tomorrow at the museum at nine sharp."

Like a marionette, my right arm raised an acknowledgment and then flopped down to my side. I stood there feeling somewhat limp, repeating her sentence in my mind. I turned to catch up to Dad who was already ambling along the walkway. I caught him by the elbow and slowed him to a stop in time to catch the tail end of a sly smile. The look on my face forced his silly grin into a straight, no-nonsense line.

"What?" He shrugged his shoulders.

"Let me add to that. *What* have I missed?"

"Nothing really. Just don't be late. She hates it when people are late."

"Late to what? What have you gotten me into?"

"That's a lot of *whats*." While he chuckled at his own wit, I wanted to growl. "Relax, son. It's innocent. When you excused yourself to the men's room after the meal, I mentioned the new Modigliani acquisition by the Guggenheim and your offer to take her with you for a viewing."

"But I never offered to take her. Of course, seeing the portrait is top on my list before we leave Venice, and I plan to reach out to the curator for a private viewing. But no thanks to you, I can do that on my own and if you want to come along—"

"Don't mention it. I took care of it for you."

"You did what?"

"There's that what again. You really should nip that vernacular habit in the bud."

I forced myself to take a deep breath, a mini time out, to conduct myself adult-to-adult with my dad instead of reeling back to acting like a horrid toddler, or worse, a hormonally imbalanced teenager.

"It took a little doing and a few weeks in advance, but I set up a private viewing of *Woman in a Sailor Shirt* . . . only it's not entirely private." He winked. "Olivia will be joining you."

"Dad, you're not answering me."

"Besides, she needs firsthand information about Modigliani." His broad smile was genuine now—like a proud, beaming parent when his kid wins the spelling bee, and in my case, the art history-o-rama. "What better scholar than you to dispense the knowledge she's after?"

"True. But this all seems so calculated. Besides, she's an expert. I'm sure she knows everything I could tell her about him."

"Oh, she's good. Actually, better than that . . . she's superb. But she doesn't have the depth of your knowledge about Modigliani, and she especially doesn't have the ethereal connection you have with the man." He paced in a small circle. "For crying out loud, you're passionate about the man as if you're half him." Dad rubbed his temple—a habit that signaled his brain was working on overload.

I wondered for a moment if he had remembered to take his blood pressure pill with the change of time zones, but then he calmed and lowered his voice to a whisper. "She wouldn't have shared with me . . . on the down-low, that is . . . that she's anticipating being stumped by this case she's got waiting back home. There's something about it . . . without even me knowing the details, that I can tell has her on edge."

Now I rubbed my temple. Like a dog having a bone dangled in front of its mouth, I couldn't help but be enticed to share about Modigliani with Olivia, even though my meeting with her was the equivalent of a pre-arranged prom date. But the notion that her new case could possibly involve a previously unknown work by my dear Dedo . . . admittedly, I began to drool.

With a curt head jerk, I mentally pulled myself together. "I know full well this isn't only about helping fill in the due diligence gaps for the mighty Ms. Danford. You were concocting something for weeks, probably months, between us."

Dad acquiesced with a slight nod. "Perhaps even a year . . . but don't worry, she doesn't know your dad made the arrangements. She thinks it was all you."

"Gee, thanks, that makes it all better." I grimaced.

He gave me a good ol' boy pat on the shoulder and locked eyes with me. "Plus you might have another shot at redeeming that ridiculous handshake back there."

All I could do was sigh and lower my head in defeat. "Good thing I love you, Dad, or I'd throw you in the canal myself . . . along with a Matisse, real or not."

I put my arm around him, and as we walked along the lamplit cobblestones, I couldn't resist holding his sagging shoulders a bit tighter—two lonely travelers, deeply caring for one another's heart.

CHAPTER SIXTEEN

Olivia ~ Response & Spontaneity

I kicked off my low-heeled sandals and slipped out of my black dinner dress. The hotel's satiny robe felt cool against my skin as I reflected on the evening with Marcus and Liam. The conversation had been intentional and intellectual, and their company was refreshing—my kind of people—good for the mind and good for the soul.

Now, if only May's phone hadn't gone to voicemail for the third time within the last half hour. It was midafternoon in Pennsylvania, and she should have been at the gallery, especially now that she didn't have to care for Thomas. Not to be ignored, I'd call the direct number for Kennett Square Art, Artifacts, and Antiques—the Triple A as the locals called. It would be easy to find online.

The quaint gray clapboard building on Main Street was loved by the locals for its coffee and cider bar, and heavily foot trafficked by tourists when the fall leaves rioted with color. Back when May was in her early twenties, the owner had taken a liking to her, or at least a convenient flirtation, hired her to run the shop, and then basically skipped town and left my childhood friend somehow feeling responsible for the well-being and future success of turning profit on quasi-tourist crap, mediocre artwork, and seasonal pumpkin spice lattes. I think May always hoped the forty-something owner would return to our quiet little town, announce he had missed her horribly, wanted nothing more of the big city, and ask her to marry. But later, it was rumored the absentee shop owner was sharing his plaid Vineyard Vines pressed shirts and whale imprinted Bermuda shorts with a boyfriend and living the high life on the Jersey Shore.

May swore she never had feelings for the guy. She counted herself lucky that Mr. Preppy kept his penny loafers in another state—far away and out of her way from the Triple A—as long as it made a little money. But in an enabling sort of way, the shop became May's baby and she's been stuck there ever since, purchasing, stocking, displaying, and selling tourist trinkets, knickknacks, and a few worthy items crafted by local artisans. She even lived in the apartment upstairs. "A convenient walk to work," she'd say.

As I punched in the store's number, the sun-bleached handwritten sign taped in the front window, *Original oil paintings by the famous, elusive, and mysterious local artist, Thomas Danford,* focused in my mind. Next to the public and somewhat distorted proclamation of my father's reputation, a red and black "Open" or "Closed" sign flipflopped depending on whether May was in the mood to deal with the flow of shoppers, folks usually more interested in the whereabout of a potential sale display.

Even though she coddled and nursed the shop through the stagnant off seasons by hiring local musicians to strum Neil Young tunes and offering wine and art nights to wannabe artists, the Triple A would never be May's idea of a real art gallery. Instead, she dreamed of a space with an evocative mood and paintings spotlighted against stark, clean walls. The artwork would be labeled with names of known artists, titles with deep and profound meaning, and prices followed by several zeros. The artists, dressed in savvy black, would garner shoulder-to-shoulder crowds of patrons sipping wine and nibbling fancy hors d'oeuvres as they coyly outbid another's offer for a must-have piece of art.

A raspy voice answered. "Hello. It's May at the Triple A."

"Hey, it's Liv." I paused, waiting if her response would be friend or foe.

"Oh, hey." Pause.

Perhaps she was doing the same, checking the barometer of my demeanor. Our last conversation hadn't gone well, although it was predictable considering how poorly we both deal with stress. May reverts to curt, choppy phrases like a child pounding hands on piano keys. Me? I kick into blabber mouth mode, diarrhea of the mouth she calls it. Neither response is very pleasing.

"How's the weather back home?" *Like I really care.* "It's beautiful here. Lots of sunshine and even when it rains in the afternoons, it's clear by dinnertime." *Like she really cares.*

"It's nice . . . that's nice."

"How are *you*, May? I've been thinking a lot about you."

"Fine."

"I know all there is to do with the estate, dealing with the house, taking care of your store . . . and by the way, I hope you haven't gone into my mother's cottage. I need to deal with that on my own."

"It's all yours, Liv."

I sighed, probably too loud. "Okay . . . I know you think I'm over here playing around, wining and dining and being a spoiled brat. I'm actually working, May. Despite everything we need to do to clean out all of Dad's crap so we can sell the house, the paperwork and legal hula hoops . . . I still need to make a living.

"Looking at art?" Her sarcasm oozed and I wanted to scream. "Really?"

"What's that supposed to mean? Of course, I'm looking at art. You know that's what I do for my job. I work my butt off so I never had to go back to the hell hole of a town I once called home."

Silence. I breathed deeply. "Hey, I'm sorry. I didn't mean that the way it came out." My face felt hot. "I'm worn out, May. There's been a lot to attend to here and I'm just spent. Even though you've been part of my life forever, it's not your responsibility to take care of everything with the estate. Even though he had so little, there's—"

"Let me know when you're back home . . . oh, I mean back in the *hell hole.* If you're looking for me, I'll be the one with the red pitchfork digging through the *crap.*"

I stared at my phone, unsure what to say. Ever since May was a kid, she had a hot temper, but this was scalding. Before I had time to reason with my business self, I whispered into the phone, "I'll leave tomorrow . . . as soon as I can change my flight." I ended the call and slumped onto the bed.

*****

My body yearned for rest. Thoughts swirled, chasing one another in my mind like an old fashioned cartoon with the dog chasing the cat, then the cat turning on the dog, until they both dissolved into a big blur of black scribbles.

What's up with her? Did another relationship with some local guy turn sour? What in the world? Why is she in such a hurry to get the house sold? It's not like she doesn't have more free time than me. She can make runs to Goodwill or toss what's trash. Changing my flight is going to cost a fortune. Shoot! I'm supposed to meet Liam at nine . . . and a candlelit dinner at the Danielli with Grant at night and then . . . My thoughts slowed and focused as I spoke aloud, "Geez, May. I deserve some fun . . . even a little romance."

My cell rang and I fumbled for it through the stack of downy pillows. Maybe May was calling to apologize, or worse, really let me have it.

"Hello?" I answered cautiously.

"Olivia, it's me, Grant . . . I know we have plans to see each other tomorrow night, but . . . well, take a look outside your balcony."

"What are you talking about?" I slid out of bed and padded to the shuttered window, secured with a burnished gold handle.

"Just look out and then down toward the water."

I unlatched the handle, pushed open the wooden shutter and peered toward the canal. Like a mythical sea creature arising from the depth, a gondola slowly bobbed in the dark water. Grant lifted a lantern in my direction, his wide smile illuminated.

"Your ride, my lady . . . and only available until midnight or it turns into a pumpkin." He gestured toward the gondolier, who in turn tipped his small hat and nodded.

"Grant Richard, you are . . . wonderful." Despite my yawn that followed, I smiled to myself. Perhaps I needed a little moonlit serenade. "Sure. I'll take a spin around the block. Give me minute and I'll be down."

I pulled on a light sweater and jeans and tiptoed down the stairs like a schoolgirl sneaking out of the college dorm after curfew . . . and it felt so good.

*****

Our boat floated effortlessly along narrow side canals, passing under arched bridges and in directions that didn't matter. At this late hour, the typically singing gondolier was quiet, instead humming a private tune to pass the extra time on the job that surely had cost Grant a small fortune.

Whatever tension pooled in my neck and shoulders during my conversation with May now dissipated with the gentle rocking of the boat. The stress and worry over the past weeks' events seemed to lift and float away as I leaned back into Grant's embrace. Beneath the blanket, his arms wrapped around my waist and I closed my eyes, allowing myself to slip into a different place—devoid of the responsibilities, reputation, and even regrets that defined me all too well.

"You know this interlude goes against all professional judgment." My attempt to summon a last dose of sound reasoning waned when his lips brushed along my neck. "And when we return to D.C., this needs to be forgotten and agreed—"

"That it never happened." He turned me toward him, our faces inches apart. "Olivia, tonight never happened." Then, as if two lost souls found each other, our lips met—any unseen layers of ice thawed and fell away as I melted at his touch. We may have floated for minutes, hours, or years . . . it didn't matter.

Only a slight bump and the ceasing of forward motion signaled we'd returned to the harbor of reality. As promised, the gondolier tethered to the dock outside my hotel just before the clock tower would strike midnight. Grant handed him another token of appreciation for helping to make the night perfectly romantic. Then, as if from a dream, the black and white stripe-shirted man gave a slight wave, pushed from the stone wall, and disappeared into the night.

I stood on the stone walkway, a literal reminder my feet were back on solid ground, and where my head needed to be. "Thank you, Grant. That was . . . a fun rendezvous."

"Only fun?" He furrowed his brows. "It was more than merely *fun* to me." He cocked his head as if calculating the next words. "Olivia, it was special . . . you're special to me."

I crossed my arms as a cool breeze blew off the water. "I'm not minimizing what happened. It's just that you're my client and we can't mix business with—"

"Pleasure?" He extended his hands toward me. "Olivia, you mean much more to me than merely pleasure. I know it's crazy . . . we don't really know each other all that well, but I have feelings for you. I have since I saw you in the conference room standing next to the window . . . you captivated me from that very moment."

He stepped closer and wrapped his arms around my shoulders. Whether I shivered from the night chill or once again his touch, Grant Richard was more than just *fun*. He was charming, intelligent, extremely handsome, and . . . holding me in Venice, a world away from anything real.

"Tomorrow night at the Danielli . . . the evening will be just as magical. I have a special table reserved overlooking the Grand Canal." He stroked my hair as he whispered in my ear. "Candlelight dinner, the best food and wine Venice offers, me with the most beautiful woman in Italy."

"Oh, Grant." I shook my head, disgusted with myself for caving to May's temper tantrum and cutting my travel short. "Tonight's been so wonderful, I didn't want to bring it up . . . I'm returning home tomorrow on the earliest flight I can book."

Grant's shoulders slumped. "You're kidding me, right? There are still two days left of the Biennial and I'm sure you and your art advisor friend need to meet again. Besides—" He squinted his eyes as if pained by the thought of our time together ending.

"I am so sorry. It's May. Her life's a mess anyhow and now this added stress with my father and her needing—"

He pressed his lips to mine, silencing any more words that, at that moment, were unnecessary. Instead, noting my knees were unusually weak, I gave in to his embrace. *I'm still in Venice and tonight is my life, May.*

Then, holding both of my hands, he extended his arms, his eyes roaming my body. "A masterpiece. You are exquisite. Olivia, I can't get enough of you."

With resolve, I pushed my job, my reputation, my father, and May thousands of miles even farther away. In their place, I gently tugged Grant's hand and stepped toward the hotel front door.

Once we arrived at the top of the narrow staircase, I fumbled with my room key—nerves mixed with exhaustion had set in.

Grant rested his hand on mine as I inserted the key into the lock. "Liv, I feel better you're safely to your room now. Not lost in this cavernous city." He kissed me lightly on the top of my head. "And, believe me, there's nothing more in the world I desire than to be with you tonight." He took a slight step back. "But you have a big day tomorrow getting home."

Now I really felt like a school girl—a naive and silly one. "Oh . . . " my mouth went dry and I was thankful for the dimly lit hallway hiding my reddened face. "Yes, thank you for walking me to my room . . . the perfect gentleman." I forced a grin. "I do have a big day and I'm sure we'll resume our talk about the Modigliani, or at least the purported original, when we're both on American soil again."

"Olivia, please don't think—"

"It's all good. The Venetian charm got the best of us this week . . . especially tonight." I turned and fussed with the key until the door creaked open. But before I stepped inside, Grant caught me by the shoulder.

"You're right, Olivia, there will be no mixing business with pleasure." He turned me to face him. "But when *The Girl in White* is displayed in her rightful spot at the Richard Museum, along with other authentic paintings, then our business will be done and perhaps our adventure we started here can continue."

I straightened my back, a false attempt at locating my true north after the evening's events. "Grant, there is much to determine about the portrait. After that, maybe there will be the chance to discern what happened here . . . perhaps it was only an illusion."

He gave a wry smile. "I can assure you, Ms. Danford, there is more than meets the eye as to what has happened between us." He brushed my lips with his. "Safe travels and until we meet again." Then, just as the gondolier had faded into the night, Grant descended the stairs and disappeared into the darkness.

CHAPTER SEVENTEEN

Liam ~ Picture of Perfection

Dad lifted his steaming coffee cup and peered over his readers. "Don't keep her waiting. She likes to be—"

"On time."

"Early." His brows raised definitively. "And I wish I could join you, but you'll enjoy your time alone."

"For Pete's sake. You make it sound like we're going on a date." I grabbed my worn leather journal—my companion when I'm viewing art. "We're looking at a painting. That's all."

"Ah, but together, and it's not just any painting. It's a Modigliani, and I know how you are when in its midst."

"And how would that be?" Determined not to be late, I opened the door leading to the narrow hallway in the pension.

"Smitten." His beamed as though sending me off to prom. "Enjoy your time with both beauties."

I closed the door, hurried down the stairs, said a quick "Buongiorno" to the front desk attendant. Despite the locals and early morning tourists waking up in slow motion, I half jogged toward the

Grand Canal and the Dorsoduro Sestiere. After all, I had a *date* at the Guggenheim Museum.

*****

I'd spent thousands of hours of my childhood with my parents in museum galleries, surveying paintings by both famous and largely unknown artists. While other kids were at amusement parks, zoos, movie theaters, and pizza parlors, the three of us were lapping marble-floored and cavernous institutions, content spending time with the creative outpourings by dead people.

Now, as the petite, smartly dressed docent ushered Olivia and me into the museum foyer and relocked the heavy door until it would reopen to the public in an hour, I was in my element. I was in my happy place and preferred habitat. By the look on Olivia's face, she was in hers, too.

Like school children, we trotted behind the woman as she wove through several white corridors and gallery rooms adorned with contemporary paintings and sculptures. It was nothing short of a miracle that Marcus was able to set a private appointment at the Guggenheim with the busyness of the Biennale and thousands of art patrons and tourists swarming the must-see museums.

We took a sharp left, entered a warmly lit room, and stopped face-to-face with *her.*

"E oro eccola qui, Le femme en Blouse Marine." The woman extended her hand toward the portrait in formal introduction.

"Yes, here she is, *Woman in a Sailor Shirt*," I whispered in a reverent tone.

Each time I see a Modigliani portrait, it's as if our eyes lock. This time was no different. The young woman with dark bobbed hair accentuating her oval face stared at me with moody, large brown eyes. Against the deep blue shirt and nearly black background, her warm pink face and rose-colored lips projected forward as if she was eager for conversation.

"She joined us in 2016. The portrait was in the collection of Luisa Toso in Venice for fifty years. The master painted this rare oil in 1916. It's believed the model is the same as in another of Modigliani's portraits."

I nodded. "Yes, the model sat for another he painted the same year, *La Servetta Seduta*."

"The Seated Servant Girl." Olivia's spot-on translation rolled off her tongue. "The image of the same young woman wearing a black blouse and striped skirt is familiar to me. Since *The Girl in White* surfaced, I've combed through art books and articles digging for any unknown nuggets about the artist and his works." She stepped closer to the painting and continued. "I suppose I'm part bloodhound . . . insatiable when it comes to getting to know everything possible to solve a case."

Olivia glanced at me over her shoulder. "And, Liam, thank you for arranging this viewing and sharing your extensive knowledge."

"Absolutely. My pleasure." Well, a partial fib . . . it was a pleasure to spend time with her.

Again, her attention was focused on the painting. "Clearly, Modigliani was an enigma. Not only impressionable, but there is something about his work that feels—"

"Personal." I stood beside her, both of us fixated on the oil painting presented before us.

"Exactly," she whispered.

"Ah, then the two of you are intimate with Modigliani?" The docent cleared her throat. "Perhaps you can teach me."

I caught Olivia's quick wink—a gracious reminder for us to step aside and allow the other expert to expound over her museum's treasure.

Positioning herself next to the painting as if on stage, the docent continued, "*Le femme en Blouse Marine* appeared in Modigliani's solo show organized by his dealer Léopold Zborowski at the Parisian gallery of Berthe Weill in December 1917. However, paintings of female nudes in the window caused a scandal and the show closed prematurely." She covered her mouth with her fingers and whispered, "It's said that the nudes literally stopped traffic."

Olivia and I exchanged a glance. I'm sure we both thought how times have changed.

The woman clasped her hands. "The painting was subsequently bought by Paul Guillaume and shown only occasionally thereafter. It's listed by the Italian State in recognition of its high artistic and historical value."

She beamed at the portrait as if it were alive. "During the restoration a thick layer of non-original varnish that had been applied during a previous intervention was removed. The process revealed the original cold blue and gray tones as well as the peach-colored face . . . which prior, had deteriorated to beige."

As though remembering there were three of us in the room, the docent turned toward us. "With that said, I suppose with many paintings we may never know what the artist originally intended." She raised her wrist and looked at her watch. "Oh, if only we had all day to wander the halls together . . . however, our time is over."

As we briskly walked toward the exit with the petite woman in the lead, I imagined a large windup key protruding from her suit back. Surely, if this museum employee wore a pedometer, hitting ten thousand-plus steps a day would be a snap. *Funny what some of us do . . . all in the name of art.*

"Liam, thanks again for letting me tag along to see this painting. The perfect timing of your private viewing was meant to be."

I cocked my head. "Why is that?"

"It's really unfortunate, but I have to fly home this afternoon. There's some personal things that can't seem to wait." She shrugged. "I'm sure there's so much more you could teach me about our friend Modi." She smiled. "Another time? Soon?"

"Yes . . . very soon." I returned the smile, wondering if the awkward pause was just me. But when her eyes avoided mine and a faint blush colored her face, I wondered if the prominent Olivia Danford was actually as introverted as I.

CHAPTER EIGHTEEN

Olivia – Something in the Air

"You're different, Liv." Joel rested his hands on my desk and leaned in . . . too close. "And I deduce it has something to do with your vacation?"

"It was work, Joel. Not a vacation."

"Then tell me why you keep staring out the window like you want to be some place other than here." His eyes narrowed. "Or with someone other than me."

I shot him a quizzical look.

"Okay, that's *not* what I meant. But Olivia, I know you well enough to know you're distracted. Is he Italian?"

"You're ridiculous. There's just a lot on my mind. This Modigliani case . . . it has me off-kilter for some reason. The initial observations look promising." I tapped the thin folder that contained notes of my first impressions of the portrait. "Like that piece really could be the real deal, but my gut isn't buying it."

"Well, Grant Richard won't buy what your gut says. That man is determined he's unearthed a hidden treasure." Joel leaned against the wall and crossed his arms. "And he strikes me as someone who knows how to beat the odds to get what he wants."

At the mention of Grant's name, I felt my face flush and turned to focus on the computer screen. Which document it displayed didn't matter. Silently, I admitted my head was in the clouds since my return from Venice even though my thoughts were grounded on Grant.

"Just like us, Mr. Richard will learn the truth about the portrait when the truth is known. She's either a rare and original Modigliani that will be the talk of the art world, or she is a clever forgery. Just like I've taught you, Joel, it's one or the other—no gray in between."

"Then what is your next step, Sherlock?"

"A visit to Winterthur and a meeting with William Barrett at the art conservation lab. The man's a chemical genius." I glanced up from my computer in time to see Joel's eyes widen.

"*The* William Barrett? I thought he's been long retired. He was the chemist on the Pollock project with you, right? Helped link the polar bear hair from the artist's rug that was embedded in the actual painting."

"The one and only."

"Amazing. Who would have guessed a lock from a long-dead Arctic animal would end up in Pollock's last painting and be the key to its authenticity? Fact seriously is stranger than fiction."

"Agreed. Especially in our business." I pushed away from the computer.

"When are you meeting Barrett?"

"I'm driving to Winterthur tomorrow." I stood and took my turn to lean across my desk toward Joel. "But first, I need you to do something for me."

His eyebrows raised in unison.

"Call Mr. Richard and tell him *The Girl in White* is going on a little excursion with me to Winterthur. She needs to be wrapped and ready for me to pick up at the back dock by eight in the morning. The security guard can pass her off safely to me and she'll be home in time for dinner."

"And you think he'll be okay with that?"

"I'm not sure what his choice is since he's chomping at the bit. Anything to move this investigation along for the chance to hang a real Modigliani in his museum is fair game." I walked around my desk and patted Joel on the forearm. "Plus, as he should, he trusts me and knows the painting will be in good hands."

"And Barrett . . . is going to do the scientific analysis?"

"I'll know more when we meet. He consults at the lab when a project stumps the other conservation scientists. Did I ever tell you he was my college chemistry professor?"

"Teacher's pet." Joel laced his fingers.

"Trite, but probably true. Regardless, he's been around a long time and has an uncanny nose for sniffing out what's genuinely old and what reeks of new. As soon as my gut began to flipflop on this case, I called him."

"I assume he knows a good deal about Modigliani? Knowledgeable about Expressionism and the early nineteen-hundreds?"

"Trust me. He's good. Really good." I smiled. "And he can hardly wait to meet *The Girl in White* in person."

Joel exhaled. "At least I can finally tell Mr. Richard you're making headway. He called me directly and asked for an update since you haven't returned his latest calls." Joel smiled, his lips pressed tightly. "And, if you'd like, I'm happy to put the dozen red roses in water that arrived at the front desk about an hour ago. The sender?" Joel scratched his head. "I've run a thorough mental check, and there's no one currently sending me roses."

"You are so thoughtful. Now, we wouldn't want those poor flowers to wilt." It was childish, but I side-stepped my office chair and pretended to rummage in my file drawer.

Later, after the case of *The Girl in White* was concluded and the final report was written, I would come clean with Joel about Grant coming on to me in Italy . . . or, *was it I who had eyes for him?*

CHAPTER NINETEEN

Olivia–Visiting Professor Barrett

The two-hour drive up Interstate 95 toward Delaware was a welcome respite. I needed time to think, and the typical flow of East Coast traffic—slow and steady at first, and then an eventual release of congestion with the city in the rearview—was the perfect remedy for my cluttered brain.

What if The Girl in White *is authentic? If she's not, I've wasted Barrett's time. He'll think I've lost my nose for stiffing out the real deal. Is it business as usual between Grant and me . . . or is there more? Why can't I get him out of my mind? And what in the world is going on with May and why is she being such a brat? What did I do to her except be her best friend forever? Would Dad forgive me? I know I didn't spend enough time with him. But he didn't have to die alone. He was drunk every time I called. It was his fault. He drank himself to death.*

I lowered the window and tipped my head toward the breeze. Yes, a change of scenery and fresh air was needed to unfold my thoughts—like hanging laundry on the line—inviting refreshment and renewal.

Why are the damp sheets hanging on the clothesline tossed and tangled, and Mom is yelling at me that it's all my fault?

Surprise attack! The memory hadn't surfaced for years. Now, it was as vivid as if the wind streaming in the car window was the same humid air on the suffocating hot summer day when Mother lost her temper . . . again.

May and I were only playing—wrapping the white sheets around our shoulders as we pretended to be princesses at the ball— spinning and twirling, reserved only for beautiful girls dancing with their princes. But the dance ended abruptly when Mother yanked the sheets from the wire and slapped me across the face.

"You've ruined them." Her face was flushed and eyes wild. "You ruin everything."

May glanced at me with sad eyes and then, as she always did, scurried away into the woods toward her home and into her own nightmare. I tried to help Mother rehang the sheets, but she shooed me away, shaking her head and muttering, as she always did after a rage, "Sorry, dear. I didn't mean to."

I glanced at the speedometer—eighty-five and rising—in tandem with my beating heart. The temptation to press my foot harder on the gas pedal subsided when flashing red and blue lights flickered in the rearview mirror.

"Oh, no!" I changed into the right lane, slowed, and pulled on to the shoulder. "Deep breath, Liv." I inhaled and blinked away tears.

After several minutes, a stocky policeman appeared alongside my car door. In response to the officer's gesture to further lower the window, I forced a smile and obliged.

"Ma'am, do you realize you were driving over the speed limit?"

I nodded. "Yes, and you caught me red-handed."

"Appreciate your honesty but not how fast you were going. Sixteen miles per hour over." He peered behind my driver's seat where the back seats were lowered, accommodating the amply foam-wrapped frame and painting. "Why are you in such a hurry?"

"Just trying to make it to a meeting."

"That important, eh?"

"Excuse me?" I felt my face redden and I fumbled my words. "At Winterthur . . . the museum."

"Ah, headed to Winterthur Museum, are you?" Thin lips curved slightly upward at the corners. "Beautiful place. My wife and I go there at the holiday time when it's all decorated."

"Yes, it's a lovely place, especially that time of year."

"We've been known to spend a fortune in that gift shop, you know, great place for Christmas shopping—always pick up a book or two for myself. Saw an exhibit a while back about famous art crime cases and the masterminds behind them all. Fascinating book about those forgers."

"That's me."

"Really?" His momentary smile disappeared. "Have I caught an art thief?"

"Hardly." I couldn't refrain a smile. "I specialize in art forgery."

Eyebrows raised above his glasses, and for a moment, I wondered if the silver cuffs dangling from his right left hip would be my new jewelry.

"No, it's not what you're thinking. I curated that exhibit."

The policeman cocked his head to the side, most likely contemplating the authenticity of my story.

"I authenticate real art and weed out the fakes . . . it's my profession." I nodded toward the back seat. "I have some precious cargo in here . . . at least I hope so. The people at the museum . . . you know, the good guys . . . they have the tools to find out. I'm meeting with the team in the Scientific Research and Analysis Lab as soon as I make my way there."

Now I was speaking his language. A smile returned, and this time it was broad.

"Wow. I'll have to tell my wife about you. Confidentially of course. And . . . " He gestured toward the wrapped package. "I hope for your sake, it's a real deal. Sure wouldn't want some knucklehead pulling a fast one on any of us."

"You . . . " I paused, "read my mind."

"Well, you're getting a warning this time, but take it easy the rest of the way. We don't want any accidents to happen." He cocked his head toward the rear of my car. "You might have a masterpiece riding with you."

*****

As usual for a pleasant weekday, a steady flow of visitors streamed into the elegant entrance of the Winterthur Museum. Since 1951, patrons of the museum came to view the current artist series, period decorative art exhibit, enjoy tea in the lovely Cottage Tea Room, or as the police officer mentioned, find a treasure in the high-end gift shop.

What most visitors didn't know about the cluster of old buildings was the existence of a state-of-the-art scientific research and teaching facility.

My destination on the thousand-acre site of woodlands, meadows, ponds, and the famous sixty-acre DuPont garden was a conventional three-story old brick structure adjacent to the public museum a short walk away. From the outside, it appeared bland—

perhaps an administrative or storage facility. However, I and those who worked inside its walls knew differently.

I pushed the intercom button.

"Hello. Name, please."

"Olivia Danford. I have an appointment with William Barrett . . . Professor Barrett."

"Just a moment, please."

After a pause, the metal door clicked, and I pulled the heavy door open and stepped inside. A security guard checked my identification, produced a temporary badge, and pointed down the corridor toward the stairway.

"Thank you." As I walked down the wide hallway lined with multiple closed doors, I smiled to myself. I knew exactly where I was headed. Third floor, take a right, and then another to the end of the hallway. The unobtrusive nameplate on the door to the left, *Professor William Barrett*, marked the portal into a world where art and science intersect—where the expert chemist and art historian could help discover, and perhaps explain, the oddly off-kilter intuition growing in me each time I looked into the eyes of the little girl dressed in white.

"Olivia, how wonderful to see you." William wrapped his bear hug arms around me and squeezed. "In anticipation of your visit, I've hardly slept."

"I have a feeling your excitement is more about meeting *The Girl in White* than seeing me." I gave a sly wink.

"Never!" He chuckled and raised both hands in mock surrender. "But you know me all too well. Always have been and always will be a sucker for a good looking painting."

Memories of being under the tutelage of the brilliant Professor William Barrett during my grad school years came flooding back. I worked endlessly on my art history studies, chemistry course and lab work, and discovered I shared the same intense passion and intrigue about the world of visual art as the esteemed professor.

By the close of Barrett's first session of *Masters & Masterpieces—A Concentrated Study of French Artists,* I knew the white-haired man with smudged half-readers in the navy suit and yellow bow tie would be the inspiration for who I aspired to be in my own career.

I was determined to become a modern-day detective to unearth authentic masterpieces, many long since forgotten, lost, and even stolen. Secretly, I considered myself a cultural warrior. French favorites such as Rodin, Monet, Matisse, Cezanne, Degas, and Gauguin beckoned me. Dutch-born Van Gogh and Rembrandt, Spanish Picasso, and America's bad boy, Pollock—each artist helping to orient my newly discovered self around the world.

I knew I was destined to ferret out and expose the fakes, just like Professor Barrett did for the past forty years. His cases were documented in a multitude of professional and academic journals and international news features that detailed his heroic feats in the multi-layered and multi-faceted world of art. Even after hours upon hours of homework, I devoured the articles as if they were my sustenance. For people like us, the long hours in books and in the forensic lab was a moral duty—a mission of sorts. Side by side, we were fighting for truth and honor in a world filled with too much deception and greed.

"Let's take a look at her. My assistant, Bertrand, will bring the piece up from the dock. Olivia, you did drop her there, right?"

"Just as you instructed, although it felt strange leaving her alone."

"Feels like dropping your child at summer camp."

"Never thought of it that way, but then again, I don't have children."

William gave the thumbs up to the young man wearing a linen work apron speckled with a rainbow of hardened oil paint. "Use kid gloves with her."

"And why you've never married, Olivia . . . " Barrett shook his head. "Hard to imagine why a wonderful man hasn't reeled you in."

"I suppose I'm hard to catch." I focused my eyes on the array of lights, bottles of linseed oil, ethanol, acetate, and instruments lining the shelves and tabletops. "Plus my work has always been my love. The artists, the artwork, the history and story behind them all. Whether authentic or brilliant fakes . . . that's where my heart is."

"I understand, but don't tell my wife." He snickered and then gestured to the wall. It was adorned with multiple paintings—George Washington on a white steed, villagers gathered in a town square with carts and baskets overflowing with vegetables and fruit, a round-faced mother with a just-as-plump infant cradled in her lap, a placid lake with an adrift canoe, and another sorrowful rendition of the crucifixion.

"I keep thinking it's time to officially retire . . . take up fishing, golf, or some other earthly pleasure, but then I can't think of another place or company I'd like to keep other than here with the art." He chortled. "Besides, my nameplate's still outside the door."

"We are two peas in a pod." I pointed to the crucifixion. "Imagine how many times this scene has been painted." I stepped closer to the cracked and faded icon. "My guess would be more times than any other subject matter in the history of the world."

"And yet each time, I am consumed." Barrett paused and stared at the small painting, particularly two-dimensional and simple. "Perhaps a better word is humbled."

"How so?" I peered closer. "The icons have such a simplistic and predictable composition. The pigments in each are similar and—"

Barrett shot up his forefinger as if a moment of genius overtook him. "Indebted! Yes, that's the word."

I held up three fingers. "Consumed, humbled, indebted. Quite a powerful triple-play of words for a common painting."

"Ah, but one more." He raised four fingers. "Forgiven . . . and loved."

"That's five." I winked. "But I'll give you the last one. I suppose it's always a good thing to be loved."

Barrett placed a hand on each of my shoulders and gently squared me toward him. He had thinned over the years, but his six-foot-plus stature still loomed, and for a moment, I felt somewhat childlike in his presence.

"And all these people, including the artists who captured them with paint and brush . . . they're gone." The creases in the corners of his eyes deepened. "This world is strange and fleeting, Olivia. My advice, if you don't mind the offer. Don't try to navigate it alone forever . . . it is a good thing to be loved."

The door opened and Bertrand, along with another apron-clad assistant, braced the carefully wrapped painting between them. Their timing was perfect as it saved me from responding to Professor Barrett. That too was a good thing, as I was without words.

*****

Now it was Barrett's time to be silent. As he carefully helped me remove the wrap, I watched his eyes widen as *The Girl in White* was slowly exposed.

She was beautiful. When I first saw her in the museum, there was something alluring about the young child. Though most likely a portrait of someone not much more than a year or two old, there was something about her that seemed to look far wiser, an ethereal presence that emanated from the aged canvas. Each time I looked at *The Girl in White*, she drew me in deeper, wandering further into her mysterious past . . . who is she?

"The eyes." Barrett lingered.

"And?" I leaned closer to the painting, careful not to press into the frame, its crackled patina revealing decades of small chips and slight areas worn thin from bumps and bruises gathered along life's journey. If this painting was a real Modigliani, it most likely lived a squalid life in his artist's dingy studio in the Montparnasse district of Paris.

It would have shared floor space with other oil pieces propped on the warped wooden floorboards. Possibly, if it was elevated to a favored status, it hung from a scrap piece of wire or twine on his studio wall. Either way, if this precious creation was an authentic Modigliani, its past existence was cold, dank, dark, and dusty—not a temperature-controlled, ambient-lit environment that the famous painter's work now enjoyed in a specially designated room on the first floor of the National Gallery of Art and the Museum of Modern Art. Whoever the real little girl was, she had been painted a hundred years ago. Even if she has lived well into adulthood, she would no longer be living.

Barrett pulled his magnified spectacles from his lab pocket, and then hovered a few inches over the child's face. Again, his silence continued as he appeared to have a stare down, as if waiting her out for an acknowledgment as to where she had been, what she had been up to all these years, and who she really was.

"Hollow . . . like the trademark eyes in his other portraits." He paused. "But not dark. Instead, a lovely blue . . . softer . . . perhaps even hopeful."

Barrett slowly raised into an upright position, then arched his back to counteract years of bending over observation tables.

Like a child anxious to open her birthday presents, my excitement got the best of me. "Do you think she's real?"

Barrett rubbed his chin with thumb and forefinger, a customary gesture I'd come to know of him when his brilliance kicked into high gear. "Let's put her to the test."

I sighed, releasing the air in my lungs in anticipation of the professor's gut inclination. "I was hoping you'd say that."

"If she proves to be the real thing, we have an extremely valuable Modigliani on our hands. If she's a fake, she is the product of an excellent forger."

"I agree." Circling the table, I viewed her from various angles, looking for the slightest oddity, perhaps something off-kilter that would call her bluff.

Barrett did the same, pacing behind me—two truth seekers orbiting in space.

I stooped closer, hovering over her face. For a moment, I wanted to lift her from the canvas, embrace her in my arms, and kiss her cherub cheeks.

"You're smitten with her, aren't you, Olivia?" Barrett had stopped as well, now eyeing me across the table with a half-squinted look. "You're looking at her like a mother gazes at her child."

Quickly, I avoided his glance. Why did a peculiar pang of sadness lash so cruelly? And yes, why was I so enamored by this little girl with blue eyes and wearing a white dress?

I muttered a truth. "I suppose I wouldn't know . . . never been a mother . . . most likely won't be. After all, the proverbial clock is ticking." I forced a laugh, attempting to redirect attention from me back to the painting.

Barrett took my cue, cleared his throat, and motioned to Bertrand to dim the lights. "Let's get her under the ultraviolet and see if she's been hiding anything all these years."

While he adjusted the settings on the imaging equipment, I added, "From the surface level, the composition, brushwork, and canvas stretcher appear accurate to the period in which it would have been executed, around 1917, maybe a year or two later until Modigliani's untimely death in 1920."

Barrett smiled. "You've been doing your research, haven't you, Miss Danford?"

"Of course, like always." Thoughts of Liam and our visit to the museum in Venice to view *Woman in a Sailor Shirt* rushed in. Our brief time together had proven him as an invaluable resource on the master Modigliani. His keen knowledge and passion for the artist's work had ignited my own motivation to learn more about this intriguing and somewhat mysterious painter.

"I've discovered a solid mentor. Liam Elliot. He knows a great deal about Modigliani, in fact, so much, he fondly refers to him as his mother did—Dedo."

"Ah, the term of endearment for the artist who was both naughty as a child and a wild child as an adult." Barrett added, "Yes, I'm familiar with Mr. Elliot. I've read several of his publications. Brilliant historian."

"Once again, the art world proves to be a tightly knit one. Liam's the son of a good friend mine, Marcus Elliot, an outstanding art appraiser. The three of us met in Venice recently at the Biennial . . . the perfect place for a crash course in the life and times of our artist at hand."

"Let's see if Dedo is really in the room." Barrett flicked on the ultraviolet light. "And if there's a chance of that, we haven't even touched on the provenance of this piece, and you and I know that's crucial to prove its authenticity."

I nodded. Yes, if the materials characterization leaned in favor, or even nearly proved the authenticity of the painting, its history of ownership and its whereabouts for the last hundred years needed to be established.

"Oh, my." We uttered the words in unison as the painting illuminated.

"The telltale fluorescence . . . there." I pointed to a faint image on the canvas.

"A pentimento, I believe." Barrett shifted his weight, repositioning himself for a closer look. "It's possible . . . we might be seeing an underlying composition by the master himself."

My heart raced at the suggestion, but I countered the thought with my professional skepticism. "Painters do that all the time—paint or draw over an original piece and then the earlier images, forms, and even strokes emerge."

"Absolutely. Especially ones like Modigliani with little or no money for new canvases. It was common practice back then, probably more so than now."

Like archaeological explorers perched over the entrance to a treasure-filled tomb, we stared in silence, I think neither one of us wanting to jinx the possibility that we were in the presence of a veritable Modigliani.

Finally, Barrett broke the silence. "There's definitely something here . . . another image . . . distinct brushwork."

"And the question is, do these elements coincide with the master's painting style?"

We pushed away from the table, both of our professional bellies filled with intrigue, curiosity, and wonder about *The Girl in White*.

From one teammate to another, Barrett patted me on the shoulder. "I suggest you stay in close touch with Liam Elliot. He could prove to be just who we need to help unravel this mystery."

"Most definitely." I needed to follow up with the soft-spoken and awkwardly charming art historian soon.

"Olivia, I assume you have the permission to keep her here a few days for more tests. She'll be highly secured."

"That should work. I told Mr. Richard the scientific testing can't be rushed. I may have to do some convincing, but I think he'll be okay with a week."

Barrett returned the familiar squinted eye response. "You and I know the necessary patience for completing a full scientific inquiry on a questionable work. That director will have to wait."

"Of course, but he's a pushy one. He has a lot riding on this piece." I shook my head, recalling Grant's words of enticement and too early promise to the museum board members that a newly discovered Modigliani painting would soon grace the premier gallery hall and fill the front pages of the most respected art world publications.

What I didn't share with the professor were the secret sentiments Grant shared with me in Venice—his need to prove himself not only as a competent and capable museum director and curator, but a valued and honored gemstone in the Richard family crown.

"Then push back if need be." Barrett crossed his arms like a defiant schoolboy. "You can't let a museum director's persistence, and in this case from what I've heard about him, entitlement as a Richard heir, sway any professionalism."

"He's actually a very nice man. We've gotten to know one another quite well."

Immediately, I recoiled at my words and Barrett's lifted brows confirmed he could still read me like a book. "*Professionally*, that is."

"Well, I know I don't need to say this, but—"

"The provenance remains an issue. Yes, I've told him that and he assures me he's on it."

"Good." Barrett gave a slight clap. "And am I correct that the private seller remains anonymous?"

"That's correct." I gathered my bag and gave the professor a daughterly hug. "You'll be my first call, when and if that secret is revealed."

As I began down the hallway away from Professor Barrett's research lab, intuition tapped me on the shoulder. I stopped and looked back from where I had come. Barrett stood in the doorway, his lips pursed, perhaps holding back a final thought or word of advice.

I opened my arms, surrendering to what I imagined he wanted to say. "Go ahead. What's on your mind?"

"Two great minds think alike." He smiled briefly, but it quickly faded. "But seriously, Olivia, be careful. You and I know better than most that things aren't always what they seem."

I nodded slowly, then turned and walked farther down the dimly lit hallway.

CHAPTER TWENTY

Olivia ~ Proposition

Perhaps against my better judgment, especially since I did not have a definitive answer regarding the authenticity of the painting, I decided to phone Grant before I started my drive back to the city. After all, *The Girl in White* was his baby, so to speak. As museum director, he did have the right to receive an update and know her whereabouts.

Before I could dial his number, my cell rang.

"Olivia, I'm glad I caught you." His voice was upbeat, not the nearly curt tone he had when we met at the museum loading dock earlier in the morning to secure the painting into the back of my car. Grant had seemed edgy, and quite frankly, pushy to get me on my way to Winterthur. *Everything rides on this piece, Ms. Danford—for both of us.*

I hadn't thought much about his statement until now. I figured he addressed me professionally in front of the dock workers, as he should. And of course, he needed to know I'd be more than careful taking her away from the secured and temperature-controlled museum. But now, I wondered what he meant about so much riding on this particular piece of art for both of us. In my years of proving artwork either authentic or forged, I'd worked with pieces of equal value and prestige—Matisse, Pollock, Renoir, even a DaVinci.

No doubt, the purported Modigliani was a big deal, especially if it truly was an original painting by the often misunderstood and mysterious painter. And if it was a fake, it was a magnificent one with a highly skilled forger behind it.

"Olivia," He cleared his throat. "I've been thinking about you since you drove off this morning."

"Is that so?" I grinned at the thought of his charming smile. "Thinking of me, or the Modigliani?"

"To be truthful . . . a little of both, but if I had to weigh in, you beat his most beautiful masterpieces. But hey, now that you brought it up, how did our girl fare with your professor friend? My gut's telling me she's real, and I'm usually spot on."

"I'm not ruling it out—and I, too, have a good track record of initial gut feeling."

"Best news I've—"

"But there's comprehensive testing to be done. Professor Barrett is pulling together his best team of conservation scientists and chemists for early next week."

"Next week? The wait will kill me."

"In our business, we can't go off good feelings, and we certainly can't rush the process. When I have more information, we'll set a time to meet and I should be ready to share the results of the elemental and molecular analysis. Until then, there's nothing more to do, unless of course, convincing evidence of the painting's provenance is found. As you know, that remains a critical missing link."

"Fact." He laughed, reminding me of our time in Venice and the carefree moments we spent walking the hidden pathways together. "Okay, fair enough. You work on the science, and I'll continue to hound my source for proof of provenance . . . like hand in glove, the perfect collusion."

"Now, that's an odd word choice."

"True. Perhaps association is better suited. Maybe combo?" He chuckled. "But, actually, I have an idea for the perfect combo."

"How so?"

"Meet me in New Jersey. A friend has a beach house he trades with me for special access to donor events." Grant was witty, and his boyish good looks and charm added to the allure to accept the invitation.

"Sounds like he gets the short end of the deal."

"Another fact, especially when you take in the ocean view at sunset tonight."

"Tonight? That's short notice."

"I like to think of it more as spontaneity. I'm heading to Cape May now and figured I might catch you before you made it all the way back to the city. It's only a couple hours' drive from Winterthur."

"I should get back to the office—you know, check in on things. Joel probably has things for me to do."

"Olivia, you own your business. You can make some time for other things once in a while."

"Funny, but I've been told that recently."

"Good, then I'm taking that as a yes. Today, tonight . . . whenever you can get there." He paused. "If we're honest, I think both of us need a break from work and there's nothing like a walk on the beach in Cape May and a good bottle of wine with dinner."

"Sounds like a date . . . uh, I mean, we, Mr. Richardson, you and I do have a professional relationship in the works."

"We seemed to have that in Venice as well . . . and I proved to be the perfect gentleman, right?"

I breathed deeply, recalling the evening that it was me who desired to be kissed and held in his arms. "True, you were. And by the way, I never thanked you for the last evening."

"For what?"

"For simply escorting me to my hotel room and saying goodnight." I paused, recalling the moment when I felt off-kilter. "A little wine went a long way with me that evening."

"Understood. It happens to the best of us." He chuckled. "Olivia, I only have pure intentions for us to enjoy good conversation and a lovely sunset view of the ocean. Besides, I miss my Pacific views, so the Atlantic will have to do."

Now I chuckled. "You, sir, have a beach and dinner companion. Just keep it low on the wine."

"Fair enough . . . and easy since most restaurants in town are BYOB. You know, Liv, it's okay to allow yourself some fun once in a while as well."

To that I had no response. In fact, my college roommates had often pulled the same line when I chose to stay home on a Friday night and study instead of meet boys at parties and bars. Even Joel, my hard-working assistant, tried his best to have me close up shop at reasonable hours and treat myself to a nice dinner on the canal in Georgetown or a performance at the Kennedy Center. But with whom? For years, that seemed to be the ongoing plot structure in my personal reality show, The Missing Link of Liv's Life.

I can have fun. I am fun. "Text me the location and I'll do my best to be there before dusk. I have an important stop to make before I head your way."

"Where's that?

"I'll fill you in tonight."

"Perfect. See you then."

"Oh, should I bring some wine for dinner?"

"Just bring yourself . . . your lovely self."

"See you in a bit, Grant."

I ended the call and opened the car window. *My, how the weather has warmed.*

CHAPTER TWENTY-ONE

Olivia ~ Key to the Cottage

Asking May to meet me at my father's house would have been the right thing to do. Besides, proving to her that I was all in to help with the enormous job of getting the house ready for sale would gain both good daughter and good friend points.

However, this time I needed to go alone. As the reality of items to do regarding Dad's belongings and selling the house became apparent from May's frequent texts and voicemails, another unspoken and private issue loomed—unfinished business with my mother.

As I pulled on to the gravel drive, I was relieved May's rusted truck wasn't under the carport. She must have been here earlier as two trash bins were filled to overflowing, positioned at the end of the drive for the garbage collectors to haul away more evidence of my father's disarrayed life.

After digging in my handbag, I found the front door key and opened the lock. An odd thought crossed my mind as I stepped inside. *Why bother to lock the house when there is nothing of value to be taken?* It was evident May had already removed my father's completed paintings. The strewn piles of canvases were gone now, leaving an eerie sense that he had never been here at all. What remained seemed inconsequential—the faded couch and dusty end tables, outdated newspapers and yellowed books. Even the wooden easel, once the center stage of his existence after he'd been laid off from his DuPont day job, stood awkwardly near the window like a faithful dog, somehow knowing his owner wouldn't return.

I considered the possibility of taking it to my home. Besides, the only items I kept from the house were my father's paint palette and the mysterious unfinished note. The easel was large, heavy, and gangly. It would have to be dismantled to fit in my car and then dragged through the carriage house where I parked and carried up the steps into my home in the city, only to be reassembled again. And then what?

For me, minimalism was better. Less clutter, organization. Organization, predictability. Predictability, control. Directing the moving parts of my life equaled happiness. *Happiness, happiness, happiness.* The word echoed in my mind as if bouncing off barren canyon walls. Was I happy? And what exactly defined such a cliché word?

I had solid finances, a profitable and respected business, my own home in a prestigious and pedestrian-friendly city. I even had a flourishing garden box on my back patio—growing perennials was something I never thought I could do. Approaching forty, all the walking has served me well—clothes shopping was easy, and the results often earned compliments. But *happiness* . . . the concept was illusive as if something essential was missing.

I rubbed my temples, pushing away further self-psychoanalysis. *Olivia Danford, you have more important things to do right now.* After staring at the easel for a few minutes and contemplating the situation, it was clear it would be better off given away to some other passionate and most likely starving artist like my father.

I walked into the kitchen. Apparently, May had made progress as boxes littered the floor, filled with kitchen odds and ends—a mismatched set of dishes and utensils, a brown-stained Mr. Coffee maker, and cooking and baking items that most likely hadn't been used in years.

A few days ago, May texted, informing me that she assumed she had found the key to my mother's studio cottage. It was discovered tucked in a chipped Winnie the Pooh coffee mug in the back of a kitchen cupboard. Now, the mug sat on the kitchen table. She assured me she didn't try the lock and would leave that task up to me.

I pushed the kitchen curtain aside and peered into the backyard. Across the lawn sat my mother's silent and petite cottage—the same structure that I had learned to ignore, pretending it didn't exist after she ceased to exist. Now, the mug, inscribed with the words from Pooh's melancholy song, "I'm just a little black rain cloud"—a fitting tribute to the state of Mother's mind—tiptoed through my memory. Gingerly, I lifted the cup and removed the silver key—an appropriate invitation for me to step into my past.

*****

She must have retreated to her writing studio extra early that day. I recall awaking and wandering around the house in my pink nightgown looking for her, but everything except for my growling stomach was silent.

I looked out the kitchen screen door, checking for the customary *secret sign* that it was permissible to visit my mother in her cottage while she worked. Pushed aside curtains meant I was allowed to gently knock on the door until her sing-songy voice called out a greeting. The invitation implied a quiet entrance, not speaking unless spoken to, and promptly leaving if she gave a backhanded wave toward the door.

This morning, the pale yellow curtains were open. As I skipped across the lawn toward her retreat, the morning dew was cold on my feet and the weekend's grass clippings stuck to the hem of my nightgown.

Rehearsed many times since I was old enough to walk and talk, I called out, "Mother, may I come in?"

"Good morning, sunshine!" Her voice was particularly on pitch that morning.

I turned the knob and stepped inside, grass clippings and all, stowed away on the tips of my toes.

She had glanced up from her typewriter. "Your hair . . . you have wild dream hair." Her words were matter-of-fact. Then pretty pink lips turned up and robin's egg blue eyes squinted in a happy, smiley way. "Your dreams must have been wonderfully lively and exciting . . . just like your hair."

I nodded even though I didn't remember my dreams from last night. I hoped they were wonderful.

Though my stomach was calling for a piece of toast with butter and jam, I was content sitting on the floor next to my mother's desk as she wrote her stories. *Tap-tap-tap, ca-ching, tap, tap, tap, ca-ching* . . . the rhythm and repetition of the typewriter notes were my sweet lullaby.

After a while, she pushed away from her desk, slipped off her shoes, and sank into the sofa near the window. Soon, her breath was audible, and she was sleeping. I wondered if she would wake with wild dream hair.

I climbed onto her upright wicker chair and settled onto my knees. Mimicking her poise, I hovered and wiggled my fingers above ABC typewriter keys. I dared not touch them. Occasionally, Mother would slip a blank piece of paper behind the roller and let me peck the round keys. Under her watch, nonsense and strings of random letters and symbols weren't allowed. I liked to hold the shift key and type, !@#$%^&*, or search the scattered letters and type out the alphabet as I sang the song I'd learned in school. However, Mother insisted I create words. Simple words. Not fussy. But, still, words, as she said, mattered . . . peace, love, happiness.

She appeared peaceful, napping in her downy sofa next to the window, legs outstretched, and her head back like a cat reclined in a favorite sunspot when I decided to make her a picture—a happy one, maybe of flowers and trees and smiling butterflies. She'd be surprised to find the artwork next to her typewriter when she awoke, and before she continued to work on whichever children's book she was creating at the moment. Hopefully, my gift would make her smile like the butterflies. I didn't realize the ink would bleed through my drawing onto her papers.

The warmth of the sunshine streaming in the windows must have lulled me into an early nap. I was dreaming, a beautiful vision of butterflies, flitting around my head and tickling my nose. But I awoke with a start, Mother's face hovering over mine, her eyes narrowed and wild, and displaced hair brushing against my face.

"You little beast! What have you done?" She tugged my arm and launched me off the braided rug where I had fallen asleep, curled at her feet like a faithful pup.

"I'm sorry, Mama. I'm sorry." Tears welled in my eyes.

"You have no business being at my desk . . . or in my private space . . . ever again!" Grabbing my drawing from atop her desk, she tore and crumpled the paper, then stuffed it into the small wicker wastebasket on the floor.

"Stop crying. I'm the one who should bawl. You've ruined my writing." She raised her hand to strike and I instinctively cowered, bracing myself for a swift slap to the back of my head that often followed one of her rages, or *episodes*, as the doctors called it.

"You ruin everything . . . everything!" She stormed to the window and stood, hands on her hips.

I stood silently, contemplating whether to slip out the door as she instead slipped into her dark and lonely world—a place where she went by herself more frequently.

Her shoulders hunched and trembled, then sobbing began as she whispered through gasps for breath, "Everything is ruined . . . the writing . . . the dreams . . . life."

My heart swelled and surged as I watched my mother. I swallowed hard. "Mama, I tried to color a picture to make you happy. I'll never do it again. Promise."

Her response was only louder sobs and muttered words.

I wanted to find Father—tell him Mother was sad again. As the ritual played out, he would shoo me away to play with May, or insist it was time for the dog and me to go for a walk down the lane.

But this morning, Father was already at work at the DuPont factory on the outskirts of town. As usual, he left the house when it was dark and returned when porch lights were on, especially when he had to drive back from one of the museums in the city where he worked a second job as a freelance restorer.

"Just helping to fix old busted up pictures so rich people can stare at them on their walls." He provided the same explanation time and time again when I asked why he wouldn't be home to eat dinner with Mother and me.

He added that he liked the countryside at dawn and dusk.

"Liv." He'd wrap his arms around my waist and plop me on his knee. "When shades of gray blanket the sky and hints of the sunrise and sunset peek through all those trees . . . it's like looking into a kaleidoscope. Remember the one you got for your birthday? Magical, Liv . . . magical."

"But it's dark, Daddy. How do you see where you are going?" I remember looking at him with wide eyes. "Aren't you scared out there all by yourself?"

"Nope." He cupped my face in his big hands. "That's when you see best . . . that's when you trust your heart and mind. You have to rely on yourself to get you where you need to be."

That morning, I learned the hard way that it was best to leave Mother's fits to Father. And, if he wasn't home, follow his rule. "Let her be, Liv. She'll wrestle it out with her own demons."

Instead, I was determined to fix my mess—collect my pen and papers and tidy up her desk so she would begin to type again. While she stared out the window, wiping her eyes and blowing her nose into a pretty white kerchief, I quietly slipped onto her desk chair. My plan didn't include bumping her teacup with my elbow. It clattered on its china saucer as if sounding an alarm.

Mother spun around. "You!" She raised her hand, pointing at me with a shaky finger. "Get out of here. You're not wanted here . . . or anywhere, anymore!"

Slowly, I slipped off the chair, facing my mother as if I was a cornered animal. I stepped toward the door, reached for the knob behind my back, and inched the door open. Her accusatory finger, still raised, begged me to wonder what exactly I had done to be unwanted.

At the threshold, I turned and ran, and as I found my familiar path into the forest, I heard Mother's voice calling after me. "Olivia, my child . . . I am so sorry. Come and let me hold you."

As my instinct and her past episodes dictated, I kept running. Like Father said, it was better to let Mother finish her wrestling.

I remember the crackling leaves and snapping twigs as my mother stomped along the path that led from our house to the pond down the hill. Holding my breath, I tucked myself into a little ball inside the rotted out stump in the grove of ferns. The gritty sawdust dug into my knees, but I kept still. Mother's voice grew fainter as she followed the path that led to the lake.

Father will be home tonight . . . and then everything will be all right.

*****

With white knuckles, I grasped the faded curtain. Tears trickled down my cheeks, washing the memory away, at least for now. I blinked several times as the blurred cottage across the yard came into focus. I released my grip on the curtain, pulling it back in place and tucking the past away. With the silver key secure in my purse, I rushed out the front door.

"Olivia!"

I nearly ran May down as I skipped the top front porch steps.

"Liv, what on earth . . . you look like you've seen a ghost." May grabbed my elbow, steadying me from shaky knees. "You okay?"

I regained my balance and forced a smile. "I'm good . . . you?"

"Well, better than you." She released my arm. "Didn't expect to see you here, though."

"No, kind of an unexpected visit. I was at Winterthur . . . for work. Thought it might be helpful to check on the house."

"Sure, but you could have called me." May frowned.

"For permission?" I stepped back, still feeling the adrenaline rush.

"Geez, Liv. What the heck's wrong with you lately? You don't need my permission to go into your own dad's house." May crossed her arms. "Unless your guilty conscience is getting the best of you."

Now, I crossed my arms. "What's that supposed to mean?"

"For starters, you barely return my messages." Her forefinger twisted strands of hair. "Texts or voicemails."

"You know I'm busy. Running a company isn't easy."

"And cleaning out someone else's family home isn't either." May dug her heel into the gravel.

I kicked a pile of loose chippings. "Then I'll do it. I'm sure I can handle it."

"Good! I have a life, too. Not that you'd care to know anything about it!" May shouted.

"Not true!" I screeched, startling both of us as May's eyes filled with tears. "Oh, gosh, we sound like we did when we were little—"

"Arguing over who got the prettiest Barbies—"

"Or favorite stuffed animals." I shook my head, mainly at myself. "I'm sorry, May. You're right, I don't know what's gotten into me."

"Probably both of us." She reached out her hand in a gesture of truce. "I suppose I miss the old days when we were part of each other's world."

Instead of accepting her handshake, I stepped forward and embraced my dearest, and in some ways, only real friend. Finally, she wrapped her arms around me, and we gave each other a much-needed hug.

"Sorry I got so angry, Liv."

"Me, too." I squeezed my friend. "Loneliness has a way of saying weird things."

"I get it." May took my hand and smiled wide. "And I have a great idea. Let's go into town, the historic district—grab a beer or two. We haven't done that forever . . . maybe ever."

"Oh, May, I have to drive to Jersey this afternoon." I pulled my phone from my bag, remembering I asked Grant to send the location of the beach house. "I'm supposed to meet a friend there for dinner."

"All the way in Jersey? Must be some kind of *friend* to drive so far just for dinner."

"Well, he's . . . "

May raised an inquisitive eyebrow. "I get it. Ditching the ol' friend for a guy, huh?" She tried to smile, but it was obvious the sarcasm was a poor attempt to cover disappointment. "I'm a big girl now, Liv. I'll grab a beer on my own. We'll catch up another time." She turned and walked toward her truck.

"Sure. Another time sounds fine." *I can play this game, too. I don't need to feel guilty about going to see Grant.*

I opened my recent texts. Grant Richards. 25 Gurney St., Cape May. See you at sunset. G.

"Cape *May*," I uttered. "Seriously?" *Guilt, guilt, guilt . . .*

As May revved her engine and began to back out of the driveway, I called out, "Hang on, I'm coming with you."

She stopped the truck and leaned out the window. "What'd you say?"

I propped my elbows on the open window, my nose inches from hers. "I said, I'm coming with you. Besides, I really need a beer."

May leaned her head back and laughed. "Oh, don't we both? Hop in, you nut."

I ran around to the passenger door, jumped in, and pulled the creaking door shut.

"Let's do this job!" It felt right to change course so suddenly—something I rarely allowed myself to do. The adrenaline rush felt good.

"Geez, Liv. You sound like a bank robber."

"We are a little like Bonnie and Clyde in this old truck, don't you think? Remember we used to watch the original movie with Thomas—"

"While quoting the best lines."

"And we were both in love with Warren Beatty." A sigh followed in unison.

"I suppose." May revved the engine again. "As Clyde said, 'I'm even better at runnin' than robbin' banks.' Let's do this!"

May peeled out of the driveway, leaving my childhood home and Mother's cottage to wait for a while longer for my return.

CHAPTER TWENTY-TWO
May ~ For Old Times Sake

Though stately buildings and quaint homes reminiscent of the Colonial Revival and the Late Victorian age continued to define the Kennett Square Historic district, it had changed for the better in recent years. Several inviting restaurants and enticing shops lined narrow streets. Flower baskets filled to overflowing brightened the mood as people strolled, wearing relaxed grins. Small town country air was good for all souls. And, even though I vowed at several of life's junctures to spread my wings and discover other places, I continued to call what was known as the Mushroom Capital of the USA my home.

I motioned to the familiar Liberty bartender and ordered us another round.

"Liv, do you need to at least call him?" Admittedly, my curiosity was sparked as to who Olivia was supposed to meet for dinner. Surprisingly, she hadn't shared any insight, especially after one beer with my noticeably lightweight friend.

"Oh, my gosh! I can't believe I forgot to tell him I'm not coming." Olivia jumped from her barstool and grabbed her phone. "Give me a minute while I call and explain." Her eyes widened as if caught telling fibs at school. "Gosh, May. I'm losing my mind. Completely spaced out calling him . . . so not like me."

I watched Olivia outside the bar window, shifting her weight side to side and talking with her free hand in an animated sort of way. *She must really like him. I guess I should be grateful she blew him off for time with me.*

As my friend returned to the bar, I couldn't help notice a few heads turn toward her. She always was the pretty one. I suppose some things never change.

"How'd the call go?" I took another sip of cold beer. It went down well, better than when drinking alone.

Liv positioned herself on the barstool and took a long gulp.

"I assume not so well?"

Liv released a burp and I had to giggle. That wasn't customary for my sophisticated and cultured friend.

"Well, he understood . . . a little. I told him I was with my best friend and we had some things come up at my father's house that needed to be addressed right away." She wiped her mouth with the back of her sleeve. "I told him I'd make it up to him another time."

"So, you lied to him?" I raised an eyebrow.

"I'd say half a lie. I'll see him another time and you and I, well, are sort of attending to the house."

"Nope, you pretty much lied." I squared up to the bar, avoiding eye contact with Olivia for the moment. "How about if you simply told him you wanted to spend time with your oldest and best friend?" My words sounded childish, but once again, I was Olivia's second fiddle. Second in line. Leading Liv, and Minor Role May.

"Come on, May. I stood the guy up to be with you. Doesn't that count for something?" Liv tapped the counter with her finger. "Besides, we came here to have fun and catch up with each other, right?"

Along with a swig of beer, I decided to swallow my pride. "You're right."

Liv swiveled in her chair toward me.

"Okay, you first," she said. "Tell me your plan. Are you really thinking about moving and opening your own gallery?"

"I am." A mixture of excitement and anxiety rushed over me. "I've been looking online at a few places in Santa Fe and Taos. It's a whole lot different than here, but it intrigues me for some reason."

"Totally new landscape, lifestyle, and the art scene is unique. Lots of cultural influence."

"True, and the area attracts plenty of talent—"

"And clientele with deep pockets."

"You know, it's funny." I turned toward Liv. "I never thought I'd be drawn to art much different from Andrew Wyeth and the others who captured this area so well. But now I'm mesmerized with Georgia O'Keefe and landscapes of wide-open spaces." I smiled. "It's refreshing, Liv. It's time I'm set free."

"From?"

Like a darkened storm cloud, my response lingered—hovering above a sea of unknown—doubt, fear, and unruly memories.

Liv leaned closer. "What are you escaping, May?"

"Sixty-two Blackberry Lane." If a heart can skip a beat, mine did at the mention of my childhood address.

Liv's fingers instinctively covered her mouth. Clearly, the memory of what happened on our high school graduation day lingered for both of us all these years.

"She promised to come to the ceremony. Clap for me when I walked the stage and got a diploma. She even bought a new dress . . . a yellow one . . . her favorite color."

I squinted, homing in on the vivid memory of returning home alone after other families had gathered in the school auditorium for photos of smiling graduates and clusters of best friends.

The yellow dress lay crumpled on the floor outside the closed bedroom door. Behind the door, giggles and moans rose and fell in an off-beat rhythm. The putrid sounds signaled why I flew solo on my special day when other students took flight in a grand send-off from what we'd known as familiar for the majority of our childhood lives.

With my closed fist, I had banged on the door. The sounds ceased. Footsteps shuffled on the wooden floorboards and the door creaked open, exposing my mom wearing only a loosely held bedsheet.

"May, baby." My mother's red-lipstick lips puckered. "What ya' doing here? Yer supposed to be at school, darling."

"I was, but it's over." I stepped back, distancing myself from the waft of whiskey. "My graduation ceremony."

Mom cocked her head, returning only a blank stare. Finally, as if a light bulb illuminated a faint path through her foggy and intoxicated brain, her face scrunched.

"Darling, I am so, so sorry . . . must've overslept again." She extended one hand toward me as the sheet partially slipped from her body. "Forgive me, honey?"

"Come on back to bed, sweetie. Getting cold in here." The gray-haired man appeared behind my mom, wrapping both arms around her.

I took another step backward.

"Hey, May. What's new?"

I wrapped my arms around my own waist, wishing away the rising nausea in my gut. "Not too much . . . just graduated from high school an hour or so ago." Sarcasm and anger boiled in me like poison.

"Well, goody for you. Congrats." He smiled a crooked, stained-tooth smile. "You know what that means, don't ya?"

I slowly shook my head.

"Yer on your own now. Time to get booted out the nest." He squeezed my mom and she giggled. "Right, babe?"

My eyes locked with my mom's glassy eyes as I waited for her response.

After what seemed a lifetime, she finally whispered, "That's right, honey. Just like in the bad winds, the nest is knocked down and the babies gotta fly or die."

I couldn't tell if her eyes filled with tears of sorrow or of joy. I suppose it didn't matter.

The diploma I'd been holding dropped to the floor. The tears I'd been holding as I scanned rows of seats, spotting familiar mothers, but not my own, let loose. I turned and ran out of the house to the only place I knew to escape—Liv's home.

My mom ditched town that day with the scraggly haired guy whose only fame was being caught on national news at Woodstock fifty years earlier in his birthday suit and living on and off the streets ever since. Liv and I vowed never to mention or even walk near the rickety house that was eventually bulldozed and left vacant for the ferns and woody trees to overtake.

Liv took my hands and squeezed them. "May, I'm so sorry. I didn't know about the dress."

"Because we swore to never talk about it."

Liv nodded. "But maybe that wasn't the best way to heal from all that happened."

"Probably so." I sniffed and forced a smile. "But secrets are meant to be kept. Right, my friend?"

"Indeed." This time it was Liv who motioned for the bartender.

"I like this side of you, Liv. A little less serious, a lot more fun."

Liv propped her elbows on the bar and folded her hands together. "Then tell me how I can help you make your dream come true . . . leave this place if that's what you want. Get a fresh start."

"I might need some extra money. You know, just to get things started. I have a decent amount of savings. My hourly wage still stinks, but the rent is cheap for my room above the gallery." I lifted the fresh beer and took a deep swallow. "Of course, I'd pay you back once I get established."

"That could work." Liv lifted her beer to mine. "To your new adventure. May, renowned gallery owner extraordinaire."

"Cheers." It felt good to smile a real smile.

CHAPTER TWENTY-THREE

Olivia ~ Walnuts

After May dropped me off at the house, we shared a hug that lasted a little longer than in the weeks prior. Perhaps the tension and grief from the initial shock of my father's passing was subsiding and our friendship would be renewed.

May needed me, at least for moral and even financial help, to send her life in a fresh direction after nearly a lifetime being stuck in Kennett Square. I was happy to share some of my monetary success with my friend who always had little to nothing in life. Except for putting money back into my company, personal accounts, and a few charitable causes, I had no one else to share with or support from the fruits of my success.

Selfishly, God only knew how much I needed a friend to talk with, someone who knew and understood the complete Liv—hard and invincible on the outside, yet soft and vulnerable on the inside. Life was challenging always trying to keep the moving parts in order—successful career, stellar reputation, full travel and speaking schedule, and gracefully fending off signs of another and another year added to my birthday calendar.

My life was good, actually great, on most accounts. But I was tired . . . tired of mistrusting and second guessing the intentions of others, tired of being guarded instead of loving . . . loving deeply like I did when I was an innocent child. I was tired . . . tired of being alone.

The looming black walnut tree in the front yard must have read my mind. Its tremendous branches swayed in the wind while blackened husks covered the grass below.

I kicked a cluster to the side, the messy tannin sticking to my tan loafer just as it stained my bare feet as a child. Each autumn, Father would rake the fallen husks on to the gravel driveway, rev up his Chevy truck and drive over the hardened walnuts. *Bang! Crackle! Pop!* The sound of crushing walnuts was like fireworks, and much to Mother's disgust, the driveway was a mess for weeks. But despite the lingering black stain and bits of husk that forced me to wear shoes after a long summer's freedom, the bounty Father and I pulled from each walnut husk was worth it.

Mother usually watched from the front bay window, but often at this point in the process, she'd join us outside, slip on gardening gloves, and help place the nuts in water. Any that floated got tossed into the trash.

"The nutmeat didn't form properly," Mother would say. "Lay all the others out to dry . . . indirect sun, two weeks, maybe three. And, Olivia, be sure to scare the squirrels away." I wondered if she'd been secretly harvesting black walnuts for centuries.

When the walnuts were finally dried and brittle, Father and I spent hours cracking them open and retrieving the delicious nutmeat. Mother never helped with this part. "Too loud," she said, covering her ears with her hands and retreating back to her cottage studio.

I kicked another pile of husks, adding another blackened smear to my shoe. I didn't care. No, I *couldn't* allow myself to care.

Despite the mighty tree flourishing and providing its bounty year after year, no longer was anyone living at this home to accept the gifts it offered.

I walked to my car, started the engine and again drove away from a tainted childhood memory.

CHAPTER TWENTY-FOUR

Grant ~ Time Out, Cape May

Taking time to pause had never been my strength. Now, watching the ocean from the deck of the beach house, I was still. The approaching and just as quickly receding tide was in perfect tempo and direction with how my life rolled, at least up to this point. Success, failure, success, failure—the pattern was the ebb and flow of my past. However, taking charge of my family's museum and the good fortune of meeting *The Girl in White* caused a seismic shift. From now on, she would be my good luck charm.

I removed the smooth green jade stone from my pocket, caressing it between my thumb and forefinger as I had done for many years. My mom had sent it to me after she split with Dad. I suppose it was her shot at a peace offering for wrecking our family. It had arrived via mail in a crumpled envelope, doodled with peace signs, hearts, and butterflies. The scrawled note inside stated the stone held magical powers—promised to bring me happiness and success. Looking back, I think she must have been high when she wrote it.

I stood and surveyed where the sand met the aquamarine blues of the water's edge. Life was different now. I'd moved on from wishing for mediocre. Instead, it was the big leagues now and a little pebble wasn't cutting it any longer. I cocked my arm, winding up to throw the stone into the sea. I stopped. Instead, I set the stone on the broad arm of the Adirondack chair. *Maybe it's best to first make sure that Ms. Danford comes through for me with this case.*

Settling back into the chair, I dialed Olivia's cell. "Hey, it's me, Grant." I hated to appear anxious to see her, but there was more at stake than missing out on time spent with a beautiful woman.

"Oh, hi, Grant. Glad you called. Again, I apologize for not making it to the Cape today. I planned on calling you later this evening after I get back to the city."

"Then you're still part way up the coast?"

"Just leaving Kennett Square. I had business to take care of at my father's house. Met with the caregiver who helped take care of my father. Lots of loose ends still."

"Nothing that can't wait one more day?"

"I can't imagine all that's piled up at work. Although Joel said it's been fairly quiet the last few days."

"Then turn around and come meet me. I'm still at the beach and you could make it before dark . . . besides, I have an update on the provenance for the painting."

"Really? Now you've caught my interest."

"Ouch." I chuckled. "Not even a slight interest in me?" An awkward silence followed. "Liv, I really want to see you. Sounds cliché, but we could at least hold hands and watch the sun set."

Another silence and then she spoke, "Cape May. Hmm? I think my best friend, May, would approve."

"Then I'll see you in a few hours?" The rise in my voice surely gave away my excitement—both to see Olivia and find out the progress on securing *The Girl in White.*

"On my way." She paused. "And, Grant, only holding hands sounds just about right, especially if there's business talk to be had."

"Scout's honor." I held up two fingers. *Or was it three?*

Prolonged ocean gazing would have to wait. I had housework and grocery shopping to do. Impressing Ms. Danford trumped anything else on a typical vacation agenda.

*****

As if I ordered the perfect sunset, juicy orange faded to cotton candy pink with hints of lavender just as Olivia pulled up to the beach house.

Like an anxious schoolboy on a first date, I opened her car door and extended my hand. "Quick, there's still some left."

"My bag and—"

"I'll bring it in afterward." I smiled my best white-toothed grin. "There's a surprise."

Olivia took my hand and together we jogged along the short path around the house where it met the silky sand. "Here, leave your shoes."

She slipped off her mules and we stepped barefooted toward the sea.

"Oh, Grant. This is absolutely lovely!" She spread her arms wide as if embracing the view.

"Look what else," I gently took her face in my hands and turned her toward the beach house. Admittedly, I had outdone myself. The patio was adorned with a table set for two—pressed tablecloth, vase filled with freshly cut purple hydrangeas, and softly glowing candles. "Dinner soon, but first . . . " I took a few steps and beckoned her with my finger. "Let's enjoy."

Minutes before she arrived, I added a final touch with a sprawled beach blanket, a picnic basket filled with a baguette, grapes, an expensive cut of my favorite Roquefort, and an even more expensive bottle of cabernet.

I watched her as she settled on the blanket and took in the subtly changing hues of the sunset. The pastel palette played off her smooth complexion, illuminating her ocean eyes. *She is stunning.*

It felt oddly natural sitting quietly next to her—no need for small talk or nervous chatter. Instead, for several minutes, the only sounds were the lapping of the waves, the breeze carried on the water, and the waning calls of migrating ospreys. In unison, we sighed. Perhaps both of us needed an excuse to pause and simply be still.

"Of all the masterpieces I've encountered, I don't think any can fully compare with a sunset. God's craftsmanship beats them all, hands down." She nodded in agreement with herself.

"Do you think there is a God out there?" I scanned the darkening horizon. "Someone who made all of this?"

She appeared deep in her thoughts, not responding at first, but tilting her head as if calculating what to say.

Finally, she spoke. "I believe none of this was by accident. Nothing is merely by chance." I joined her as we reclined on the blanket, resting beneath the earliest hints of visible stars. "Yes, I'm sure of it. I wasn't brought up in a church . . . " She smirked. "And I haven't been in one lately. But yes, I know in my heart, even since I was a little girl, that God created everything. I don't understand most of it, but there's a purpose for it all."

"How so?" I turned on my side toward her and propped myself with an elbow. "Do you think us being here together isn't by chance? Maybe part of a bigger plan?"

She turned on her side as well, our faces closer than I expected as there was an awkward pause. She grinned and I took that as permission granted to remain in place.

"I guess, Mr. Richard, we will have to wait and see."

A warmth ran along my body, despite the cool breeze blowing in from the sea.

As the last glimmers of color faded behind the lighthouse, we shook the sand from the blanket, gathered the picnic basket and headed back to the beach house.

When I slid open the wide glass door, the pungent smoke was the first clue the rest of the evening wouldn't follow a Nicholas Sparks-inspired romantic oceanside tale.

"Crap! I forgot the salmon!" I rushed into the kitchen and yanked open the oven door. The remnants of the blackened fish greeted me. I brushed my arms through the air as I ran in a circle opening windows. "In there!" I pointed to a drawer. Olivia grabbed a hot pad, pulled the pan from the oven, and plopped the fish in the sink.

"Well, it's cooked through . . . that's for sure." She giggled as we stood together, peering at the still sizzling fish.

"Indeed, it is." I shook my head. "Painful."

"What? The fish?"

"No, my pride." I chuckled. "I suppose him, too."

"You know, I'm pretty full from the cheese and bread." She patted me on the back. "You, too?"

"I'm a survivor." I slid my arm around her waist and she leaned closer. *Funny how little mishaps lead to better things.* "Hey, I have an idea. We can go out for seafood. There's plenty of places around here that know how to treat a fish better. Or even drive a little farther to Lucky Bones. They have great brick oven pizza."

"Either works for me. You choose."

I paused. *If there's anything to a name* . . . "Then Lucky's it is." *I could use a good dose of it tonight.*

*****

Cape May Hazy Pale Ale and pepperoni pizza were the perfect combination. Conversation with Olivia was easy, not like most of the other women I'd taken on dates, and even considered having a longer relationship. She was smart, witty, and pleasant. More importantly, there was something that we shared—something unspoken and tucked away. It wasn't easy to pinpoint, but likely designated on the trodden map of both of our lives, marking points in time of deep and piercing pain. I was sure Olivia and I stepped gingerly around our past—guarded and unsure whether to let others visit that tender place.

Perhaps it was my second beer, but I decided to venture further. "How are things going with your father's estate? You mentioned there are lots of loose ends?"

"There are. Kind of silly, actually. I wouldn't call what he had much of an estate. Only a run-down house and a small bank account. I suppose he was the proverbial starving artist. Talented for sure . . . I wish I'd noticed that earlier, maybe been able to help him monetize his gift more than selling his paintings as one-offs in a local tourist shop."

"Was he always an artist? I mean, was that his profession?"

"Not always. When I was younger, he worked at the DuPont facility in Kennett Square as chemical engineer. Super intelligent man. Later, he started a side business restoring artwork, mostly paintings, for some of the smaller galleries in D.C. I think that's when he discovered he liked to paint as well. From that point on, he always had a piece in process on his easel at the house."

"What about your mom? Did she work? I don't recall you mentioning her."

Olivia took a bite of her pizza, wiped her mouth with a napkin, and then proceeded to fold it into smaller sections.

"Sorry, you don't have to answer." I leaned back in my chair, taking note of her furrowed brow.

"It's okay. She was an author . . . wrote children's books."

"Wow. I hear those are the hardest to write with so few words."

"I've heard that too. For her it was probably easy since she never had much to say . . . at least to me." Liv shrugged. "My mom spent most of her time in her writing cottage in our backyard. There were lots of times my father had to make her come out and go to bed."

"Isn't that kind of a writer's thing . . . getting so immersed that all sense of time is lost?"

"Especially if the writer is depressed and couldn't care less about her kid." Olivia's eyes widened, as if surprised by her own admission. She lowered her head and spoke softly. "I'm sorry. That was harsh. I suppose she did love me in her own secret way."

I was quiet, lost for a moment in my own past—a mixture of messed up parental love, sweat, and plenty of tears.

"She killed herself when I was twelve." Olivia's tone was matter-of-fact, as if stating the weather. "That pretty much ended any happily ever after for my family of three."

Usually able to find the right words, my brain stumbled and tripped back to my past. I reached across the table and gently squeezed her hand. "Losing a parent is hard . . . you never forget it."

"You've lost a parent?" Her voice was soft.

"Both of them, in an odd way." Was I ready to step into a personal and fragile arena?

"What do you mean? Did you lose them . . . tragically?" Her eyes narrowed.

"Lose them? Losing your parents." A slight chuckle followed. "That's a funny way to think of it."

"Why is that funny?"

"It's the semantics. That's all." I chuckled again, perhaps from nervousness that this taboo subject, by my own admission, was unleashed "Think about it. If parents lost their kid in the grocery store, or a crowded amusement park or packed sports stadium, they'd panic. They'd be terrified until the kid was found."

She wrinkled her nose, obviously unsure where my line of thought was leading.

"But imagine this. The same setting, say the grocery store, but instead of the kid, it's the parents who get lost. And over the loudspeaker a deep voice booms, 'Two parents are available to be claimed at the lost person counter . . . a middle-aged balding man with gray hair, a slight paunch, and wearing a particularly obnoxious Hawaiian party shirt. The other lost person is a fairly attractive middle-aged woman with large lips, large hips, and large, uh . . . If either or both of these persons are described as someone's parents, please claim them as soon as possible.'"

Her wide-open eyes apparently begged for clarification.

"I tried to claim them. Bring them back home, so to speak. Bring them back to their senses. But at that point in my life, I was a confused and angry teenager. Dad preferred his new, carefree lifestyle and the life-size Barbie Doll he'd hired as an intern at work. Mom, well, she couldn't handle the seismic shift in her life. She pretty much broke free from the mainland, left me on the shoreline, and has been floating in search of anything that anyone promises will bring her happiness."

"Then your parents are still both living?"

"They are. Living, but lost." He puffed out a deep breath. "Pathetically lost to their selfish dreams and desires."

I shared my rocky past with Olivia—Dad's faithfulness to being unfaithful to Mom. Her ensuing insatiability to find purpose and utopia in all the wrong places. Result? An only child who, as a result of my parents' screwed up lives, got left in the Unclaimed Kid Bin.

I felt a flush creep over my face. Now knowing Olivia's mother took her own life and her father recently died, my situation was tepid in comparison. It was foolish to wallow in things that I couldn't change.

"Do you ever talk with your mom or dad?" Her question seemed pointed.

"Not really." My mind scanned through a mental calendar. *When was the last time we spoke?* "Mom tries to call on my birthday . . . but she's got the date wrong the last several years." I forced a weak smile. "And my dad . . . I called him when I got the position at the museum. Figured he'd want to know the family news."

"And I assume he was happy for you? Maybe even proud?"

Surprising myself, I laughed aloud as I recalled his response. "Well, if I remember correctly, he basically told me I wouldn't make any money as a museum director and, more importantly, not to screw it up and disgrace the family name."

Olivia's mouth dropped open.

"I know. Pretty harsh." I lifted my beer toward her. "But hey, here's to survivors. Cheers."

We clinked our glasses, perhaps a pact to tuck away our pasts and focus on the present and future.

"So, tell me, how is our *The Girl in White?* I've been dying to ask about the initial tests."

"And I am *dying* to know what you know about where's she been and what's she's been up to all these years." Olivia smiled a sly grin. She was back in her game, and I needed to keep up with her pace.

"Aha, then you believe she has been around a long time... hanging out in Modigliani's personal studio in some dark, Parisian alley." I leaned forward, elbows on the table, inviting more information.

"Well, the team, or I should clarify, the lead researcher at Winterthur I mentioned, William Barrett . . . he and I got a much closer look with the ultraviolet light."

"Yes, go on."

"There appears to be an underlying pentimento . . . a sketch, maybe even another painting or part of one, under the surface pigmentation."

"Is that good or bad?"

"Could be either. As you know it was common practice for artists to make several attempts on a canvas, change the composition, paint over areas." She ran her forefinger in swirls on the tabletop. "The question is, does the underlying image match up with a known or similar sketch by Modigliani?"

"So we dig deeper."

"Yes, with the help of an expert on the master painter. Someone with extensive and thorough knowledge of the catalogue raisonné." Her finger tapped the table. "If there's anything in a comprehensive and annotated listing of all his known work that resembles the pentimento, then we might be on to something."

"And I'm sure you've perused everything that exists?"

"Of course, at least what Joel and I could find . . . and we're awfully good. Besides, if we already knew about the existence of a Modigliani portrait titled *The Girl in White*, we'd be miles ahead and only determining whether this one is the genuine or a clever fake. The fact she isn't recorded . . . no prior description, title, or notes about her, she's a greater mystery."

"A mystery, yes, but not ruled out that she could be real."

"True, previously unknown works of art do occasionally surface." Olivia grasped her hands together. "Grant, that's why it's imperative that the anonymous owner of the painting, even if he or she wants to stay unknown, provides proof of provenance."

A surge of defensiveness rose up in me. Maybe it wasn't too wise to leak the tidbit of information to a museum board member that I'd been given word from the seller that proof of provenance was in the works. Heck, I didn't expect the balding man in the pin-striped suit to prematurely spill the beans to the other members. The emails that poured in soon after he and I had coffee in the museum café confirmed word has a way of traveling quickly when money and notoriety are at stake.

"Olivia, if she's authentic, and I believe she is, then I know you'll do everything and anything to bring that truth to light."

Her eyes softened, the approachable Olivia I gazed at on the beach only hours earlier. "You're right, Grant. Truth has a hard time hiding in the dark for long."

I clapped my hands. "Then bring on the light, Ms. Danford. Let it shine."

"Grant, you know I shouldn't venture an opinion at this point regarding the authenticity. It's not like me at all to step outside professional boundaries and—"

"But you're hopeful." I winked. "I see it in your eyes."

She blinked. "Well, all I can say is Professor Barrett is setting up the detailed scientific testing protocols. There's chemical analysis to be done that tells us more than meets the eye. He wouldn't waste the time and resources if it was obvious we have a forgery. I'll know the testing schedule in a day or two and I'll head back to the Winterthur lab to work alongside him."

"Then I'd say both you and I have work to do . . . separate assignments but all for one worthy cause." I lifted a near-empty glass. "Cheers to the museum director and his sidekick art expert?"

She raised her glass in return. "Hopefully . . . to the three of us."

We left the restaurant, both patting our full bellies. Not only was my stomach full, but my mind as well with both doubt and hope churning as to whether my efforts would be met with success or failure.

"Hey, Liv, you mentioned the need for an expert on everything and anything Modigliani." I took her hand. "I'm curious. Who would that be?"

"Liam Elliot." Her head perked up. "And I happen to be talking with him tomorrow when I return to the city."

I watched her slender body slip into the passenger seat. "Perfect. I'm sure you'll let me know how that goes."

As I shut her car door and walked around to the driver's side, I breathed deeply and then let out a full breath. *Olivia Danford and The Girl in White...I'm not certain any longer which of you consumes more of my heart.*

CHAPTER TWENTY-FIVE

Liam ~ To Call or Not to Call

For what seemed the hundredth time, I tossed the worn tennis ball for Bella across the backyard. It was the perfect diversion to avoid eye contact with my dad.

"For crying out loud, son, put down that slobbery ball and give the woman a call. You need to take action if you want to get her attention." Dad cleared his throat. "Not trying to tell you what to do . . . but by the looks of it, you need a little advice from a seasoned gentleman on the subtleties of dating."

"Since when have you been subtle about anything?" Blond and beautiful, my golden retriever dropped the ball at my feet. "Good girl." I patted her on the head as she stared at me with pleading brown eyes. "See, I don't need advice as to how to get the attention of a good-looking girl."

Dad dismissed my comment with a wave of his hand. "I give up."

To be honest, I had thought about Olivia actually often since our morning together at the Guggenheim Museum in Venice.

Perhaps it was an odd detail to remember, but I was drawn to the slight crease that ran down her forehead as she listened intently to the museum docent describe some of Modigliani's elements of his signature painting style—long, oval faces with unseeing eyes, reddish nudes posed against textured backgrounds, slightly askew.

Olivia was smart, no doubt about it, and I appreciated her willingness to be a student, too. There were plenty of big heads in the academic art world—too many who thought they knew all and were all. I appreciated that Olivia was humble. Like Dad, the fact she'd come across so many fakes and forgeries in her pursuit of truth must have made her that way.

As though she was a mysterious painting, there was something else that intrigued me about Ms. Danford. I first noticed it when we exited the museum door, just in time for her to thank me for the meeting and catch a passing vaporetto back to her hotel. She had smiled at me, a lovely smile. But, like an ornate and beautifully detailed Venetian mask donned only once a year for the Venice Carnival, her smile seemed to hide something. As quickly as Olivia Danford had come into my life, she floated away, leaving me to wonder who she really was.

Dad patted me on the shoulder, snapping my mind back once again to my home in Raleigh, North Carolina.

"Liam, I'm calling her."

"Don't do that." I stood and stretched my back. "The last thing I need is my dad making calls for his forty-year-old kid."

Dad lifted an imaginary phone to his ear and smiled a wide grin.

I rolled my eyes. "Fine. You win. I'll call her tomorrow."

"Why not today?"

"Fine. Today."

"I'm calling her, too." He reached into his shirt pocket and pulled out his cell.

"You are ridiculous! I think *you* have the hots for her too."

"Aha!" Dad wagged a finger at me. "You admit it."

That comment was my cue to toss Bella yet another ball.

"Liam, of course I don't, as you say, have the hots for her. Your mother was the only woman who ever got my blood boiling, in the best of ways." He winked. "I merely need to follow up with her about the Matisse I'd shown her in Venice." He puffed out a loud breath. "That one still hurts . . . thought it was a real contender until Olivia determined the canvas was produced in the 1970s. The authorities don't have any leads, probably will never catch the scoundrel that passed it off to the New York gallery where it surfaced."

"Yep, that one was a heartbreaker. I know you were counting on it to be the Golden Sleeper." I returned a pat on his back. "You'll get 'em next time."

"Hope there is a next time. I'm only getting older while the crooks get better and better."

I scoffed. "Amazing, really. As time passes, there's less and less chance of the authentic masterpieces surfacing, but more and more opportunities for forgers to make a fortune."

He shook his head in disgust. "That's right. More lies, more deceit. God's told us all along . . . the dark will become darker—"

"And the light, lighter." I wrapped my arm around my dad's shoulder and gave him a hug. "You always told me truth will eventually win, right?"

"Absolutely." He gave a slow nod, and a small glimmer in his eye might have been a tear.

*****

While Bella rested in the shade of the sprawling maple tree, Dad was surely napping by now at his home only ten minutes away. I smiled and shook my head at the thought of him—loved him dearly, but seriously, I needed a little more independence by this point in my life.

Then do something about it! Even my subconscious was harassing me. *All right!* I picked up my phone and scrolled through my contacts. *I'm sure I have her number from our meeting . . . or was it a date?* "Olivia Danford." I whispered her name as I tapped the call button.

"Hi, Liam. Great to see you pop up on my phone." Her voice was upbeat. "I love it when this happens! I was just about to call you."

"Really?" I chuckled in disbelief.

"You've been on mind and we have so much to talk about." She paused. "Again, sorry I had to cut our museum visit short, especially the fascinating history lesson. I bet you could have talked about Modigliani for hours."

"And really live up to my reputation." I settled in the patio chair and crossed my legs. "The book nerd who hangs out with dead artists and has no life of his own?"

She laughed. "Believe me, I've been called the same."

"Then I'm in good company." I smiled. "So why have I been on your mind?"

"I need your help. The purported Modigliani I told you about . . . " Silence hung between us. "There's a good chance she might actually be real."

"I'm listening." As if a juicy prime rib was placed before me, my mind couldn't help but salivate. "How can I help?"

"Come to Winterthur Museum to view her. My colleague William Barrett and I have done initial tests and, from the results, we're committed to dig deeper."

"Intriguing." I sat forward, my mind racing with the possibility of witnessing the discovery of a previously unknown work over a hundred years since its creation.

"I can fill in the other details, but we think there's a pentimento, perhaps elements of a drawing. You might recognize it, or at least elements that would signify if it's from Modigliani's hand. Barrett is arranging further elemental and chemical tests as we speak."

"When do you need me?" I didn't want to seem over eager, but hey, this kind of talk was better than a high-impact action film. "I'm in the middle of a lecture series at the university and a few other speaking commitments."

"First of next week, Monday." A no-nonsense note had replaced her lively tone. "It's important we hash this one out sooner than later. There's too much riding on this piece."

"How so?" I rubbed my chin, a familiar gesture Dad often did when perplexed about or questioning the validity of a piece of art. "What exactly is at stake?"

There was silence on the other end of the phone, and I wondered for a moment if we'd lost our connection. Then I heard her clear her throat. *Did I overstep?*

"Let's just say . . . reputation . . . and not only mine."

"Hmm." Clearly, my response begged for more information.

"We'll talk more next week when you arrive."

"Let me see what I can juggle around on my calendar." Had I even agreed yet to come?

"Liam, by the way, why were you calling me?"

Good thing we had distance and a phone between us as I felt my face flush. "Oh, thought you might have questions or need more information about Modigliani's catalogue of work." I hesitated. "And . . . to say hello."

"Oh, hello, then." She giggled. "I'll text the time as soon as I have details from William. Well, see you next week."

"I'll do my best." I ended the call as Bella plopped her ball at my feet, puppy dog eyes fixed on mine and tongue hanging. "You women won't take no for an answer, will you?"

CHAPTER TWENTY-SIX

Olivia ~ Tag Team

I had learned a great deal from Liam's history lesson about Modigliani—his childhood in Italy, his doting Spanish-Jewish mother, his mostly absentee father, and his budding passion for art as a prepubescent teenager. We also spoke of the adult Modigliani, living in the Montparnasse quarter of Paris, painting and sculpting in his dimly lit one-room studio flat, often high on opium and sometimes drink. He had admired Pablo Picasso and Chaim Soutine, joining them in stylistic distortions of faces, necks, and bodies. Unlike Picasso, whose work was wildly accepted during his lifetime, Modigliani's work appeared edgy, and to some, even distasteful. But Liam had an almost poetic manner of describing the master's unique and memorable artistic style. Most definitely, Liam Elliot knew the dead man better than most.

However, one thing I learned from my time in the art world: there is always much more to uncover. Like two speed walkers, Joel and I briskly navigated the cracked and uneven sidewalks in the Dupont Circle neighborhood leading to the Richard Museum. From years of mature tree roots heaving the slabs of cement, pedestrians were wise to tread carefully in this quaint, historical area of D.C. that contained a world-renowned art museum.

For us, we were on a mission to reach the museum at opening time—not to meander the Rothko Gallery of contemporary abstracts, absorb the hues in Van Gogh's *House at Auvers*, and the moody composition of Delacroix's *Paganini*. Instead, Joel and I were going subterranean—into the museum's windowless basement that housed the archival library. Our mission was to spend time with all things Modigliani—at least, anything and everything the Richard Museum had to offer.

Typical of Joel, he lugged his bulging and worn leather bag on his shoulder. It was filled with tan Moleskin journals, black ink pens secured together with a rubber band, one-inch square pads of yellow sticky notes, two pairs of readers with varying strengths to compensate when his eyes tired from hours of researching, and his laptop computer. Mostly old school. That's why I loved Joel, and we made a good pair.

For me, I carried a small lined notebook, used primarily for jotting to-do reminders and items needed at the grocery store. I liked to travel light as my brain was constantly filled. Father claimed it stemmed from his side of the family, as I could read volumes of textbooks and recall most if not all of the information that was pertinent. My mind had worked that way all my life—elementary through high school tests were a breeze, undergrad and graduate school exams the same.

Names, faces, and even past events and places have always been etched like a fine lithograph into my mind. It's as if my brain is a sponge—read, do, experience something, soak it up, and file the information, and even many of the associated sensory details, as if I'm a human filing cabinet. In many ways, this gift as my teachers and professors called it has also been a curse. When certain memories of my past surface, I wish they could be tossed overboard, sink to the depths, and be forgotten forever.

*****

Joel and I arrived at the museum entrance just as the doors were unlocked and a sweet-smiling, gray-haired greeter welcomed us in. We exchanged good mornings, accepted a flier detailing current and upcoming exhibitions and events, and headed directly to the stairwell that led to the archives. Perusing the prized treasures of the Richard Museum would have to wait. Joel and I had work to do.

As though part of the decor, perched behind a sprawling desk was the archival librarian. When we approached, she raised her eyes over purple-rimmed half-readers and smiled. Her hair was grayed at the roots, followed by a frenzy of short orange curls that appeared to bounce with excitement when we said we were here to do research. She reminded me of a vibrant, tropical, wide-eyed bird—not what I would have expected in the depths of a hushed museum records room.

She peered around the orderly stacks of books, magazines, and filing folders.

"Good morning. How may I help you?"

"My friend and I would like to see what research sources you have for Amedeo Modigliani," I said.

"Isn't that something?" She removed her glasses, and despite the wrinkles around her eyes, they sparkled. "There's been more interest in his works lately than I can remember."

"Really?" I shot Joel a side glance. "How so?"

"Well, the new museum director . . . another Richard family member . . . he seems to have an interest in the artist. He was down here a couple days ago asking for resources." She leaned in closer and whispered, "I shouldn't speculate, but there's a rumor the museum might be close to a very valuable acquisition."

"A Modigliani?" Joel whispered back.

Orange curls bobbed a silent *yes.*

"You don't say?" *He's such a tease.*

"And then a Georgetown student working on her doctoral dissertation in art history asked to see the files as well. It's strange how past artists' popularity ebbs and flows over time. Van Gogh, DaVinci, Michelangelo, Rembrandt, Picasso . . . they'll always stay on top."

I couldn't help but insert my favorite. "And Matisse. He'll always be worthy in my mind."

"True. I *love* his work." She rolled her head as if to swoon and then clasped her hands together. "So, if both of you can sign and date the register, we can get started."

For a moment, I hesitated revealing my true identity. It felt a bit strange to retrieve any leads regarding *The Girl in White* figuratively under Grant Richard's nose. Being a professional, I have other sources to tap into than on the same turf as a client. *But this isn't a conflict of interest. I'm merely turning over any unturned stones.*

Joel had already spent countless hours at the National Gallery of Art in the East Wing, Ground Gallery. The nation's treasured Modigliani collection is breathtaking and comprehensive—one that any fan or not of the master would find intriguing. Like a bloodhound, he had sniffed out five current catalogue raisonnés in that museum as well, putting in countless extra hours looking for any clues that could lead us to the portrait's past. As usual, Joel had proven himself indispensable to the forward momentum of an investigation.

"I've been at the Richard for thirty-five years and know the books, catalogues, prints, articles . . . anything art history and provenance related . . . quite intimately."

"I can only imagine," Joel chimed in. "Thirty-five years . . . you must love what you do."

"Can't imagine doing anything else." She was short in stature, and when she came around the side of the desk, her diminutive frame was accentuated as she looked up at us. We had signed the registry, and now the librarian placed her hands on her hips, her feet set wide. For a moment, it felt as though we were to have a standoff—us against the protector of the files.

"So what specifically are you looking for regarding Amedeo Modigliani?" The name rolled off her tongue like a soothing melody. "The master of Expressionism . . . and of course, his famous nudes. I assume you've viewed, or plan to see, *Elena Povolozky* upstairs?"

"All of her?" Joel interjected with a laugh.

"Oh, she's not nude, instead, a lovely face portrait. Elena was one of the artist's best friends and supporters in Montparnasse." The librarian added, "It's believed she often provided food and money to Amedeo and his close artist friend Chaim Soutine."

I couldn't help but add, "Yes, I'm familiar with the portrait. Painted in 1917, and if I'm correct, the Richard acquired it in 1949, after a couple graphite pencil sketches in the early forties." But my thoughts were already racing to unfamiliar information about the artist's work. "We'll be sure to stop by and tell her hello today before we leave, but for now, my friend and I would like to take a look at other sources—auction and exhibition catalogues for example—anything else that speaks of provenance."

"Letters, receipts, lesser known sketches or journal entries." Joel was already unlatching the buckle on his bag. "Whatever you can provide, we'll dive in."

She nodded and then disappeared into the maze of bookshelves and filing cabinets that she assuredly knew how to navigate to locate the information we requested.

After nearly fifteen minutes, she reappeared, pushing a rolling cart heavy with legal-sized manila folders stacked haphazardly, several books and yellowed newspaper articles, mimeograph papers, and wrinkled magazines. As she parked the cart, the familiar smell of musty paper, reminiscent of aged vanilla, wafted in the air. At once, my appetite stirred, ready to devour all things history, and in this case, all things Modigliani.

"I apologize the files are in disarray. That student I told you about . . . she asked if she could take photos with her cell phone and make lots of copies. She did and then got up and left in a hurry."

"Late for class?" Joel asked.

"Who knows, but she left me with this mess." She shrugged. "People these days."

"It's fine." Joel helped me roll the cart toward a large, empty table where we would most likely spend a good part of the day. "We really appreciate you pulling this much for us."

"Any time. We art lovers know how to have a good time." Before returning to her position behind the desk, she stopped and glanced back at us. "Curious though . . . what brings the two of you in to spend time with Modigliani?"

Joel and I hesitated, and then offered in unplanned unison, "Just big fans."

"That's right," Joel accented, "Big fans."

CHAPTER TWENTY-SEVEN

Olivia ~ In Good Company, Winterthur

There's not much better than being in the company of another who lives for discerning the truth, especially when it comes to art authenticity. The only thing better is being in the presence of *two* others who share the same goal.

Liam had made the six-hour drive from his home in Raleigh to Winterthur Museum. I appreciated he rearranged his schedule to join William and me. Besides, I knew he looked forward to meeting Professor Barrett and was especially motivated to meet *The Girl in White*.

Barrett and I were already in the research lab discussing the planned scientific testing when Liam arrived. We exchanged introductions and were talking about recent articles in *ARTNews* when Bertrand entered the room with the portrait.

For me, it was impossible to tire of looking at her. That same *something* about her still mesmerized me. It was if the little girl kept a secret that was intended for me. Whether or not William and Liam were as infatuated, I watched them stare at her as Bertrand carefully laid her on the table next to the high-powered microscope.

Liam approached her first, leaning in closely and cocking his head. "She's stunning . . . better than I expected."

William joined, hovering his finger over the letters in the upper right edge of the canvas. "Modigliani. Most definitely signed in the artist's typical fashion. Do you notice where he picked up the brush between letters?"

"Yes, and only using his surname and written in all lower-case cursive." Liam pursed his lips. "It's possible the painting is authentic . . . or, a—"

"Clever fake," I interrupted.

Both men turned and looked at me. My words were abrupt with a definitive tinge of anger. Where had that come from?

I grimaced. "Sorry to be a little black cloud." I forced a smile, hoping to add levity to the conversation. "I just hate to be fooled."

William and Liam continued staring at me and I felt compelled to explain what must have been written on my face. "I don't know exactly why, but I can't seem to shake a gnawing feeling that the painting is both real and fake."

Barrett turned both palms up, teetering his hands like an imaginary scale. "Well, Olivia, it's got to be one or the other. There's no room for middle ground when it comes to what's real or not. I'd venture the three of us have learned that truth many times over in this profession."

I rolled my shoulders and straightened my back. "You're right. Let's get on with the testing and get to the bottom of this."

"Before the samples go under the microscope, I want Liam to take a close look at the pentimento we discovered." Bertrand handed William the fluorescent light and dimmed the overhead lights.

As before, a slight designation appeared under the surface of the painting—curved lines, oval spheres, and hatch marks darkening the certain areas against lighter, untouched parts of the canvas.

Liam gestured to the eyeglasses on the other side of the table. "May I?"

William handed him the magnifying loupes, and Liam proceeded to lean in as closely as possible to the painting, careful not to touch its surface. "There's definitely an image that was applied before the paint." He hovered for several minutes, scanning the canvas from left to right, and top to bottom. "I could be wrong, but the strokes and forms of the lines and shapes are indicative of him."

"Dedo?" My voice raised a little too quickly. "You recognize the marks as Modigliani's?"

Liam stood and arched his back. "I do." When he grinned, his cheeks reddened. "And they follow the contours of what he most likely would have sketched while studying the posture and features of a young child sitting before him." He set the eyeglass on the table. "The lines are loose and seem to be quickly drawn . . . but then again, how could one expect a baby to sit still?'

"Then who was she?" Though the statement escaped my mouth first, I knew we must be asking the same thing.

"She could have been a friend's child, but there is no mention of a painting like this in any records. Most likely, she is their young daughter, Rachel . . . the only living child of Amedeo Modigliani and Jeanne Hébuterne." Liam shook his head. "After all these years of studying their lives, it still saddens me that Modigliani's lover chose to take her and their unborn child's life in such a tragic way."

We were silent for a moment, perhaps sharing an unspoken moment of respect for the three long gone people of the past.

"But this is what stumps me . . ." Liam rubbed his forehead as if organizing his thoughts. "The eye color doesn't match what could have been their daughter's dark brown, like her father's. However, Jeanne's were blue."

"The eyes are definitely blue," I added. "Windows to the soul."

Liam stepped toward me and then was still. "He painted them robin's egg blue . . . just like yours."

I raised my hand to my face, realizing my fingers were shaking. Why in the world did this painting unnerve me? Why did it seem there was so much at stake?

As all empirical researchers do, William got us back on track. "It's time to learn the facts." He tapped his foot three times on the wooden floor, the same gesture he used many years ago when I was in his class and his patience had thinned with lackadaisical students. "But you're on to something, Olivia. Like you, I'm unsure why this particular painting seems to have an unusual and emotive hold on us. Maybe we're all too human and yearn to be part of something really big." He locked eyes with me. "Or maybe it's something else. Something personal? Perhaps something we aren't even sure about."

As if I had been stripped naked, a vulnerability swept over me. Had I crossed the line and allowed my feelings for Grant to persuade my professional judgment—assure his successful reputation and future with the help of my expertise? Had my feelings for him become that strong? Or, if I was completely honest with myself, did it go deeper than that? Was I so desperately wanting to find true and trusting love that I'd lost my true north?

I steadied myself on the viewing table and sighed.

"Olivia," Liam's hand rested on my lower back. "Are you okay? You look a little pale."

I shook my head and quickly gathered my internal self. "I'm fine. Probably hungry. In all the excitement, I forgot to eat lunch."

"We'll grab a bite soon." Professor Barrett was already in his element, adjusting the configuration of the high-powered swing arm magnifier for optimum viewing. "Because, as the Bible says, 'eat and drink, for tomorrow we die.'"

"Well, that's depressing." I scoffed.

Liam winked at me and smiled. "At least we'll die with a full belly."

As the four of us, Bertrand included, gathered around the observation table, I couldn't help thinking we looked like a band of Egyptologists eagerly awaiting the opening of a tomb.

Barrett was quiet for several minutes, shifting his weight from one foot to the other as he peered through the round lens. Finally, he spoke. "Olivia, take a look." He stepped back. "Tell me what you see."

As we exchanged positions in front of the magnifier, my heart raced. I gave William a slight smile, and then aligned myself with the eyepieces. "Craquelure."

"Move the lens around the painting." Barrett whispered.

Slowly, I edged to the left, then up, circumnavigating the head of the little girl. "Distinct cracking of the oil paint . . . as I would expect."

"Keep going." Barrett's voice was stern.

I continued traveling the intimate details of the painting—brushstrokes appearing like hills and valleys under the intense magnification, hues changing from light to dark, and then back again, until I landed in what seemed like a sea of white.

"Stop there." Barrett was leaning over my shoulder, and we both knew what we saw.

"It's not the same." I spoke softly. "The craquelure is different on her dress." I pushed away from the table.

"Help me out here," Liam said. "What exactly are we seeing?"

"Or not seeing might be a better question." Barrett motioned Liam to the area beneath the lens. "Do you see that spiderweb-like cracking?"

"Yes. I'm familiar with that patterning that happens with oil painting over the years. Typical"

Barrett added, "Absolutely, but move the lens. Travel around the painting like Olivia did."

Liam traversed the canvas, retracing the direction from which I had traveled.

"Do you see it?" I asked.

He was silent at first, moving slowly up, and then down again. "It's different. The cracks look different from one section to another."

Now, Liam backed away from the magnifier, allowing Bertrand time to inspect the painting as well. While the assistant took his turn, the three of us stood in a small circle, staring at one another until Barrett spoke.

"It's subtle for sure . . . thought my eyes might have been fooling me. But, the craquelure definitely changes on the girl's dress. Therefore—"

"Something is amiss." I rubbed my moist hands together.

Barrett extended his hand to Liam. "And you, very well done. To notice something that slight without conservation training. I'd say you're a natural."

Liam accepted the gesture. "Thank you, but I know we wish it didn't exist."

Barrett turned off the LED light to the magnifier and gave a side nod to Bertrand. "Well, let's not stop there. Time to go even deeper . . . to the molecular level, that is. I'll get the team to process the samples we took right away and hope for a report as soon as possible."

I nodded. "Thanks for pushing the process. I know the analysis can take time."

"We can get what we need with several fractional samples taken from the dress area, and maybe a dozen or so from other portions of the painting." Barrett pulled a pen from his lab jacket pocket and jotted some notes on the clipboard Bertrand offered. "We'll check the elemental signature of the paint mediums as well. A lot can be told from the pigments and binders used and the paint brands available in the artist's time."

"His color palette varied, but chrome and cadmium yellow, ochres, vermilion red, chrome green, and Prussian blue were favorites. Of course, he mixed rich organic colors, using lead and zinc white to change values and imply highlights."

"And what about his canvas prep?" I had already studied about Modigliani's brand preference but was curious if Liam knew otherwise.

"Lefevre and Foinet was the most typical dealer of the time. Some say the artist preferred to use pre-made canvas with an industrial primer instead of a mix of bone extracts and white primers." Liam rubbed his chin. "And we have to remember, Modigliani was dirt poor, and until his dealer Léopold Zborowski sold some of his work, our artist friend got by on minimal art supplies, not often using an easel, but nailing and painting many of his works to his plaster studio walls."

"Exactly. The *Woman in Sailor Shirt* we viewed in Venice, that painting had four slight holes, one in each corner, where he had hammered the canvas on to the wall before beginning to paint her."

Liam approached *The Girl in White*. "I just thought of something that might be on the back." William and Bertrand carefully lifted the frame, setting the portrait on its painted side. "See this black paint along the wrapped edge? That was common of many artists of the time to measure a perimeter area that would eventually wrap around the stretcher. You can see that was done here." Liam ran his finger around the four sides of the rectangular frame. "And the size . . . a standard French number ten, fifty-five by forty-six centimeters—"

"The most common size for a portrait," I added.

"Yes, especially in the early 1900s." Liam was a walking art history book, and I was sure he was only sharing his prologue of knowledge about Modigliani. "But like his contemporary, Picasso, he liked to break the so-called rules so there is nothing entirely consistent or predictable about his creative process."

William appeared to be intently listening to Liam, nodding in agreement while pacing the room. "So, to summarize," he stopped mid-sentence and changed direction, "there appear to exist signs of a painting that was potentially created after the turn of the century and into the early 1900s. The stretcher, canvas preparation, existence of a craquelure, although that remains a mystery, color choices, and even an underlying pentimento—a sketch of sorts—*could*, and I emphasize *could*, point to an authentic Modigliani is in our presence."

Now it was my turn to play the other hand. "Or, as we all know the greater likelihood, we have a compelling forgery by a proficient con artist." I took one last look at the portrait before gathering my bag. "On the surface, she looks so good."

Barrett gave me a slight hug. "But we know what lies beneath is what makes all the difference."

CHAPTER TWENTY-EIGHT

Olivia ~ Heartbreak

For two days while waiting for the forensic results from the Winterthur lab, Joel and I huddled in the small conference room at Axiom, poring over books, articles, photos of Modigliani's paintings, and even his beloved tribal-like sculptures. After hours upon hours of research, I was certain Joel's laptop was close to emitting smoke, and I made a mental note to get my eyes examined.

Modigliani captivated Joel and me to the point we, too, adopted his nickname of Modi. Even though proving or disproving the authenticity of *The Girl in White* didn't rely on how intimately we knew the artist's history, or even his known 349 known pieces of work, our appetite for ingesting as much information about him was insatiable.

Joel continued to fix his eyes on the computer screen. "Breaks my heart Modi gave away many of his paintings in exchange for food—"

"And absinthe and hash." I pointed to a paragraph and read aloud. "Even though poor, he lived a wild life . . . even known for taking off his clothes at parties when he was on one of his common alcohol or drug binges."

"True, and the fact he destroyed who knows how many canvases and drawings when he went off. What would drive someone to do that?" Joel pursed his lips.

I ran my hand over a jumbled stack of articles and copies, reminiscent of the disorderly sheets of typing paper scattered on my mother's cottage floor. *Damnit! This is awful!* Her typical sentiment screamed from the past, a prelude to the memory of her crumpling papers, sometimes blank or containing only a word or two. Other times, there were multiple sheets, most likely a completed story, abandoned and stuffed into the small wicker wastebasket next to her desk.

"Sickness," I muttered.

"Poor soul, the tuberculosis . . . bad physical health wrecked his life too early."

I breathed deeply, wishing the image of my mother from my mind. "And devastating mental illness. It's the worst of all."

"Such a shame, isn't it?" Joel's voice was monotone. "When the mind overpowers the body?"

The image of my mother remained—now on her hands and knees on the braided rug, frantically gathering the mess she'd made, determined to destroy her beautiful writing that had come from what I wanted to believe was the peaceful part of her brain.

The answer to Joel's question was obvious, but I couldn't bring myself to say it and only nodded, then stood and excused myself to freshen my coffee.

When I returned to the conference room after a mental time out, Joel held up my cell phone. "Barrett called. I told him you'd get back to him right away."

"And you didn't ply him for information?" I patted Joel on the back.

"I do my best. But you will put him on speaker phone, right?"

Again, I ignored Joel's question as I forced myself to settle into a chair. Getting the test results, either in favor or against *The Girl in White*, would be better received while sitting.

"William, sorry I missed you." My tone was intentionally calm as I reminded myself this was not my first forensic case. *You are a professional, Olivia.* "How are you? Having a good day?"

"Doing well, thank you." Barrett cleared his throat. "But I'm afraid our little girl isn't."

Across the table, Joel's eyes widened in what must have been in response to my dropping jaw.

"Sorry, I'm putting us on speaker now." I pushed the button. "Go ahead. We're listening."

"You recall the oddity in the craquelure pattern. It's subtle, but as we all observed, it exists."

"Yes, and it occurred to me it could be due to an added extender. Maybe Modigliani used a filler to increase the bulk of the paint, particularly in the whitest areas of the dress. We know artists add extenders, especially to zinc and titanium white, as the most acquainted shade."

"The team and I considered that, and in fact, an extender could easily distort the spider-like pattern from one area to another."

Joel and I nodded in silent affirmation.

"But we discovered something perplexing." Barrett paused. "Both the molecular and elemental tests point to the existence of a polymer . . . and only in the white dress."

Joel positioned a photograph of *The Girl in White* between us. For weeks, the image had been posted on the dry erase board in the office—the focal point of current cases with our to-do's, questions, and brainstorms added in brightly colored markers. Now, the eight by ten print lay on the table, her oval, aquamarine eyes staring back at us.

"Tell us more," I prompted Barrett.

"We know in the most simplistic terms, a polymer is a chemical compound that's made up of small molecules that are arranged in a simple, repeating structure to make a larger molecule."

Joel scooted his chair closer. "And there are different types of polymers: organic polymers found in nature and synthetic polymers."

"Exactly." Barrett continued. "Synthetic, or artificial polymers, are manufactured in a laboratory and have petroleum-based ingredients."

"Sure, Bakelite plastic was the big breakthrough in the early 1900s and discontinued in the forties . . . too expensive and eventually brittle in nature." I rubbed my wrist, recalling the brightly colored bangles, handed down from my grandmother that my mother wore on occasion.

"And now we have neoprene, nylon, polyester, rayon, polyethylene, and styrene . . . pretty much any plastic bag, storage container, Styrofoam cup." Barrett sighed. "Basically, most anything plastic and rubber, and even Teflon, resins, and silicone."

"And to home in on the art world, the invention of acrylic paint revolutionized the art world after the 1950s and opened an entirely new genre of painting. Though, in my opinion, it will never fully compete with the richness of oil paint." Joel crossed his arms.

I hesitated to say it, but the proverbial elephant was in the room. "If this material is anachronistic to the artist's known palette, then we have verification to question the portrait's authenticity."

Barrett was quick to respond. "Question, absolutely. Is the evidence conclusive . . . indisputable? I'm not entirely there. Even back in 1901, Otto Rohm had a patent for a polymer-based binder to help dry oil paint and lacquer."

"I thought of that." My mental file on the German chemist had resurfaced. "But the chances of it being widely used, especially in France and by an impoverished painter, would be unlikely."

"Then where does this both leave and lead us?" Barrett's question was rhetorical as he and I usually followed the same path of reason.

"I'd say we are left at a dead end and it's time to move on to another case. I'll call Liam and fill him in as well. We don't want to waste any more of his time thinking about this." It was my turn to clear my throat. "What would you suggest I say to Mr. Richard? I can't keep him in the dark any longer."

Barrett was silent for a moment, most likely choosing his words thoughtfully as he always did. "Tell him about the polymer and that the scientific analysis is complete. I'll email you the report tomorrow. And if I were you, I'd emphasize the results imply a clever, and I might add, masterfully painted forgery . . . especially before he gets even more ahead of himself and purchases what he promised to the museum to be a real Modigliani."

Joel rolled his eyes. "Excellent point. That would not play out well, and the museum would be looking for another new director."

Barrett chuckled. "Let's hope not. The new guy deserves a fair start. I understand him being overly excited about this one—she's a looker for sure, and if I'm honest, she almost had me fooled. But I prefer to side with the good guys to ferret out the fakes . . . find the truth and keep Modi's oeuvre intact"

"Like Superman," I teased.

"Truth, justice, and the American way," he bellowed in baritone. "Actually, with this painting, I'm disappointed, even sad that she's not real."

The thought of Grant being devastated, and possibly even disgraced at the outcome of *The Girl in White*, profoundly saddened me. I didn't want to admit it, but I'd allowed myself to step over my professional line. Being involved on a personal and even intimate level with an artwork in question . . . or person . . . was something I'd sworn never to do. *Olivia, you fool. You know better than to ever share your heart . . . it's only meant to be broken.*

CHAPTER TWENTY-NINE

Grant ~ Good News, Bad News

Tie, or no tie? I looked myself over in the office bathroom mirror, buttoning a freshly pressed shirt and baring my teeth to make sure no food remnants remained after a rigorous brushing. The earlier breakfast meeting with a "concerned museum board member" had gone as . . . expected. Apparently, word on the boardroom street was a growing agitation among the members that the new acquisition I promised to be revealed at the annual gala event was still missing.

"Mr. Richard, when can the members plan on viewing the acquisition?" The bottle-blond, blue-suited woman's question was no casual question. Her follow-up smirk confirmed I was running out of time to pull the rabbit from the hat. No doubt, *The Girl in White* existed, was not a figment of my imagination. However, proving her authenticity through material testing and unearthing the provenance remained key. And if Olivia didn't come through for me, the seller would be forced to provide solid provenance. A history of the painting's whereabouts for the last hundred years would have to be enough to calm further dissent. After all, too much was riding on this.

I grabbed a navy tie from the hook, effortlessly securing the perfect knot. I'd done the dance enough times in my adult life to realize how a piece of fabric around one's neck implied the seriousness of a situation. However, despite the importance of the approaching lunch date with Olivia, I didn't want to appear overly professional, and certainly not anxious—a tweed sport coat and slacks trumped a suit.

She insisted we meet at the members-only George Town Club. The restaurant and bar, known for its long history of high-powered, high-society, and high-stakes meetings over prime rib, lobster tail, and the finest bottles of wine and whiskey, weighed in favor of a boy's club. However, I had no doubt Olivia Danford held her own in the sea of attorneys, doctors, investors, and politicians, and surely turned a head or two each time she walked in the door.

Her text arrived last night as I was driving home, barely surviving another commute while swimming upstream to Alexandria. I try to make a practice not to read texts while driving, but getting word from her about the tests was top on my mind. I'd been patient enough, and it was overdue time for good news. Besides, I knew the next encounter with a board member, or possibly, the entire committee, would be like stepping in front of a firing squad. Responding to Olivia's invitation, I pushed the thumbs up emoji on the text, then continued to make my way home through the crowded civilian jungle.

*****

Now, back at the office after a restless night's sleep and needing to be both prompt and peppy to meet the board member, I was determined to be on time to meet with Olivia at noon. I accepted one call but made a point to avoid running into Shirley for my daily rundown of schedule and must-do's. Stealthily, I slipped out the back stairwell of the museum and sped away.

Despite my best efforts and miraculously finding a parking spot only a block away from the club, Olivia was already standing in front of the entrance. She was on her phone, head tilted in the same fashion as when I first saw her standing next to the conference room window. Admittedly, she was more stunning each time I saw her—a timeless beauty that brought out my schoolboy grin and left me weak in the knees.

I stopped a few feet from her and spread out my arms in a hug. She looked up, spoke into her phone, and then tucked it away in her purse.

"Grant." She returned an air hug that begged me to take her in my arms.

"Thanks for the invitation." I gestured to the blue awning, accentuating the main door of the two-story red brick corner establishment. "I've had the pleasure of eating here only a few times. My membership recently got approved."

Olivia gave me a sideways glance. "Ah, good to know they did a background check. They don't let everyone in."

I followed her inside where we were greeted by the maître d' who escorted through a cozy bookcase-lined sitting area, past a polished grand piano, and into a larger dining area adorned with intricately carved mahogany tables and finely upholstered chairs. An array of members and guests, both the young and upcoming, and the seasoned and most likely wiser, filled the room while sharing lively conversation over midday cocktails.

"Ms. Danford, I have you over here in the alcove, just as you requested."

"It's perfect, thank you." She smiled as he pulled out her chair.

"Enjoy your lunch." He nodded at me and retreated to his post near the front door.

I surveyed the crowded room from our set apart respite. "Busy place."

"It usually is." She unfolded her linen napkin and laid it in her lap, reminding me to follow suit. "I try to come here at least a couple times a month, sometimes for pleasure, but mostly for work."

"And what would today be?" I shared my white-teeth smile. "I'm hoping for a bit of both." As I sipped my water glass, an ice cube dislodged and a dribble rolled down my chin. As suave and sophisticated as I tried to be, moments like this were reminders that I fit best on the beach, sipping a pina colada from a straw in a plastic half coconut cup.

Before she could answer, the waitress arrived, wearing black pants and a starched white blouse. "Hello, Ms. Danford. It's always a pleasure to see you." The attractive dark-haired woman nodded toward me. "Welcome. What can I get the two of you to drink?"

A double shot of bourbon on the rocks. But of course, I deferred to Olivia to answer first.

"Thanks, Stacey. I'm fine with water today." Olivia pointed to the leather-bound drink menu. "Grant?"

"Water is perfect for me as well. Thank you, though." As much as a stiff drink sounded delightful, a sharp mind was necessary. I was clearly in Ms. Danford's territory.

While I perused the menu, Olivia was quiet, perhaps allowing me focus to read the ample offerings. However, when I closed the book, her lips were pressed together and her brow furrowed as if in deep thought.

"You okay?" I cocked my head. "Something on your mind?"

She took a deep breath and rolled her shoulders. "Oh, you know me, always thinking about something—"

"Good, I hope." I reached across the table and gently held her hand. "And by the way, you look as beautiful as ever. I've been thinking about you ever since you texted."

"The same." She removed her hand from mine. "Busy schedule today at the museum?"

"Not too bad. Hanging out with dead people tends to keep a slower pace."

Her blank stare confirmed she didn't follow my lame museum joke.

"The artists . . . you know . . . the painters and sculptors . . . most, if not all of them, aren't around anymore."

She grinned and gave a slight nod.

"Besides, there's nothing on the day's agenda that's more important than being here with you."

I wasn't begging for the same response, but a little positive affirmation would go a long way.

With eyes cast downward, her manicured forefinger ran along the handle of the dinner knife. If her motion hadn't seemed absentminded, I would have been paranoid that I was about to go to the slaughter.

I leaned forward and whispered, "Olivia . . . is something wrong?" Despite the steady conversations and bouts of laughter in the dining room, a silence hung in the air as thick as if we were dining in a cigar smoke-filled room. "You seem a little . . . off."

She crossed her hands on the table and locked eyes with me. "The painting . . . *it's* off."

"Off?" I shifted my weight in the chair. "What exactly do you mean? The *deal* is off?"

"Grant." Her eyes narrowed. "I didn't realize we had any sort of *deal*. On behalf of the Richard Museum, I've been hired to authenticate or not a piece of art. I don't consider that working a deal."

I leaned back in the chair, crossing my arms with my hands tightly in my armpits. "Forgive me. That was a poor choice of words, but frankly, your verbiage is perplexing. So what specifically makes the painting *off*?"

"My apologies as well. Off is an ambiguous word. Perhaps a better choice is—"

"Unusual?" As if glued to my armpits, my hands remained fixed. A flickering memory of my college psych 100 reminded me of the reality of body language. My defensiveness was surpassing a safe water mark, but I didn't like the direction of our conversation.

"Yes, there is most definitely something unusual about the portrait." She smoothed the already smooth tablecloth with the palm of her hand. "Grant, this is hard for me to admit, but I've become too close to this case."

"You're done?" My voice rose an octave and my mind began to reel. "With *me*? Is this about us?"

She shook her head. "No . . . I mean, sort of." Her face was flushed, and mine felt the same.

"Olivia, I am so confused." I breathed out, allowing my hands to finally retreat to a locked position on the table. "What are you saying?"

As if her spine lengthened by several vertebrae, she straightened her back and sat up tall. "The painting is most likely a forgery . . . a very professionally executed one, but still, a fake."

If stomachs could actually slip into one's feet, mine would have oozed out of my shoes. I forced myself to grow a few inches in my chair as well. "And why is that a possibility? You did say *most likely*, so that leads me to believe you and your team of experts are not positive."

"You are correct on two counts. First, even after a series of thorough scientific tests that document our suspicions, which are being detailed in the written report as we speak, there remain unanswered questions that make us curious and continuing to research."

"I see a glimmer of hope." I grinned, but Olivia wore her game face and didn't return my smile. "And two?"

"Between Professor Barrett and his organic chemists and conservation scientists at Winterthur, Liam Elliot's vast knowledge of Modigliani's style, materials, and catalogue raisonné, and under my tutelage, I assure you, we *are* experts in the field."

"Touché." I gestured a mock sword thrust toward my heart. "I wasn't implying that at all. Obviously, I hired your firm with the knowledge you are the best in the business. But you can't blame me for being disappointed that the tests are questionable."

"There's a polymer detected in portions of the painting that most likely didn't exist during Modigliani's lifetime."

"There's that *most likely* again."

"Yes, but remember, he died in 1920 and manufactured polymers didn't exist until much later. There's also a crackling pattern found in aged oil paintings that isn't consistent across the painting. That's a red flag as well." As if holding an invisible pen or pencil, she drew curved lines on the tablecloth. "But what I can't get out of my mind is an underlying pentimento . . . a sketch beneath the surface painting, that the team, especially Mr. Elliot, says would be in line with our artist's style of drawing and even preparatory work on a canvas before beginning the actual paint application."

"And the brushwork, colors, composition . . . all highly consistent with the artist's work," I added.

She raised an eyebrow. "And you've been doing your own research?"

"Moonlighting, my dear. Always working."

She returned my smile.

"But seriously." Her game face returned. "The proof is in the testing, and without proof of provenance, the painting will never stand as an authentic Modigliani." Now, the creases between her eyes softened and the Olivia I held on the beach and gazed at over a candlelit table returned. "Grant, you do realize it's both of us that want her to be real."

"I do." *Though I have much more riding on this than you.* My stomach had settled but was still doing slow-motion somersaults. "And if you'll give me a few days, promise to hold off on delivering the final report and conclusion to the museum . . . I'll have something that could turn this whole case upside down."

Olivia scooted her chair and leaned in to the table. "Now I'm confused."

"Provenance, baby. The seller is ready to produce papers proving the lineage of our painting." I smirked. "We're about to find out where our little girl played hide and seek all these years."

"Why are you just now telling me this? And there's still the polymer and the craquelure to consider. Don't forget science plays heavily into this hand."

"Ah, but there's always a wild card."

As Olivia smoothed her hair, I knew she was thrown off with my news. It was refreshing to finally have a hand up during this lunch meeting.

"Shortly before I was leaving to meet you, I got a call from the seller. Actually, a person who oversees business dealings for the seller. He, she . . . who prefers to remain unknown, is ready to provide proof of provenance so that the sale can move forward. God willing, let's hope it happens soon." I rubbed the back of my neck. "To put it mildly, the museum board members are getting restless."

"Well, I hope they aren't beating you up badly. You know better than anyone that they too are responsible for the museum's money and reputation." Olivia wagged a finger at me. "Don't say I didn't warn you. Don't promise them anything until we know more."

"Then you promise to keep the report under wraps for a few more days." My voice was flat, yet firm. "If the provenance turns out to be fraudulent, then I'll concede the science, confirm the painting is forged, and approach the board with my tail between my legs. However, if the paperwork is solid—"

"Then my team and I will scrutinize our analysis and take the next necessary steps."

I extended my hand across the table and we shook. *Now, we do have a deal . . . and I prefer to win.*

I looked around the restaurant. "By the way, and not to sound rude, but is it odd that the waitress hasn't returned for our order?"

Olivia winked. "I'll wave her over. This staff works hand in hand with the members when negotiations, and even not-so-palatable discussions, are at hand. I figured the news about the report would have spoiled your appetite and I could save a buck or two." She smiled.

I stretched back in my chair and patted my stomach. "Oh, I'm hungry . . . in fact, I'm starving."

CHAPTER THIRTY

Olivia ~ Meeting with May

I exited the highway and followed the winding roads toward Kennett Square. Thick forests of rich palettes of greens and browns saddled both sides of the road as sunlight peeked between the canopy of trees. I lightened the pressure on the accelerator, taking in the lush surroundings. Despite meeting May and the attorney in fifteen minutes to sign papers to finalize my father's estate, I breathed differently.

Seamlessly, over the past twenty years, I had adapted to the fast-paced city life of D.C. Axiom thrived while building a steady and reputable client base. At the same time, I enjoyed attending theaters and museums, frequenting a vast array of restaurants and boutiques, and keeping a committed schedule at the pilates studio near my renovated and immaculate federal row house on Book Hill. But even with a full schedule, I wondered if my life was complete.

Now that Thomas had passed and May was no longer his caretaker, it felt good to reconnect, hopefully reestablish, an old friendship that had tarnished over the years. The shiny and bright camaraderie we'd known as children and even into our awkward teen years had been neglected. And to be honest, most of that was on me. Perhaps my father's death would be the catalyst for new life for both May and me.

I parked my Lexus next to May's old truck, noting the rust around the pickup's fender and numerous dents. Parked side by side, our vehicles were the perfect metaphor of our lives—May's rough and tumble, and mine sleek and smooth, at least on the outside. I fumbled with my purse, tucked away the keys, and quickly went inside.

"Hey, Liv." May was seated in the waiting room, flipping through a magazine. "How was the drive? Bad traffic?"

I glanced at my watch. "I'm on time, right?"

"You're good." She closed the magazine, stood, and gave me a hug. "I figured you'd be late fitting this into your day."

"No, I made a point to clear my schedule. It's important we wrap this up so I can focus on selling the house."

"And I can move forward with Santa Fe." May pushed her hands into her jean pockets. "It's not getting any cheaper to find a place to live and rent gallery space while I wait around here."

"True." I tried to smile, but I couldn't fake it. "You know I'm excited for you . . . and supportive, too. Of course, these aren't the best circumstances for us to spend time together . . . " I gave a side nod to the attorney's office door. "But I'm really going to miss you. We need to make a point to stay—"

"I'll miss you, too."

The office door opened and a petite, young, dark-haired woman greeted us. "Hello, May. Ms. Danford." She extended her hand to me. "I'm Janice Bell, your father's attorney for the past, oh, I believe six or seven years. It's a pleasure finally meeting you. I'm sorry about your father's passing."

Finally meeting me. Whether intended or not, the guilt jab continued to poke at my conscience. "It's nice to meet you, too." *You look as if you're still an undergraduate. Or am I getting that old?* I nodded toward May, "I've been very fortunate to have my friend taking good care of my father's estate."

"Absolutely. It's good for all involved to have a competent executor." She invited us to sit at the small conference table as she opened a manila folder and distributed sets of copies. "Another good thing is Mr. Danford's will is straightforward and in order. One can never underestimate the importance of planning ahead and having personal business in order." The attorney smiled, most likely at her own sales pitch. "May and I have reviewed the documents and need to go over them with you. Then we need some signatures to finalize the process."

"That's fine." I pulled my readers from my purse, holding them to the ceiling light, and then wiping them with the cleaning cloth in the eyeglasses case. I needed a moment to gather myself. As the only child and sole heir of Thomas Danford, it was awkward to learn of his wishes for his assets and possessions only now. I wasn't surprised his will was uncomplicated. My father, though a hard worker and committed husband and family man, preferred to live a simple life— no bells and whistles. However, by my own admission, I chose to ignore the details of his life while I attended to mine. Now, sitting in the illuminated lawyer's office, I was the one who was in the dark.

After reading through the standard last will and testament of Thomas Danford, the woman asked if I had any questions. The document was mostly as I had expected. Being the only child, Father had designated me as the sole beneficiary to his assets, including his remaining pension from his years at DuPont that he had been receiving to cover his minimal living expenses, a small balance in his checking and saving accounts held at the old Santander Bank in the town center.

The home mortgage had been paid off several years ago, when in conjunction with his pension income, Thomas built up a solid business restoring artwork for several East Coast museums and galleries. The hours were odd, often working on projects late at night and on weekends, filling what I suspected were the lonely gaps when he missed my mother's companionship.

Now, the house would be sold—his messy, living room art studio, my mother's secluded and secretive writing cottage, and the surrounding two acres of dense forest with a small pond would pass on to someone else. I hoped the new occupants, perhaps a family with a little girl, would make better memories than mine.

"We have one more important document to go over." The attorney handed May and me each a single-sheet copy. "This is your father's tangible personal property memorandum. As you can see the date and his signature, he completed this about four months ago. Per law, the document would not be legally binding if he had completed it at home, but fortunately, May was able to drive him to my office for him to sign and have it notarized."

"I'm a little surprised I wasn't aware of this addition." I looked at May. "Especially if you made a special trip to have the document signed."

"He thought it best to have the original in the attorney's file." May shrugged. "And looking back, he was pretty sharp still in the late winter . . . before he began slipping closer to summer."

The itemized list, though handwritten, was precise and legible— different from the mysterious note I'd found in stacks of papers on his desk the day of his funeral. The penmanship of this list was articulate and focused—similar to how he approached his realistic paintings.

Instead, the scrawled words on the discovered note, though artistically stroked, were abstract and emotive—seemingly created from an artist's mind versus that of a person attending to business at hand.

"Olivia is the sole beneficiary, but Thomas had a few items he designated to May. Even though the two of you are longtime friends, this was wise of him to document his wishes. You can see on the first line at his request, that May receive his inventory of oil paintings."

"Yes, and Olivia graciously had me take those from the house when we began clearing things out." May folded her hands on the table. "Several already sold at the Triple A here in town. Once word got out he was no longer around to paint, people snatched up his work. Like you suggested, Liv, I've kept a handful to add to my initial gallery stock when I get moved and settled."

I lowered my eyes, considering my words carefully. "If you end up with an extra painting, I might like to have a piece of my father's work . . . especially before they're all gone." A lump filled my throat. "I should have talked with you about that. I figured you'd sell some but keep the special ones."

Though surely not uncommon in an estate attorney's office, an uncomfortable silence filled the room.

Finally, Janice spoke. "Let's continue. Bequeathed to May, three gold American Buffalo coins, valued at approximately five thousand dollars. Of course, the monetary value is dependent on the current market."

"I didn't know Thomas was a pirate." I forced a smile, attempting to ease the tension.

"And a notorious one at that." May chuckled. "You okay with this one, Liv?"

"I don't need the money." As soon as I spoke, I regretted my words. "And anyway, it was his decision. Even if he had a treasure chest filled with gold, he and I could never repay you for the care and companionship you gave him."

"Only a few more line items. Let's see . . . A Corona manual typewriter . . . for Olivia. All inventory of children's picture books authored by Anna F. Danford." Janice stared at me. "Fascinating. I've always wanted to write children's books. I assume a close relative?"

"My mother." I swallowed hard. "Anna Danford was my mother."

"How special. I bet she read great bedtime stories."

I exchanged a quick glance with May. Silently, we shared the reminder that it was Thomas, rarely Mother, who tucked two little girls in bed and read one of Anna's happily ever after stories.

Janice bobbed her head between May and me. "These items must have special meaning . . . hopefully you know where they are?"

We nodded, and I could only imagine May too was thinking of Mother's silent cottage with closed-curtained windows and a locked door that would soon need to be opened.

*****

The meeting with the attorney to sign papers went well, no glitches or issues that would prolong finalizing the estate. However, the familiar tension between my shoulder blades had returned. The momentary peace I'd enjoyed while driving to the appointment had dissipated like the lifting of the morning mist. Instead, thoughts of having one foot in Kennett Square to deal with selling the dated and dilapidated house while still contending with the Richard Museum case put me on edge. Hopefully, May's insistence that we grab a coffee before I drove back to work would give me the pep I needed to effectively have my feet on two shores.

We sat at an outside bistro table near the planter boxes filled with orange and golden mums. I took a deep breath, taking in a tinge of cooler temperatures and the crisp aroma of fall—plants, trees, and leaves dying—a scent of morbidity disguised as my favorite time of year.

"Liv, I'd like you to stop by the gallery and take one of Thomas's paintings. There's some really pretty autumn landscapes, and you might see one that you'd especially enjoy . . ." She sipped her cappuccino. "Even though he left those to me, it seems you should have a piece of his artwork."

I surprised myself that I even paused to consider the offer. To have one of my father's oil paintings displayed in my home would be nice—a small piece of him nestled into my daily existence—an unspoken means to think of him often and what he loved to do most. A single piece would be enough, having prided myself on being a minimalist—only necessary household items and certainly no visual clutter.

But to be honest, May's gesture was bittersweet. Why didn't my own father leave what little he had to his own daughter? It should be me gifting a painting to May, not the other way around. Instead, the tangible items that held the most intimate and authentic qualities, hopes, and dreams of my father had fallen from the family apple tree and landed in the basket of another's bounty.

My mind wrestled—justifying my blood lineage versus childish jealously. *Defer to neutral ground.* "That's sweet of you. I'll think about that."

"Well, don't wait too long. My plan is to leave town in a couple weeks. If I have a chance of opening even a small gallery before the holidays, I need to get on it. Plus everything is so expensive to rent. I plan to look around in some outlying areas as well."

"Have you thought of buying?"

May rolled her eyes. "Are you serious, Liv? I'm not made of money like you."

"Oh really?" I wanted to make light of her comment, but her words were weighted with envy. "But I did say I can help you get started. A friendly loan to make a gallery deposit or on a place to live. You can pay me back once you get on your feet."

"Hate to do that . . . and of course, you'll get your money back as soon as possible."

"When you have a chance to do more research, let me know the amount you might need and I'll see what I can do." I sipped my coffee and pondered my offer.

As children, I often played the motherly role with May when her real mother was incapable. It was me who retrieved the bread, peanut butter, and jelly from the pantry and made sandwiches. It was me who pulled a clean t-shirt and shorts from my dresser drawer, offering them to May and reminding her to add her stained and dirty clothes to the laundry pile for me to wash when my mother did not. It was me who ran a brush through May's matted and tangled hair, her flinching as I whispered it would be all right.

Thirty-some years later, sitting across a table from my friend as she shared dreams of launching into a new life, I still wanted to help. Even though having May around to check off the to-do list to sell the house would have been beneficial, it was time for May to fly. If I could help her jump, just like when the creek on our property swelled with the springtime rain and made it hard for May to cross, it was worth it to coax her into taking a running start and leap wide.

May twisted a strand of hair around her forefinger and then rummaged through her handbag. She pulled out a package of Eve

Slim cigarettes and a matchbook and plopped them on the table. "Are you up for taking a to-go cup? I really need a smoke."

"Actually, I don't need more caffeine or I'll be up all night." I pressed into the table, eyeing the matchbook. "Hey, I know this place." I pointed my finger at the dark blue matchbook, etched with the familiar gold logo lettering. "George Town Club. That's my private club. When have you been there?"

May's finger returned to her hair, twirling layered locks around and around. "*Your* private club?" Her sarcasm was obvious.

"No. I'm just surprised you have that matchbook. It's exclusive and—"

"Too nice of place for a girl like me?" May shoved her cigarettes and matchbook back into her bag. "Geez, Liv, you know how to make a person feel low."

"May, that's ridiculous." I folded my napkin too many times and tucked it under the saucer. "I'm just curious when you were there. I guess I didn't know you'd been in the city."

"Apparently, there's lots you don't know about me." May turned up her chin. "I'm in D.C. a decent amount . . . spend time with a guy who loves to tour the art museums and check out new exhibitions. He's a big foodie, too. We love to try new restaurants . . . and oh, he belongs to that same club as you."

"Really?"

"I've gone there with him once. We shared oysters on the half-shell." May ran her tongue across her lips. "Really tasty."

"I wonder if I know him. What's his name?"

May zipped her bag and then bottomed out her coffee with a long swallow. "Bruce Anderson. He's in finance."

"Huh, doesn't sound familiar. But there are lots of members, and *lots* of money people." I smiled, not wanting to turn the conversation south with any false assumptions on my part. "Well, good for you. Maybe we can all catch dinner at the club and I can meet him."

"Most likely not. He and I might or might not hang out again." May stood and pushed in her chair. "Remember, time is ticking and I'll be out of here soon."

We walked back to our cars, which were parked side by side, exchanged a hug, and promised to call each other in the next day or so. Before May was even settled in her driver's seat, smoke billowed from a cigarette dangling from her mouth.

I called out to her as I unlocked my car door, "I thought you were done with the smoking." I wagged a finger in the air. "It's not good for you."

May threw her truck in reverse and leaned out the window. "Thanks for the reminder, Mom. I'll work on that." She smiled a wide grin and drove away.

CHAPTER THIRTY-ONE

Olivia ~ Proof in the Provenance

The offer was tempting to join Grant in Cape May for the weekend. Setting the phone aside to fake an interruption from Joel so I could wrestle with my common sense reminded me again that I am consumed by work. The salty ocean breeze, painted sunsets, and sand between my toes sounded heavenly after a particularly busy week at work, especially if time away would be shared with Grant.

However, the call with Grant felt disjointed. He was insistent that we head north for a brief getaway at the beach house, promising good conversation, great food and drink, and even a surprise. For me, despite the obvious and taboo attraction to my client, a nonromantic setting was best to confirm the news about the portrait.

I'd held off longer than typical in delivering solid scientific results that *The Girl in White* hadn't passed the litmus test of authenticity. Even if the seller provided a source of provenance, there was too much evidence in Barrett's report that the portrait was forged. *I can't wait any longer.*

As I did often, I turned my desk chair around and looked at Elmyr de Hory's forged Matisse, which beautifully graced my office wall. From past experience with clients hopeful that they possessed a priceless treasure, the objective empirical disclosure was best conducted in the conference room at Axiom—where truth is revealed, whether to the liking or disdain of the client, and business is done at its best.

Admittedly, when Joel stepped in my office to tell me Mr. Richard had arrived for our appointment, my face flushed. I fumbled with the stack of folders on my desk, hoping Joel hadn't noticed.

His wide grin proved otherwise. "It's game time, coach."

I stood, smoothed my dress, and walked into the foyer.

"Grant, thanks for agreeing to meet with us and coming to the office." It felt odd offering a handshake, but we were on professional turf this time. "This works great for us. Joel and I have been slammed with new cases . . . a fascinating Matisse that's promising. And a O'Keeffe that could change the deceased artist's narrative if it proves to be real."

"Enchanting." Grant accepted a water bottle from Joel. "These dead artists seem to constantly pop up . . . no luck keeping them in the grave."

"And keep us in business." Joel raised his bottle in a toast. "Cheers."

"Cheers." Grant returned the gesture. "And I still wonder why I stepped into this wacky art world. Seems surreal much of the time."

"Ah, you must be hanging out with Salvador Dali," Joel quipped.

"Come again?" Grant scrunched his face.

"Sorry, bad art joke. My boss reminds me daily that I'm a failed comedian."

"True." I nodded toward the conference room entrance. "Shall we get started?"

As Joel led the three of us along the short hallway, Grant leaned his head alongside mine. A hint of his familiar cologne sent a tingle down my back. "You have great digs here, Liv, but the beach house is better."

I gave him a slight smile, tucked my hair behind my ear, and followed Joel into the room.

We settled around the table, Grant across from me and Joel to my right. The final report from Winterthur and my professional summary were on the table, bound neatly into Axiom's signature style report, one copy for me and one for Mr. Richard.

Since my company's inception over ten years ago, I'd captured the hearts of my clients with the news they hoped to hear and unfortunately broken the hearts of more. Art forgery was a lucrative business and there would never be a shortage of fakes that made their way into galleries, museums, collectors' homes, and even the purported family one-off treasure—a priceless painting bought my Grandma Sue at the garage sale down the street. Whether good news or bad, the common denominator in all situations: . . . human nature ultimately desires to know the truth. Today was Mr. Richards's day to learn the hard way.

"So, Mr. Richard . . . Grant." I offered a copy to him across the table. "I realize you and I have spoken informally about the case results. However, in a minute, we'll go over the details of the scientific analysis that support the conclusion. But let's first take a look at the summary. Working backward often makes the most sense."

I slipped on my readers and opened the document. "You'll see on page—"

"I have a better idea." Grant clasped his hands together.

Joel and I exchanged glances.

"Instead, let's work forward." Grant slipped his hand into his jacket. "I've never been one to backpedal." He pulled an envelope out of the pocket and waved it in the air. "And there's no sense in wasting time when I have a better hand to play."

My eyes locked with Grant's. "I didn't know you came here to play a card game."

"Isn't reality just a house of cards?" His eyes narrowed—the usually dreamy hue turning a shade darker.

Joel, perhaps feeling the levity of the moment disappear, sank back in his chair.

In turn, I leaned forward, and propped my elbows on the table. "Are you concerned the house is about to come tumbling down?"

Grant grinned. "Not a bit." He laid the envelope on the table between us. "Solid rock . . . we're standing on the firm foundation of the master builder." He folded his hands together. "In this case, the *master painter*."

I eyed the sealed white envelope, slightly bent from being shoved into a suit jacket pocket. "I suggest we go over the report first and then—"

"No need." Grant tapped the envelope with his forefinger. "Ms. Danford, this is the proof of provenance we've been waiting for . . . received yesterday from the owner of *The Girl in White*."

My ears perked, but I kept my voice leveled. "Well, this certainly is a surprise."

"I promised you just that, and here it is . . . though of course, presenting this over a lobster dinner would have been much more climactic." Grant smiled. "Sorry, Joel. No offense nor intention to leave you out of the excitement."

"None taken. But I am intrigued since the in-depth research I've been doing to find any sort of provenance for the portrait has turned up empty. Quite disappointing, really."

"Well then, I'm thrilled I can help you out." Grant looked from Joel to me. "Apparently, the painting has been in the seller's family for three generations, acquired back in 1920, shortly after Modigliani died."

"So, we now know the seller?" My question was more rhetorical than not. If family history was involved, the seller would surely be ready to disclose his or her identity and explain the lineage of the portrait's ownership and whereabouts for nearly 100 years.

"Not exactly. Whoever it is, he or she is certainly private and I'm assuming very affluent. I pushed to meet in person, or at least speak on the phone, but no luck. All business has been conducted through private courier service directly to my office." Grant nodded at the envelope. "But, in the end, it doesn't matter. We finally have enough of the portrait's history to know she's the real deal."

"Date and location of purchase, sales receipt, a listing in a reputable catalogue raisonné?" Joel interjected. "That would be helpful, especially since Olivia and I have scoured any existing catalogues of Modigliani's work."

"Of course, the two of you are the experts, but I believe you'll find what you're looking for to finally make everyone happy, including the pesky museum board members." Grant's smile widened. "We can finally rest easy that we've struck gold with a real Modigliani."

"May I?" As I reached for the envelope, Professor Barrett's words played in my mind. *There's so much that's right about the portrait, but the existence of a polymer . . . doesn't add up, Olivia.* I'd never doubted the aptitude of my former professor and his team of scientists. But just this once, I wished they were wrong. How incredible it would be to confirm a never-before-found painting by the bad boy of Paris— the genius rebel artist. And at the same time edify and elevate Grant Richard—the bad boy of the Richard family lineage.

Carefully, I unfolded the paper. It was a small paper—not an American size, 8 ½ by 11-inch sheet that was standardized in the early 1980s by President Ronald Reagan and used for nearly all written work since its inception. The paper I held was slightly smaller, similar to a common European standard used for writing, business notifications, and transactions. The edges had yellowed and felt thin and fragile. The faint smell of aged paper, reminiscent of the time Joel and I spent in the museum archival library, elevated my senses.

I adjusted my readers, making note of the faint writing that appeared to have faded over several years. The words were written in cursive script, most notably in a style characteristic of handwritten French. "Gallerie Paysage . . . on St. Germain Boulevard. The logo imprint is readable, however, I can't recall a gallery with that name . . . at least one that still exists."

Joel opened his laptop. "I'll do a quick search and—"

"No need." Grant interjected. "I did some of my own. The gallery was open only a few years, sometime between 1917 and 1922. I would have contacted them myself to check records if the company was in business. It was small at best, but apparently the gallery acquired a handful of Modigliani's paintings from Paul Guillaume, an art dealer who the artist met through Max Jacob and agreed to attempt to showcase the artist's work. As we know, Léopold Zborowski was Modigliani's main art dealer, who by the way was also an artist, poet, and close friend . . . he did his best to develop interest in the paintings. However, this piece is unique in that a different dealer was involved with its initial purchase."

"A possible reason for part of the difficulty in finding provenance." Joel rubbed his chin. "A hundred years doesn't seem that long ago when you consider the centuries of art creation, but it's all relative. Lots can get lost, stolen, and even forgotten in shorter periods of time."

"Impressive information." I eyed the paper closer and then laid it on the table. "La Fille en Blanc."

"Or, on this side of the ocean, *The Girl in White.*" Joel pressed forward. "And if I'm seeing correctly, acquired by the gallery in 1920—"

"From Guillaume." Grant pointed to the signature, and then reclined in his chair. "There you have it . . . the portrait of the same name, time period matching the painter's life, and a gallery location that aligns with where good ol' Guillaume could have hocked some of Modigliani's work. Both amazing and sad. The poor guy didn't live to make a penny off his work, yet here we sit years later with proof of his genius."

"Sad and tragic." I stood up and walked to the window. I needed a moment to gather my thoughts and decide the next move in this perplexing game. I always enjoyed the view from the conference room window—the Potomac River flowing effortlessly, predictably, and constantly. On any particular day, whether the current was slower or faster, gravity, a greater power, forever guided the water onward to its destinations.

Perhaps it was my gut instinct, or perhaps from an even greater power that I'd found myself calling upon more and more since my father's death, I was determined not to cry. Instead, I wanted only truth. Was it possible my father, despite his less than perfect lifestyle, did believe in God who hears and answers prayers? *God, please show me what is real.*

I turned and bobbed my head at Joel. "Well, Mr. Richard has provided fascinating news. Hasn't he?" Though his eyes widened, my assistant nodded in return. I would clarify things with him later. "I suggest we put a hold on the final report and summary . . . give us some time to digest the provenance findings, take a closer look at the gallery receipt, and then, if necessary, make any edits to the report."

"A quick ultraviolet test should tell us if the paper is authentic to the time period, or at least that it's not a contemporary fake." Joel took a swig from his water, careful to set it on the bureau behind his chair. "Don't worry, Mr. Richard. We'll take good care of the receipt."

Grant stood abruptly, forcing both hands on the table. "I need to have the report, confirming the authenticity of the painting no later than Monday. The board convenes that afternoon and I plan to present them the good news."

Usually, a client would not gain ground with me by forcing a deadline, especially if the timeline was unrealistic or rudely pressed. However, the quick change in Grant's demeanor confirmed my worst suspicion. I too could play a strategic hand.

"And a joyous occasion it will be." I smiled. "Joel will hand deliver the report to your office Monday morning. He'll be the bearer of good news, so to speak."

"Perfect. Joel, I'll see you then . . . and Ms. Danford, if you should change your mind, I'm heading straight to the beach house now to enjoy the weekend. The invitation is still open if you'd like to join me." Too easily, Grant's boyish grin had returned.

"I'll have to decline this time. Like I said, work trumps fun for right now." I gave an easy nod and winked. "A future celebration dinner is most definitely in order."

I led the three of us to the office doorway where handshakes were exchanged. After Grant exited and the door shut, I leaned against the wall and sighed.

Joel stood in front of me with arms crossed and brows furrowed. "I am miffed." What was that?"

"I can't believe it," I muttered. The rush of emotions—sadness and confusion, mixed with a bile taste of anger and disbelief—were overwhelming. I held my stomach, hoping to calm a wave of nausea.

"Wow, Liv. You'd better sit down. You look ghastly."

I took Joel's extended hand as he led me back to my office and settled me into my chair. For a moment, I felt as if I'd aged a hundred years. I'm sure I looked it as Joel stared at me with narrowed eyes.

I lifted my cup and swallowed the remains of the early morning coffee. It didn't matter that the drink had turned cold. Nothing seemed to matter now.

Joel ran his fingers over his chin in his customary, deep-thinking manner. "You don't think it's real . . . the receipt, that is? I have my suspicions, too. Did the seller pull a fast one on our friend, Mr. Richard?"

I squeezed my eyes shut, wishing to push the truth away a final time, but with no luck. "Joel, I'm afraid our friend tried to pull a fast one on us."

Joel's fingers stopped and his jaw dropped.

"I'm afraid the director of the museum falsified a copy of the receipt from his own museum . . . the receipt kept in the archives for the museum's only original Modigliani painting."

Joel began to pace. "*Elena Povolozky*, painted in 1917. The portrait Grant's great-grandfather acquired in 1949."

"Good recall."

He pointed his finger at me. "And yours, even better. I shouldn't be surprised you remember a detail like that . . . but are you sure?"

"The paper is aged and sized just the like the other. The gallery insignia matches as well, Gallerie Paysage . . . the one that went out of business."

"A little odd that the same gallery is linked to both paintings."

"My thoughts as well." I closed my eyes again, remembering the small details of the receipt we'd viewed in the archives. I hadn't taken a photo of the piece of paper as it seemed inconsequential at the time.

Joel and I were following our noses on a different path—searching the vast catalogue raisonné for similar style, composition, a matching sketch, or even mention of a small child wearing white in a letter or journal entry.

As I opened my eyes and refocused, a fine detail came into clear vision. "The size."

"Of the receipt?"

"No, that's the same." I slapped my hands on my desk. "The original Modigliani portrait of *Elena Povolozky*, the one hanging in the Richard Museum is twenty-five and a half inches by nineteen and one-eighth inches. Those are the dimensions noted in the museum exhibition details." I quickly punched in the numbers on my calculator. "I thought so . . . in centimeters that converts to sixty-four and three-quarters centimeters by forty-eight and a half centimeters."

"I'm assuming just like noted on the receipt. Obviously, metric measurement would only be used on a receipt issued in Paris. And?"

"Take a look at the receipt we saw today." I slipped the envelope from the file folder and removed the receipt. "Look at these dimensions."

Joel leaned in closer and read aloud. "Sixty-four and three-quarters centimeters by forty-eight and a half centimeters." He stood and stretched out his arms, first in height and then width. "If my European roots serve me well, those measurements would make *The Girl in White* larger than she is."

"Right. Our painting is only twenty-two by eighteen inches, or in centimeters . . . " I tapped the numbers into my phone calculator, making a quick conversion. "That would be fifty-five by forty-six. A standard French number ten figure canvas."

"I'd say someone is bad at math." Joel quipped. "And assuming *The Girl in White* is the same size as *Elena Povolozky*."

"And forging provenance."

"I just noticed one more glaring error." Joel pointed to the title. "I may not be French, but I know what's feminine and masculine. The title reads *La Fille en Blanc*."

"Yes, and where's the error?"

"Just a minute." Joel trotted from the office, returning a moment later with a magnifying glass in hand. "My eyes may be tricking me, but take a closer look."

I hovered over the paper, adjusting my position to capture the best focus of the handwriting.

"Do you see the tiny mark above the *à*, slanted from left to right? It's called an acute accent. The problem is, in French, an acute accent is only used over an *e*. Besides, in the usage of *la*, to indicate the feminine form of a word, there is no accent at all."

"Excellent catch." I shook my head. "The French would never make that mistake."

"Exactly. I'd say someone is also bad at French."

"Tell me this. How are you sure this dastardly deed was done by Mr. Richard? Why not the anonymous seller who could make a haul with this sale?"

"Possibly, but unlikely. I don't believe the seller would make a sloppy calculation error with the dimensions, and he or she certainly would be careful to get the title correct. Whoever this person is, he or she has had plenty of time to get the *i*'s dotted and *t*'s crossed if producing provenance meant making things up. Plus, why wasn't the provenance provided when this whole thing started?" I drummed my fingers on the desk, a habit that drove myself nuts when my mind worked overtime.

"Agreed. And yes, Grant's highly, or I might add, overly motivated to acquire an authentic Modigliani. Obviously, his reputation at the museum and within his family circle are at stake. It's no secret he is the outlier in his family clan. But what lengths would he personally go to . . . to pull off passing a fake for the real deal?"

"Faking that he's in love with me." The words spurted out before I could rein them in, and the wave of nausea returned. I had been duped before on a few cases—concluded pieces were real when they were not, and even vice versa. However, this time veering off my true north sent me reeling, reminded again that things aren't always what they seem.

CHAPTER THIRTY-TWO

Olivia ~ Doing My Own Due Diligence

For the third time, I scanned the ultraviolet light over the surface of the receipt and a blank piece of copy paper. I was looking for optical brightening agents—chemicals added to paper only after World War Two. If the receipt was indeed vintage, it would appear dull versus the other that would literally appear to glow. I passed the UV pen light over the papers one more time. The pieces responded completely different—like chalk and cheese.

"At least he knew to use vintage paper." I clicked off the power. "I'm sure it wouldn't be hard to locate a blank piece of old paper, or at least a section from a book or journal to use to make a copy."

"True. The archives emanate all things old." Joel flicked on the room lights and removed his safety goggles. "I know what you're thinking. We're going—"

"Back to the Richard Museum archives right now." I grabbed my bag and started for the door. "And, to answer your unspoken question, I'll buy you lunch when we're finished."

Joel swung his backpack over his shoulder with an animated grunt. "More likely dinner the way I know you work."

*****

As if a déjà vu, the same librarian was perched behind her desk, head down, purple half-readers roosted on the tip of her nose. For a moment, I wondered if she actually lived in the depths of the Richard Museum, but her bright, lemon-colored blouse lit her like sunshine.

"Hello, how can I help . . . " She raised her head and peered over her glasses. "Oh, I remember the two of you. Back for more of Modigliani?"

I approached the desk and lifted the pen to add my name to the sign-in sheet.

"No need to do that, . . . Ms. Danford." She smiled. "I did a little research after you left. Sorry, can't help myself when it comes to acquiring information." She shrugged, "Anyway, I had a hunch who you were, especially with an important acquisition on the line." She looked to Joel. "And you must be Ms. Danford's assistant."

"The one and only. I'm Joel and it's a pleasure to be back in your library."

"He's certainly my better half," I added and extended my hand to the librarian. "Please, call me Olivia. And you are?"

"Marcia Burns." Like a small canary, she shook my hand in a quick, fluttered motion. "Friends call me Bernie."

"Then . . ., Bernie, what's the recent museum talk about the acquisition?" If anyone knew the latest buzz amongst the museum employees, especially the docents and board members, it would be Bernie. The only other person who would have the pulse of the museum happenings would be Grant's secretary, Shirley. After decades of tenure at the museum, these women certainly weren't in the dark when it came to museum gossip. Instead, they could prove to be quite illuminating. *I need to pay Shirley a visit sometime soon.*

"Well, we know the piece would be a substantial and much-needed acquisition. Obviously, the museum hired your firm to help the process . . . that is, if the Modigliani is real. As you can imagine, not only the board of directors and Mr. Richard are hoping for the painting to be authentic, but all of us who consider the Richard Museum our home."

Bernie continued to talk as she began to walk into the maze of shelves. Joel and I following like hungry mice.

"For years, the Richard legacy has faithfully pursued and attained fine pieces. The representation of well known and immensely famous artists exists in all the exhibits, and for a private museum, our reputation is known worldwide." Bernie pushed her readers on top of her nest of curly hair. "But to be honest, it's been too many years since we've had a new acquisition to set the public interest on fire. The problem is the donor base is getting older and the younger patrons either don't have as deep of pockets or are unwilling to support the arts unless something is overtly in it for them."

She tossed up her hands in mock disgust. "If you want my opinion, I think that's why the Richard family got the young Grant to take over. Not that he has the track record like his predecessors, but he has the good looks and pizzazz to garner a new following of supporters." Bernie pressed the back of her hand against her forehead as if she was about to faint. "He has charisma, that's for sure. You should see the women in the gift shop and ticket desk all aflutter when he wishes them a good morning or afternoon."

"I can only imagine." My whisper didn't go unnoticed.

"Excuse me?" Bernie called out over her shoulder as she turned and scurried down another aisle.

"Oh, I said I can imagine. Mr. Richard is charming. It's been a pleasure to work on this case with him, right, Joel?"

"Most definitely, but we'd better get to work on what we came here to do today." Joel gently squeezed my elbow and whispered in my ear, "And what exactly did we come here to do?"

When we finally caught up to the librarian, her readers were back on the tip of her nose as she scanned a section of books and stacked files. "Last time, I brought the Modigliani material to you on a cart so you could really dig into it on one of the large tables. I'm happy to do that again if that's what you need, but to be honest, after that grad student got her hands on all of this . . . " She motioned to the bookcase and adjoining file drawer. "I've spent hours putting all of the material back in order and still have a few more files to go."

"That student must really be enthralled with Modigliani." I ran my fingers over the row of books. "Was there a particular aspect of his work or . . . his life that she was intent on researching?"

Bernie pursed her lips. "Not that I am aware of . . . though I'd say she was definitely doing a deep dive. She must have looked through all the catalogue raisonnés we can access, plus all these files. Seems pretty overwhelming to me. Tons of professional research papers written over the past, I'd say, eighty-plus years. But, they're mostly the same material churned out from different perspectives. Lots of opinion articles about his paintings, sketches, and early sculptures. You know how art academia works . . . always speculating on whether an artist's style and content had deeper meaning than what's on the surface." She lifted an overstuffed file from the top of the pile. "And then there's this material. I need to reorganize all of this . . . old exhibition listings, gallery showings, letters, receipts—"

"I'd like to take a look at that file."

Bernie lifted the file, first tucking loose paper edges back in place before handing it to me. "If you don't mind the mess."

"Not at all. We'll take a quick look and return it right where you had it." I glanced at Joel. "We shouldn't be too long, right?"

"Right. No needle in a haystack for us." Joel rubbed his stomach. "Plus I'm starving."

Bernie clasped her hands together. "You know where to find me if you need any help." She disappeared down another aisle.

Neither Joel or I spoke as we situated the file on top of the cabinet and began to flip through one piece of paper at a time. The familiar aged, vanilla scent wafted from the contents as we sifted our way through the odd-sized forms. Every piece of history we had observed, noted, and recorded from our first visit to the archives, though in different order and organization, remained . . . all except one. The gallery receipt, the priceless provenance for the portrait of *Elena Povolozky* that hung on a museum wall, floors above the basement archives, was missing.

Joel broke the silence. "The void that can't be filled."

"My feelings exactly." I carefully closed the file, making sure no stray papers slipped out of the edges. "I'd like to believe the receipt accidentally slipped out and will turn up under the dutiful eye of Bernie. That, of course, is wishful thinking."

Joel and I made our way back to the librarian's desk to find her once again, roosted.

"Already finished?" Her head bobbed. "If there's anything else I can do to help with other research or information related to the acquisition, please let me know."

"I am curious about something." I was about to drum my fingers on the desktop but stopped myself. "The graduate student you mentioned. She sounds like a fascinating person, I mean, going through the Modigliani resources in such depth, taking photos and all. I bet she'd be thrilled to have firsthand knowledge about the newly discovered painting, especially if it's authentic. Can you imagine how incredible that would be to include in her graduate thesis? Who knows . . . maybe she'd be interested in some volunteer work at the museum to add to her post grad resume."

"Refiling her mess in the archives?" Joel chirped.

"Well, that's *incredibly* thoughtful of you to include an aspiring art professional, but I'm not sure how to contact her." She flipped through the recent sheets of the sign-in clipboard. "Ah, here she is . . . Amy Green. No contact number though." She uttered a *tsk-tsk*. "I need to do better at collecting visitor information. Very unlike me."

"I wonder if I know her." I gave Joel a slight elbow. "Occasionally, I teach a graduate art history course at Georgetown University. What does she look like?"

"Petite woman, brownish hair . . . definitely a little older . . . not your typical straight out of undergraduate to graduate program student." Bernie looked over the rim of her glasses. "She does wear cool readers similar to mine, except red. I noticed them right away."

"Hmm, not sure I know her then." I adjusted my purse on my shoulder. "Bernie, thanks again for your time. I'm sure Joel and I will be back to do more research on upcoming cases. You have quite a treasure trove under your watch."

"I do indeed." Bernie beamed, and in her yellow garb, she looked like a ray of sunshine. "How wonderful it would be to have the precious little girl . . . the portrait that is, added to our treasure chest."

"Then you've seen her?"

"Not in the flesh, so to speak. Mr. Richard's secretary, Shirley . . . she's been here as long as me. She shared the mockup of the program for the upcoming gala. The Modigliani portrait is on the cover. It's stunning. Such a beautiful work of art by one of the twentieth century's most brilliant artists."

Bernie rubbed her hands together as if savoring the image. "I can hardly wait to see it in person. It must be exquisite, and of course, I'm dying to know who she was. After all, Modigliani mostly painted friends, their children . . . common people. He focused on people in his daily life. I think that's largely what makes his work relatable. Even behind the mask-like eyes and odd body shapes, there are real people." She cocked her head to the side. "Don't you think?"

I nodded. The cherubic face of *The Girl in White* played across my mind. In all the hurry and pressure to hopefully determine the portrait's authenticity for Grant's sake, I hadn't allowed the gnawing feeling that I desperately wanted to know her myself. I glanced around the cavernous room, noting shelves upon shelves of books and documents—an exhaustive accounting of mankind's desire and drive to create over the centuries. At first, I didn't realize my hand was resting on my heart, because in my soul, I sensed I knew the little girl in white.

CHAPTER THIRTY-THREE

Olivia ~ Hunch & Heartache

While Joel worked on devouring his hamburger with ample toppings, my physical appetite was nonexistent. However, my brain was uncomfortably stuffed, struggling to digest the disturbing information discovered in the archives.

"Olivia, can I be frank with you?" A dollop of ketchup slipped from the bun, landing on Joel's pressed white shirt. "Well, shite! That's a bugger." He grabbed for a napkin and began to furiously rub his shirt pocket.

"You're not going to take no for an answer." I did my best to suppress a giggle as the red substance smeared into a larger stain. "Goodness, Joel. You look like you've been shot."

"Very funny." With his chin to chest, he surveyed the damage, and then looked up and smiled. "Well, what do you expect? This business we're in . . . it's risky. Apparently, we're dealing with shady characters. At least one for sure." He wadded up the napkin and tossed it on the table.

"Seriously, Olivia, this isn't like you to let the louse get the upper hand. I know you were more excited about a relationship with Grant than you let on . . . and for good reason." He lifted a pickle spear from his plate, dangling it back and forth in front of me. "It's a professional pickle to mix business with pleasure."

I raised an eyebrow at Joel—a subtle reminder for him not to overstep.

"You know what I mean . . . and most assuredly you've kept any budding romance from going full bloom."

"Since when did you become a dating expert? I can't recall the last time you've been in a relationship of any substance."

"Ah, there's much you don't know about me." He grinned. "Much more than meets the eye."

"Lately, that seems to be happening to me quite often." I stared at the melting ice cubes in my water glass and gave them a quick swirl.

"Regardless, and in my opinion, he wasn't good enough for you anyway. You deserve better. In fact, I see you with someone more organic, down to earth. Smart for sure, likes to have fun and not too stuffy. Maybe even a little older, though not too much. Fit and—"

"I get it, Joel. Really, I'll work on it." I crossed my arms, feeling a bit childish. "But, Joel, what if Grant was set up? What if he isn't responsible for falsifying the receipt?

"Do you really believe he had nothing to do with it? We saw with our own eyes that the original receipt from *Elena Povolozky* is missing from the files, yet its duplicated form showed up with him in our office this morning as a supposed receipt for *The Girl in White*. Clearly, someone lifted the original from the archives and either made a decent copy or altered the original . . . albeit with some stupid mistakes." Joel tapped his fork on the table as if it were a judge's gavel.

"And who else but Grant Richard would have that kind of access to take a recorded piece of provenance from his own museum?"

Outwardly, I didn't respond. However, Joel's question was valid and from common sense and professional experience, he and I knew it. Sadly, the beautiful world of art had an ugly side as well. Fame, power, and money had proven to make even well-intended people step into the dark side. No doubt, Grant had much riding on acquiring a showcase piece of art for the museum. He'd acted impulsively by telling the board about it too soon in anticipation of the gala.

"From the beginning, he must have wanted it so desperately that he convinced himself the portrait is real." Joel interrupted my thoughts.

I shook my head. "For heaven's sake, why did he put her on the cover of the gala program already?"

"It's obvious. He never intended to take no for an answer." Joel pushed from the table. "And one more thing . . . since when do you teach at the university?"

"One can only aspire." I fidgeted with my unused fork.

"You're not answering, and you're acting weird. What's up with being concerned about a grad student's final paper?" His eyes narrowed. "And you gave me an elbow."

I pressed my lips together. It was out of character for me to keep case information from Joel. We worked together like the cliché well-oiled machine. However, the gnawing feeling in my gut had to remain unspoken. First, I had some detective work to do, and I prayed I was wrong.

*****

Joel didn't press when I asked him to drop me off at home instead of returning with him to the office for the afternoon. I had prepared to feign a headache, but now my temples were beginning to throb as I picked up the phone and called the George Town Club.

"Hello, this is Olivia Danford."

"Yes, Ms. Danford. Good afternoon. Will you be needing a reservation for the evening?" The familiar voice of the maître d' was soothing, deep and resonant like my father's. A surprising pang swept over my heart.

"Not tonight. I'm hoping you can help me with something else." I cleared my throat. "I'm trying to recall the name of a club member who needed a business contact. I promised to get back to him as soon as possible and I seem to have misplaced his business card." I laughed softly. "Hate it when that happens."

"Believe me, I understand. My wife reminds me all the time that I lose and forget things. Getting older has its challenges."

"I'm beginning to realize that." I paused, making mental note of the past several months and how much life had suddenly changed. "Anyway, the member's first name is Bruce and I can't remember his last name for the life of me."

"Hmm. Off the top of my head, I know there's a Bruce McPhearson . . . comes here often."

"No, that's not him. Any others?"

I waited as I heard his fingers tap on a keyboard. "Bruce Sanchez? He's the only other Bruce that comes up in the member registry."

"Oh, it just came to me . . . Anderson. Bruce Anderson." I paused. "There must be a member under that name."

The keyboard sounded again. "No, only a William Anderson . . . goes by Bill. He's been coming for Wednesday lunch and Saturday dinner for years. Good man."

"Odd. I'm usually good with names." I rubbed my temple. "His correct name will most likely come to me in the middle of night."

"When it does, happy to help."

"Thanks for your time."

"Always a pleasure. Hope to see you soon, Ms. Danford."

I ended the call, set my phone down, and rubbed both temples. *No member at the club under Bruce Anderson. Interesting. Or, is it possible I'm losing my mind? Maybe I am working too much.*

Hiding away in my bedroom with shades pulled and a much-needed nap would be the best medicine to calm my pounding head. Instead, I grabbed my keys off the kitchen counter, snatched an apple from the glass bowl, and dashed to the garage. Late afternoon's traffic out the city would be horrendous, but bottling up my suspicions would be far worse.

CHAPTER THIRTY-FOUR

Olivia ~ Clarity & Conviction

Sugar maples and birch trees were beginning to relinquish shades of soothing greens. With the cooler temperatures and October approaching, vibrant yellow, burnt orange, and red glimpses were cast across the forest canopy. Autumn had always been my favorite season.

As a young girl, I'd run through the thick trees to May's house, beckoning her to come out and dance in the fallen leaves with me. For us, piles of raked leaves became princess beds and falling leaves caught in tangled hair were our crowns. May and I always felt special in the newly fallen leaves—our kingdom of color that we would play in all day.

The recent drives north to Kennett Square had become a cathartic exercise in sorting out my past, the present, and perhaps even the future. After I'd left for college, delved into my career and life in D.C., it was easier to sugarcoat my roots in the Pennsylvania countryside. Whenever asked where I grew up and had family, I readily answered, ignoring that the beautiful scenery was peppered with pain and loss.

However, it seemed that with each excursion away from the busyness and crowds in the city, a sliver of my adult self was shedding. I couldn't deny there was a part of me that yearned for a simpler and less stressful life—not necessarily a return to what was—because in actuality my childhood was often tumultuous with Mother's frequent mental illness episodes. I sighed. *What I would give to play in the leaves again.*

As I sped past the last dense grove before entering my hometown, the blurred collage of color confirmed a conviction that I hadn't felt before. *No more just passing through life, Olivia. It's time to live. Truly live.* I breathed deeply, relieved my headache had eased.

Surprisingly, getting out of the city in rush hour went better than expected. I glanced at my watch, pleased that I'd be able to catch May at work. The gallery shop would still be open and she'd most likely be tallying up the day's earning from the steady flow of tourist shoppers. Since I didn't call to tell her I was coming to town, hopefully she wouldn't have plans and we could go out to dinner. The apple I'd nibbled on the drive didn't suffice. I was hungry for food, but also much-needed clarification from my friend as to what exactly had been going on.

I didn't have a plan or any clear indication of what to say or ask her about the things on my mind. I did know May was still my best friend in the world and nothing lately was making sense. I wasn't ready to fill her in on the details of being duped by Grant. That was fodder for another day after I had time to digest all of that. But I did want to find out more about her life. Maybe I really had been so caught up in my own world for so many years that I had no clue what was happening in hers.

It took a few laps around the block to find a parking spot near the shop. Tourist season always boomed as the leaf color peaked.

Autumn was only beginning and several more weeks lay ahead for color-gawking visitors. The streets, sidewalks, shops, and restaurants would be brimming with people before the town would fall into its winter slumber. It struck me as odd that May planned to leave town in the next few weeks while the gallery owner needed her help during high season. *Maybe she's tired of seeing her life pass by as well.* I smiled to myself. *I get it. Good for you, May.*

I opened the squeaking screen door and stepped inside. I hadn't been in the store for a long time and memories of my father seemed to spill from the walls. Several of his paintings were displayed, tucked next to other local artists' work, ceramic windchimes, and wood carvings. Kitschy framed quotes—tossing out random words of humor, wisdom, and inspiration—filled the gaps in a visual overload.

As I was scanning the walls, looking for more of Thomas's work, an elderly woman bumped into me as she headed toward the door.

"Oh, I'm so sorry, honey." She smiled warmly. The creases around her mouth and eyes made her face resemble a dried apple. "I'm a wrecking ball getting this painting out of the store."

A bald and wrinkled man followed behind her. "Yep, let's hope it makes it home in one piece. Here, doll, let me have that thing. We've done this dance many times before."

I was about to offer to carry the framed painting to their car, but they fumbled the piece between them until he successfully held it by the hanging wire. Yes, I was sure they had indeed danced through life together.

"How wonderful to take home a new piece of art." I gestured to the sixteen-by-twenty-inch canvas.

The man turned the painting around so I could see the picture. "It's a beaut . . . a Thomas Danford landscape. It's a shame there won't be any more of them."

The couple exchanged frowns, and then the woman added, "We've been buying his work for years . . . mostly smaller pieces but—"

"This time we stretched to get a larger one." He nodded to his wife. "We've eyed this one for weeks."

I stared at the painting—a thick autumn forest of birch trees. Fiery red leaves contrasted against white and gray speckled trunks, tossing a muted reflection across a pond of serene water with cattails tickling its shores.

"I know that place," I muttered.

"What's that, honey?" The woman leaned closer.

"What's that she said?" The man echoed.

My eyes focused on the water's edge where I remembered slipping off my shoes and dipping my toes in the cool water. "I know that place. I used to live there."

"Then you must be from around here." The man beamed. "The artist painted scenes from this area. Such a shame he passed away earlier this summer. Had an amazing talent for capturing the changing seasons. After all, he was local and—"

"My father." The quick statement surprised me as well as the couple. Now, both beamed ear to ear.

"Well, isn't that wonderful!" The woman reached for my hand and squeezed gently. "But of course, our condolences on his passing."

"Yes. So sorry, my dear. We'd heard he had a daughter who lived with him, or at least spent a great deal of time helping him with his failing health."

"That was sweet of you to care for him." The woman slid her arm around her husband's waist. "There's nothing more important than taking care of those you love."

If a wash of guilt was wet, I would have been soaking by now. For a moment, I considered sharing the truth—admit I was the absent daughter, living life away from my father as someone else watched him die. Maybe this was my eternal penance—banished to the far side of pond, only to be forever reminded that I let my father lose his moorings and drift away under another person's watch.

I forced a slight smile and then turned and opened the door. "Here, the least I can do is hold the door open."

Still attached, and with the painting clutched in the man's free hand, the couple teetered out the door.

Through the screen, I watched them slowly make their way a short distance down the sidewalk. They stopped next to an older beige Buick where he leaned the painting against the car, opened the door for his wife, and brushed her forehead with a kiss.

Will I ever have that kind of love? The question dangled in the air, taunting and teasing. "Yes." The word, spoken aloud, was resolute. *If I can trust again.* The unspoken words were raw—ripped from the deepest part of my soul. "Yes," I said again, this time louder.

I was startled by a girlish voice behind me. "Hello, ma'am." When I turned, a freckled girl smiled. She was most likely in her late twenties, but her long braids, bell bottom jeans, and butterfly tattoo on the side of her neck made her look much younger. "I'll need to close the store in a few minutes. Can I help you with something?"

"Hi." I gave a slight wave. "I stopped by to see May."

"If it's store related, I'm your person."

"No. May and I are longtime friends. I came in from out of town and was hoping to catch her so we could have dinner tonight."

"Oh, she's not here . . . left just a while ago. Probably starting her night off at Two Stones Pub." She stuffed her hands into the front pockets of her denim apron. "It's my first chance to close up the shop on my own. I've been in training this week since May is quitting soon."

"Good for you." I nodded toward the door. "And looks like you made a nice sale to that sweet couple who just left."

"I did. They were really stoked to get that piece since they seemed to know a lot about the artist." She furrowed her brow. "Danson . . . or something like that. I guess we have quite a few of his paintings in the store."

I glanced around the room. "I'd say so."

"Nice work for sure. But me, I prefer more abstract . . . you know, art that makes you feel things . . . think deeper."

I couldn't help but grin. If this young woman only knew the depths to which my father's paintings journeyed.

"Well, nice to meet you . . ." I extended my hand. "I'm Olivia Danford."

The girl's blank stare confirmed my surname hadn't jostled the name of the gallery's most popular artist.

"Crystal. Like a gem." The girl shook my hand in return. "I'd tell May you stopped by but she's taking the next few days off. Said she needs to start packing." She raised her forefinger. "Wait a minute. She left her laptop." She trotted behind the cashier desk and returned with the computer. "Do you mind giving this to her? That'd be a drag if she had to come by and get stuck here if it's super busy." She rolled her eyes. "Sure hope I don't screw things up and get fired."

"I'm sure you'll do fine." I gave her a thumbs up. "Sell more of those Thomas Danford paintings and you'll be golden."

I tucked May's laptop into my bag and waved goodbye. There was a good chance I knew where to find May . . . bellied up to the bar at the Two Stones Pub.

CHAPTER THIRTY-FIVE

Olivia ~ Confusion

The day wasn't over, and it had already proven to be a roller coaster ride of emotions—surprising and conflicting information left me with a jumbled mess of questions. The librarian's description of the grad student, followed by learning there was no George Town Club member under the name I was searching, had me on edge.

Fortunately, the relaxing and scenic drive to my hometown had a calming effect. Then, the innocent comments of a dear elderly couple and a clueless new salesperson had the reverse effect. As a ripple of stress grew wider and wider, substantial doubts and questions expanded in my mind.

I closed my eyes and leaned my head back on the car seat headrest. Was I prepared to drive to the pub, find May more than likely well past tipsy, and expect a coherent and truthful talk? If the grad student really was May, which seemed a huge stretch, could it be possible that she really was taking classes through the university? She loved art, especially its history. And what if I got the name wrong of the man she was seeing? It wasn't like me to forget details. Was I that detached from my friend's life that I failed to listen well? To top off the day, my headache returned. This time it was relentless.

"I've got to get something for this." My head pulsed as I started the engine, pulled onto the street, and headed to Walgreens. If I had a chance at surviving what could be a rough encounter with May, I needed to calm the storm raging in my head.

As I made my way to the pharmacy section, I grimaced under the glare of the fluorescent lights. It was a year ago, but I recognized the gray-haired pharmacist behind the counter. Last fall, I had stopped by my father's house for a quick visit before a presentation at Winterthur about a newly surfaced Matisse forgery. It sounded like a good idea—quick visit, say hello, and then off to a high-profile engagement.

Instead, Thomas was determined to show me a patch of wild blueberries growing past the edge of the lawn. Besides blue-stained fingers, I ended up in a tangle with poison ivy and desperately needed ointment to ease the itch and pain. By the time I made it to the drugstore, the poison had spread from my legs, up my torso, and along my arms like wildfire. I remember waddling to the counter, legs apart, arms spread wide, and grimacing in pain. Now, the way the pharmacist eyed me, I was sure he remembered me as well.

"Hi, it's probably over the counter, but can you suggest the most effective medicine for a raging headache?"

"Sorry to hear that. Headaches aren't any fun, and you look like you have a doozy of one." He stepped around the counter and walked to the aisle endcap. "Like the old commercials, Excedrin, the extra-strength pain reliever."

He took a bottle from the shelf and stepped behind the counter.

I winced from a particularly sharp pang as I handed him my credit card.

"Hopes this helps. You look miserable. Do you have a history of migraines?"

I shook my head. "Thank goodness, no. This whopper must have to do with stress. Maybe I'm due for a beach vacation."

"Better than any medicine I have here. Anything else I can do for you . . .?" He read the credit card. "Olivia Danford." He lowered his glasses. "I thought that was you. You look different from the last time you stopped in."

"I thought you might remember the crazed woman covered in poison ivy." It was embarrassing to be recognized from that unfortunate event, but I had to laugh at myself. "The way I looked, I probably scared you to death."

"Believe me, I've seen it all. Good to see you made a full recovery. That stuff is wicked." He handed me a small bag and the receipt. "And I'm really sorry to hear about your father. Such a good man . . . and talented artist. My wife and I have a real pretty landscape he did years ago."

"Thank you, and I'm happy you enjoy a piece of his artwork. He would be happy to hear that."

"Well, I figured he wasn't doing too well when his medicine wasn't refilled. That seems to happen when folks are failing, or they aren't able to call in prescriptions on their own."

I swallowed hard as a pit stirred in my stomach. "He wasn't getting his medicine?"

"Oh, I remember filling his meds and his caregiver picking them up pretty regularly." He straightened his glasses. "I can't recall exactly . . . maybe just a month before he passed he might have missed out."

"That's not good." My stomach reeled. "He needed his medicine."

"Absolutely. Until one day . . . which we all face . . . " He half-turned and pointed to the shelves behind him, filled with bottles and boxes of medicinal remedies. "Even all the pills in the world can't ward off the inevitable."

Whether my pounding head kept me from responding or the jolt I felt from the stark truth the pharmacist spoke, I was silent.

"Sorry if I am too direct, but in this business and at my age, you learn quickly about the fragility of life." His eyes softened. "Truly, I am sorry about your father. I bet he's painting in heaven with the Master Creator. Now, wouldn't that be something?"

I nodded slowly and turned to leave. "Yes, it would. It most certainly would."

*****

Once in my car, and after a brief wrestling match with the child-proof medicine top, I prayed. Perhaps it wasn't so much of a prayer, but more of a frank talk with God. Never in my life had I considered him my go-to confidant—the one with the listening ear and solutions to life's dilemmas. Instead, he was neatly confined to Christmas and Easter, or an occasional Bible verse that would catch my eye at a home or office. Even the paintings and sculptures by the greatest masters— DaVinci, Michelangelo, Rodin, Botticelli, Rembrandt, and so many others—though appreciated and admired for their beautiful biblical representations, for me, it was all a matter of art, not faith.

However, my insatiable need for the truth couldn't be ignored any longer. The desire extended far beyond determining the authenticity of a piece of art. Instead, I felt duped by those I trusted—Grant and May—important people in my life who had sent me spiraling into a pit of questions and ambiguity.

God, what is happening? Am I losing my mind? You know my entire career has been built on my ability to discern fact from fiction. And to be honest, I've been pretty good at it. You're the one who wired me this way. My whole life I've wanted to know the truth. Remember Santa Claus, the Easter Bunny, that silly Tooth Fairy? I hated those lies . . . threw a fit until Father came clean. Mother never admitted she was in on it, but I knew all along. But this is much bigger than childhood lies. Grant's the first man I've wanted to trust in a very long time. And May . . . my closest friend . . . why would I expect nothing else but complete honesty?

I rested my head on the steering wheel. *God, if I can't count on them . . . who am I supposed to trust?*

Despite the only response being a dull ringing in my ears, I had an odd sense that my plea was heard. I never rejected the belief that God existed—he was out there . . . somewhere. I breathed deeply in an affirmation to myself. I wanted to know him, and I prayed there was room in his heart for someone like me.

Slowly, my headache was easing. The pain medicine followed by several swigs from my water bottle helped. I was about to turn the key and speed off to find May, but I had one more thing I needed to do. I lifted her laptop from my bag, set it on my lap, and opened the screen.

Password? Once upon a time, May and I shared the cheap, frail metal keys to each other's diaries. We knew each other's favorite numbers and colors—mine, eight and blue, and May's five and pink. Nicknames were uttered in secrecy and sworn never to be told. Although I couldn't recall mine, May's remained crystal clear: . . . *Maybe,* . . . derived from the hit song "Call Me Maybe" by Carly Rae Jepsen. May and I became rock stars, belting that song out in my bedroom at night when we were supposed to be asleep. Hairbrushes to lips and singing out of tune, we became somebodies, not nobodies from the back woods of Kennett Square.

Could it be that easy? My passwords were all computer generated—combinations of numbers, letters, and symbols that resembled a computer gone mad, spitting out lengthy and convoluted sequences, impossible to remember much less duplicate. But May . . . she had always taken the simple route. Keeping track of finances, paperwork, and organization of any sort were a waste of time. "That stuff stresses me out," she said. "Life was never intended to be so complicated."

It was a stretch, but I positioned my fingers above the keyboard and typed MAYBE. The password area jiggled in defiance. I tried again. CALLMEMAYBE5. Again, the screen jiggled, reminding me that it would soon lock me out. Perhaps I underestimated my friend and she was now savvy to tech protocol. What was I doing anyway? Snooping into May's personal business, assuming she had something to hide?

Without contemplation, I typed 1-2-3-4, and to my pleasant surprise, the computer invited me in. "Oh, May, if I could only live life as uncomplicated as you."

Exactly what I was looking for, I wasn't sure. Starting with an email search from a Bruce Anderson was a start. With the application opened, I typed in his name. Nothing. If May did have dates with this person, who's to say they would have communicated via email? Seemed too formal. Most likely they exchanged texts or phone calls. Next, I pulled up the calendar app and searched for George Town Club. Again, nothing. In fact, it didn't appear that May used her computer calendar at all. Maybe she preferred to keep track of her appointments and meetings the old fashioned way with paper and pen. Knowing May, she probably didn't even keep a calendar.

Another item I couldn't shake was the crazy thought that the woman in the library poring over dusty Modigliani files and books was May. The concept was absurd, and I was acting foolish to even consider the possibility. Even in a million years, if the woman was May, wasn't she entitled to study art history and take courses at the university? After all, she was passionate about art and determined to open her own gallery.

Liv, you're acting paranoid. Get a grip on yourself and put your energy back on The Girl in White. *This case should have been done weeks ago.*

I rested my hand on the lid, ready to close the computer. "Sorry, May. I need to look for one more thing . . . a selfie of you and the handsome financier."

My finger navigated the track pad, clicked, and in a few seconds, photos filled the screen. *Well, certainly the cloud and her cellphone talk.*

Snapshots of giant sunflowers, loaded tomato bushes, and a harvest of yellow squash and deep green cucumbers filled the screen. May always loved to garden, especially when we were teens, choosing to spend hours picking weeds for my father instead of watching TV with me. *She's done a good job tending her own garden. I'll be sure to compliment her about that.*

As I scrolled, photos of Thomas's paintings followed, each one propped against a blank wall as if May was intent on documenting the inventory my father had graciously gifted to her. The quality of the photos wasn't great, but I suspected she intended to sell them both at her new gallery and online.

I scrolled up. More paintings . . . so many paintings. Landscapes inspired by every season, worn and tired barns, cows resting under shady trees, coursing rivers and trickling streams, flowers of every hue, shape, and size, fields of bounty, and fields of rest. The familiar pang swelled in my heart and my eyes moistened. Each one was a piece of my father—not merely a portrayal of his artistic talent, but a revealing of his soul. Maybe the pharmacist was right. At this very moment, Thomas might be painting in paradise.

I blinked, refocused my eyes, and swiped one more time. A different batch of photos filled the screen. I gasped.

CHAPTER THIRTY-SIX

Olivia ~
Confrontation

I t felt as though a shockwave rippled through my body. A strange
numbness followed as my hands gripped the steering wheel,
knuckles white. Now, there was no denying it—May was up to
something, and it wasn't good. I pulled out of the drugstore lot and
turned on to the main street in the direction of Two Stones Pub.

My cell phone rang just as I found a space in the rutted dirt lot.
Joel. I debated whether to pick up, but I needed to hear a familiar
voice. Plus I'd left him earlier in the day not acting like my typical
self.

"Hey, Joel. What's up?"

"I have the same question for you." His usual lively tone was flat.
"I've been concerned about you. How are you feeling?"

"Better, thanks."

"Good to hear because I stopped by your house after I finished
things up at the office. Figured you didn't feed yourself, so I took it
upon myself to bring you a kale Caesar salad from Sweetgreen."

"That's sweet of you, Joel. I love that salad. Sorry I wasn't home to enjoy it."

"Then . . . where are you?"

"That's direct."

No response. Clearly, he was waiting for an answer.

"I drove home . . . I mean, I'm in Kennett Square near my father's house."

"Is everything okay? You didn't mention you were going there today."

Now I was the one who didn't respond immediately. *No, everything isn't okay. In fact, everything is so convoluted that I'm wondering which way is up.* "Joel, I don't know where to begin right now, but I promise I'll fill you in as soon as I make sense of things."

"You're worrying me, Olivia."

"I'm all right. I promise."

"Okay . . . then I'm going to trust you." He paused. "Oh, by the way, William Barrett called. He said he tried to call you but you weren't picking up. I told him you weren't feeling great and probably had your phone silenced. I think he was a little worried about you as well. Be sure to give him a call as soon as you can."

"Will do. Nice to know I have some people who care." I smiled to myself. "And, Joel, you can trust me as well."

I hung up the call with Joel and checked prior incoming calls. Professor Barrett called when I was in the pharmacy and left my phone in the car. I needed to call him back later . . . *I have serious business at hand.*

As I entered the pub, the smell of too many beers spilled on the floor emanated from the dilapidated room. For a beautiful autumn day, my eyes had to adjust to the dimly lit area. Seventies hard rock blasted from a jukebox and loud voices laughed and cajoled over the music. A few bearded and tattooed men raised their heads and glanced at me. I walked past, intent at finding May at the bar.

"Hi. How ya doing?" The bartender was a petite bottle blond. Her hair was gathered up in a messy bun, pieces straggling above heavy, dark-lined eyes. "Can I get you something to drink?"

"No thanks. Just hoping I'd find my friend here." I scanned the length of the bar. "No luck, I guess."

"Who ya looking for?" The woman spiraled a damp rag on the pock-marked wood.

"Her name's May."

"Meriwether?"

"Yes, that's her."

"Left a while ago. Been here a good part of the afternoon . . . might be back tonight. Usually does. If you want, I'll tell her a friend was looking for her."

"Thanks, but that's okay. I'll give her a call." I turned to leave.

"Suit yourself." Glasses clanked as the woman lifted four empties at the same time and plopped them in the dirty dish rack. "Hey, you don't happen to be Thomas Danford's daughter?"

I stopped and turned around. "I am. But how would you have guessed that?"

"Oh, May and I are close. That happens sometimes between bartenders and patrons . . . just like hairstylists and their clients." Although she smiled a pretty smile, the young woman was roughened around the edges, and I understood why she and May connected.

"May told me you've been coming to town . . . now that your dad has passed. Sorry about that, by the way." She leaned her elbows on the counter. "From what May's told me, you're kind of a famous woman . . . at least in the city circles."

"I'm not sure about that." I shook my head.

"Well, she showed me an article with a photo of you. All dressed up at some fancy party." She tapped her forehead with a black nail-polished forefinger. "It was at some museum."

"Probably so. Once in a while, those events are just part of my job." I shifted my weight, feeling off balance with the perceived fame.

"May really misses your dad. That was a good job for her, you know, taking *really* good care of your him."

I squinted, trying to read through the woman's words. "I suppose it worked out well for both of them." Suddenly, the air felt heavy, and I needed to get outside. However, I needed to make one thing clear. "I really miss my father, too . . . terribly."

*****

The outside stairs leading to May's apartment above the store were dark. No other indoor lights appeared to be on, and I wondered if she was home. Regardless, I navigated the stairs, bag over my shoulder, with May's computer tucked inside.

I knocked and waited. Knocked again, and in a few moments, an outdoor light flashed across my face. Immediately, miller moths fluttered around the light in frantic flight as I waited some more. Finally, the door slightly opened, and half of May's face appeared. One wide eye confirmed she was surprised to see me.

"Liv, what are you doing here?" She opened the door and leaned against the frame. "Did I know you were comin' over? Everything good?" Not overt, but her words were slightly slurred. "Well, come on in, silly." She gave me a slight hug and stale beer breath confirmed she'd overindulged.

I followed her into the small kitchen where she opened the refrigerator and pulled out two beers. "And what's the honor I have tonight of having Ms. Olivia Danford show up unannounced?" She held a bottle toward me.

"No thanks, May. I'm good right now." I motioned to the kitchen table and chairs. "Can we sit down?"

"Sure." May slid into a chair and I sat opposite her.

"I know you, Liv, and you have your game face on." She purposely scrunched her face, making an ugly frown. "You must still be on the business clock." She read her watch. "Heck, it's after hours now. The night's started." She twisted the metal cap off her beer and took a long swig.

"I do have some things to talk with you about." I straightened my back, collecting my thoughts as to where to begin.

"Oh, great, what has little old May done wrong now?" She rolled her eyes.

"Knock it off, May." My voice was stern, and I wasn't about to play into her sassy attitude. "There's some serious things to discuss."

"Like?"

"Like why didn't you give Thomas his medicine? Why wasn't the prescription filled on time and his medicine taken on schedule?"

May reeled back in her chair. "What are you talking about?" She threw her hands up in the air. "You're freaking crazy!"

"I want the truth, May. The pharmacist told me his medicine hadn't been refilled. You know he needed you to do that for him. His health depended on taking his meds."

"And how would you know, . . . Miss Consumed with Her Own Life?"

"Low blow, May. Really low. I may not have been here on a daily basis like you, but I know what his health issues were, and I know he needed his medicine consistently." I peered at her, determined not to back down. "I want to know why he wasn't taking his medicine shortly before he died."

May stood from the table and walked in a small circle. "He didn't want to take it."

"And you gave him that choice?" My voice raised.

"For God's sake, Liv. You're acting like I killed him. He was an adult. He was entitled to make his own decisions."

"You said yourself the dementia was getting worse. He wasn't capable of making—"

"That's where you're wrong." May pointed an accusatory finger at me. "That's where you have no clue what was going on in Thomas's head . . . and his heart for that matter . . . when he knew he was close to dying."

"And what's that supposed to mean?" I crossed my arms.

May reversed direction, pacing slowly. "He loved you, Liv. He wanted to spend more time with you. You were always too busy."

"I wasn't the perfect daughter, but I loved my father." I pushed away from the table, straightened my back and stood. I'd shouldered the guilty burden long enough. "And, yes, sadly now that's he's gone, I realize that even more."

Except for the humming of her old refrigerator, an awkward silence filled the room.

May broke the silence. "He refused to take more medicine. Told me he didn't want to waste his money buying more pills when he knew the inevitable." May grabbed a dishcloth and tossed it on the counter. "Maybe I shouldn't have let him have his way . . . but that's the truth, Liv."

I nodded, more to myself than to May. My father had always had a deeply cut stubborn streak. Once his mind was made up, there wasn't much anyone could do. However, an anger still burned toward May that I knew would take time to subside. I'd entrusted her to do everything in her power to care for my father. Perhaps his determination, or more accurately, his concession to let life take its natural course had left her powerless.

"Anything else you need to talk about?" May yawned. "It's only Friday night and the weekend already feels long."

"Actually, yes." I pulled out the chair and sat again. May followed my lead as we huddled around the table. "And I need to know the truth."

"Shoot." May tapped her nose. "And it won't grow like Pinocchio's."

I hoped the same yet wondered how May would try to get herself out of this pickle.

"The man you said you've been seeing, or at least had some dates with him in the city—"

"Sure. What about him?"

"There is no Bruce Anderson who's a member at the George Town Club." I interlocked my fingers. "Why did you say he was?"

"Geez, May. What kind of question is that? He told me he was. Isn't that good enough?"

"No, it's not." I pressed in. "I'm wondering if there really is a Bruce Anderson."

"Oh, my gosh. I need another beer for this interrogation." She stood and grabbed the beer intended for me off the counter. "What, you think I don't go out? Sit at home, twiddle my thumbs and wish I had a date? Not good enough to have a man take me out for a nice dinner, huh?"

"Not at all." I swallowed. *Liv, stay the course. Don't waver on this.* "I did a little digging, and there is no member under the name of Bruce Anderson at the club. Who were you with, May?"

"Maybe he goes by an alias . . . doesn't want irritating people like you knowing his business."

"Cute." I stood up and faced her. "I think you're lying to me about things, and I want to know why."

"And I think you're paranoid." She pushed by me and yanked her purse off the hook by the door. "I think you need to get help with that issue."

She opened the door and started down the stairs. I rushed after her, determined to get to the bottom of this. There was no turning back.

"May," I called into the darkness. "I have your computer . . . I've seen the photos." I didn't want to pull out the final stop, but she left me no choice. "I'm calling the police." Darkness filled the area behind the gallery, and I wasn't sure if she heard me. If she had, she was determined to run away.

I gathered my bag with May's computer inside. Before I left her apartment, I couldn't help notice a stack of unopened envelopes, most likely bills, on the small table next to her door . . . with red reading glasses placed on top.

CHAPTER THIRTY-SEVEN

Olivia ~ Digging up Dirt

Calling Joel and filling him in was the logical thing to do. He'd been patient enough and the day's events had thrown a mammoth punch at the case involving *The Girl in White*. However, I knew exactly who I needed in my corner right now—both professionally and in a grandfatherly, wisdom-filled sort of way. I picked up my phone and called Professor Barrett.

"Hello, . . . Olivia. I saw your name come up."

"I'm sorry to call so late at night. Completely unprofessional, but I need to talk with—"

"Likewise. Did you get my message from Joel?"

"He told me you called. I'm fine, by the way . . . felt under the weather earlier today."

"Glad you're back in the saddle." He paused. "I need your help."

"I'm in, and I need yours as well."

"I took the liberty and did more research on our girl. When's the soonest we can meet?"

"I'm in Kennett Square now. I have so much on my mind, but I can sleep, at least try, at my father's house and meet you in the morning."

"I'm afraid I won't catch a wink tonight. I'm actually at the lab with the restoration team. A private gallery in New York nearly lost all its inventory to smoke damage. Sounds like a sluggard employee decided it was okay to light up on the job and caught a stack of papers on fire. There's an Andrew Wyeth piece that took the brunt of the damage."

"That's horrible. I hope you can save it."

"The team up here is one of the best. That's why the gallery sought us out and overnighted the artwork with the agreement we'd get right on it."

"Well, it sounds like you have your hands full so I can wait." I hesitated. In truth, it was urgent that I speak with the professor. "And let you go home this weekend and enjoy your time away from work."

"If you consider watching recorded shows of BBC's *Fake of Fortune*, then those aren't very exciting plans. Besides, I already know the verdict in each of the episodes."

"I bet you knew the outcome before the end of every new show."

"True. I pride myself on that." He chuckled. "Come to the lab tonight. The team knows what they're doing, and they don't need me hanging over their shoulders. We can talk and clear our overextended minds. Sounds like we both need that. By the way, I have some interesting things to share with you."

I merged onto the freeway heading toward Winterthur. It felt good to have a friend and colleague whom I could trust. Tonight, I would share the bizarre turn of events with William Barrett. *And he will hardly believe his ears.*

*****

By now, the night guard at Winterthur was familiar with my name and buzzed me into the research building. As I made my way down the long hallways toward the professor's lab, I wondered at which oddly plotted point to begin the conversation—Grant's falsified receipt, his insistence that the case report be revised, the mysterious grad student in the Richard Museum archives, the piece of provenance now missing from the Modigliani file, May's nonexistent boyfriend/club member, and incriminating photos upon photos contained on my friend's computer. All of these, bound up like a ball made of intertwined rubber bands, stretched any semblance of truth until it had snapped.

I knocked on the lab door. William greeted me and then motioned to his office. "Let's talk in there."

We settled into saggy leather chairs, most likely furnished when Winterthur opened in 1951. I glanced around the small office, amazed that so many books, journals, and documents could fit in one space. This was a thinking person's space, and most definitely, I again needed the sound thinking of my past college professor.

It took time to unpack all that needed to be shared. In his customary way, William listened, jotted some notes on a yellow ledger, and nodded on more than one occasion. When I included the revelation about Thomas's missing medicine, he instead shook his head and muttered, "Such a shame."

After all information had been shared, I was a bit surprised William hadn't said much. He asked a few clarifying questions, mainly about who May was and how long I had known her. He asked to see the photos on the laptop, which fortunately, I'd kept in my bag and brought along with me. After all that had occurred in a single day, receiving the forged receipt only this morning seemed like days ago. Although the actual piece of paper was still under Joel's watch at Axiom, I told William about the sloppy errors that someone had made. Was the dishonest deed done at the hands of Grant? Or did May have a part in this? Still, none of this made complete sense.

William tapped his pen on the pad in quick succession. Like an extension of his brain, I could tell his mind was deducing, calculating, and summarizing all that he had heard.

"Olivia, I have some surprise findings to share with you." He lowered his head and peered over his glasses. "I reached out to a retired chemical engineer buddy of mine. We play pickleball once a week."

I smiled. "That is a surprise . . . that you play pickleball."

"And you'll be doubly surprised to learn I'm very good. My wife says I have to do something to keep this old body in shape." He patted his stomach. "Anyway, I asked him to take a look at one of the samples we extracted from the portrait. We ran the chemical profile of that minuscule chip of paint through several reference databases and discovered two interesting conclusions."

My ears were burning now. I lived for this type of work—gleaning facts and insights from following the scientific process. "And?"

"The paint contained residue of ash, . . . most likely from a thick presence of smoke."

"Like the pieces the team is working on right now . . . that were in a fire."

"Possibly, but not likely since our portrait has no other damage and the residue is focused in only portions of the painting."

"That doesn't make sense."

"Exactly." His brows furrowed in deep concentration. "Unless the painting was subjected to a steady dose of smoke, say from a fireplace or someone smoking cigarettes at a certain point in its creation. Maybe certain intervals in the painting process when only part of the paint had been applied."

"Modigliani was known as a smoker . . . most everyone smoked in those days."

"True, but here's the kicker. Some of the residue contains trace elements of wax, oil, and organic fruit seeds."

"You've lost me." I rubbed my forehead. "I feel like I'm taking one of your awful college tests."

He jotted a word on his paper and then spun the pad around toward me. "Duraflame. I confirmed that's the same ingredients in those fake logs. That's why they burn so long and pop due to the cracking of tiny fruit seeds."

"Poor Modigliani surely didn't have access to those in Paris in the early 1900s. If he did, he wouldn't have nearly frozen to death on winter nights. Liam told me that Modigliani and his artist friend, Chaim Soutine, would sleep together on a dirty floor cot to stay warm."

"Yes." He circled the brand name on his paper in a sort of grand finale. "Another confirmation our beautiful little girl is, alas, a forgery."

I settled into the chair. "You know what's even crazier? I really wanted her to be real. Working closely with a real Modigliani would have been a professional highlight for sure. I admit being star struck with the possibility." I sighed. "Maybe I am going nuts, but I fell in love with that little girl . . . almost like I knew her and needed her to be real."

"Maternal instinct?" He raised a brow. "Even though you haven't had children yet, maybe one day you will."

"That's a whole other story."

"Yes, a story for another day."

"You said you have two findings." Mentally, I pushed aside my personal life, eager to hear more about the elemental process.

"The existence of a distinctive polymer in the paint." William stood and began to pace the room. "That element has really bothered me . . . been losing sleep over it."

"That's two of us."

"My friend, the pickleball player . . . when I showed him the analysis I'd done he recognized the unique chemical profile of the polymer."

"How so? It must be a commonplace polymer found in acrylic paint. One that a forger could have easily picked up at any art supply store."

William stopped. "Actually, not at all. In fact, the polymer is extremely specific and never was available on the common market. Apparently, it was developed in the late 1990s as an industrial pipe coating, meant to harden quickly in the field and in most weather conditions." William rubbed his chin. "It's either incredibly good luck or fate, but if my buddy wasn't a retired DuPont employee who helped in its development, learning the origins of the polymer most likely would have been a dead end."

I nearly jumped from my chair. *Is it possible? Absolutely not! But, what if . . . ? Nothing anymore is impossible.*

The thoughts came first, like rain before a flash flood. In a deluge, the words poured out. "My father . . . Thomas Danford. He was a chemical engineer at DuPont."

Professor Barrett and I locked eyes as I uttered the final words. "In the 1990s."

My knees weakened and I sank back into the chair.

William's eyes softened in the grandfatherly way I'd come to depend on. It was unspoken, but the aged professor and occasional professional colleague had become a type of father figure to me over the years—honest and trustworthy. Was it possible that my own father was anything but those things?

"This is absurd!" I couldn't contain my rising voice. "How could my father be involved with any of this?"

"Olivia, if you hadn't learned all the other peculiar facts you shared with me tonight, I'd say we'd still be on a wild goose chase. All we'd know is the painting isn't an authentic Modigliani and that would be the end of it. Grant Richard and the museum would receive our professional conclusion and then move on to acquiring another notable piece. But for whatever reason, very odd events have conspired to draw you in deeper than ever imagined." He stepped toward me and rested his hand on my shoulder. "And, if I know you, you won't be able to let this go until everything's in the light."

I looked up at the professor. "Do you believe my father is involved . . . even though he's dead?"

"After what I know now, the thought's crossed my mind." He gave my shoulder a slight squeeze and stepped away. "But since he isn't here any longer, I'm not sure if we'll ever know."

This time, I wasn't convinced I wanted to know the truth. It depended on which way the scale would tip—in favor, or not in favor, of my father's integrity. Was he really the upright man of substance that I wanted to believe he'd always been? My protector. The knight in shining armor that came to my rescue when Mother's moods tried to consume me. The one man that I knew I could count on . . . even when he couldn't count on me. No, regardless of the outcome, I had to know the truth. If I didn't, I'd drift even further away, a piece of lifeless wood, tossed and turned on the ocean's edge, always out of reach of someone trying to pull it in.

I stood, closed the laptop and tucked it into my bag "I have a conversation I need to finish."

"Tonight?" William pressed his lips together. "Be careful, Olivia."

"Don't worry. I'm not afraid of her. I'll call you in the morning." I opened the door. "Besides, you should go home and get some sleep. You don't want to lose your edge on the pickleball court."

CHAPTER THIRTY-EIGHT

Olivia ~ The Story Unfolds

I t wasn't surprising that May didn't pick up her phone. After all, it was after midnight by the time I rolled on to the gravel drive. Leaving a brief message was best for now. If she had the decency to come over in the morning to tell me the truth, then that was on her. If not, I had plenty of truth-seeking to do on my own.

My shin took the brunt of the hit when I tripped over the Coming Soon For Sale sign jammed into the lawn. The realtor said she was about ready to put the house on the market, but now the reality that my childhood home would be occupied by another owner saddened me. I pulled open the screen door that hung lopsided and loose on one hinge. It was likely new buyers would scrape the house, take it down to the foundation and build something fresh and new. I couldn't blame them. The house was beaten down . . . worn and wasted from too many years of neglect.

I stepped inside and flicked on the light. The house was barren, any remaining furniture moved out. A lingering smell of bleach and wood polish hung in the air, reminding me the realtor had insisted on a cleaning crew coming in to make the house more palatable. As I walked across the weathered wooden floor, an unfamiliar echo bounced off the walls. I'd never experienced my childhood home empty, and now my heart felt equally so. *What was I thinking to come here to spend the night? There isn't even a bed.*

I nearly turned to leave, but then a strange idea drew me in. I walked into the kitchen, pushed the curtain aside, and stared into the backyard. As though poised on a stage like a petite ballerina, the cottage stood silently, illuminated by an intense, full harvest moon.

The realtor had been instructed not to go inside until I had time to clean it out. Besides, the key was never offered and still tucked inside my purse.

The night air was cool against my face as I walked quietly across the lawn. Fireflies flitted in nearby bushes and a distant fox, in an eerie screech, called to its young. I tightened my grip around the key as I was about to enter either a dangerous lair like Hansel and Gretel, or step inside a fairy tale castle.

This time, I make my own story. I slipped the key into the lock, wiggled it a few moments, and the door eased open. By habit, I remembered the positioning of the light switch. I hadn't considered that the bulb was old and most likely burned out. To my surprise, the etched ceiling light lit the small room. I looked around. Everything was just the same. The only item missing was Father's weekly gift to my mother—freshly cut or in the winter store-bought flowers—filling the cobalt vase that now sat empty on the corner of her writing desk.

Finally, the fatigue from the day won. I reclined on the small sofa, barely big enough to fit my now adult-sized body. My mother's favorite quilt, still draped over one of the arms, would suffice to keep me warm. I unfolded the quilt, remembering each unique square and fabric pattern as if I'd just curled up for a childhood nap.

I ran my fingers over the threaded stitches, recalling the stories my mother told me about her mother making the quilt—long before I ever would have met her—each color, every design, perfectly placed with a purpose. "Nothing is by mistake in this life, Olivia. Everything and everyone have a purpose."

*****

I awoke to a soft ray of light coming through a gap in the curtain. I had slept through the night and felt amazingly refreshed. A cup of coffee would be needed soon, but now that I had emotionally survived my mother's cottage in the dark, I needed to face its contents in the light.

I brushed my fingers through tangled hair and surveyed the room. Near the window, my mother's Corona typewriter rested on the small table as if she had been there only moments before. A neat stack of blank paper, though yellowed, sat dutifully nearby. The wicker wastebasket was empty—no unworthy drafts wadded up and cast away.

A few steps away was her bookcase—neatly organized with books according to size. I ran my finger along the spines, rereading the titles that I'd read hundreds of times. Learning to read had come easily to me, and I'd practice "adult" words aloud wherever they could be found. *The Merriam-Webster Thesaurus, Webster's Dictionary of the English Language, Pride and Prejudice* by Jane Austen, *To Kill a Mockingbird* by Harper Lee, *One Hundred Years of Solitude . . .* by Gabriel García Márquez, and my favorite, *Jane Eyre.* I loved the brave girl, and I often wondered if Charlotte Brontë, though living in another century, could have known my plight and wrote the book just for me.

I slid the novel from the shelf and paged through the chapters. Though it had been many years since I read the book, the heart-tugging story played through my mind. Jane had been my role model. For the first time, I realized now that the fictional character had largely determined who I was to become—dignified, strong-minded, and fiercely committed to justice and sound principles. All because she put her trust in God. But why then had I become all of those things, yet I didn't allow myself to trust God? I closed the book and placed it back on the shelf. *Because somewhere along the way, maybe I let myself get too big and in his way.*

"Liv? Are you in there?"

The voice outside the window startled me even though I recognized it as May's. Before opening the door and inviting her in, for what I could only imagine would be an interesting conversation, I stopped and looked at myself in the oval wall mirror. Most likely, the last image reflected in the mirror was my mother. She was beautiful, especially when she smiled, and for a brief moment I imagined that it was her staring back at me. But I knew clearly who I was. Olivia Danford. Daughter of Anna and Thomas Danford. Loved . . . and willing to love, despite it all.

I placed my hand on the knob, stood tall, and opened the door. "May, I'm glad you've come to talk. Come in."

Gingerly, she stepped inside, glancing side to side.

"Don't worry, I haven't called the police . . . at least not yet." I motioned to the sofa. "How about you sit there?" It was more of a command than an offer. I pulled my mother's upright wicker chair from the writing table. I'd let May get comfortable in the overstuffed sofa while I remained on high alert.

"So, you want to finish last night's conversation." May twisted her hair around her finger. "Gotta admit, you caught me off guard . . . showing up unexpected like that."

I didn't respond and only raised an eyebrow.

"What do we need to talk about?" May eyed my bag propped on the floor. "And I'd like to have my computer back. I use that for work, you know."

"And other things." I willed myself to be calm. "It's time to tell the truth May . . . all of it."

May averted her eyes, looking at everything in the room except me. "I can't believe you'd call the cops. Besides, when you hear the facts, there won't be any need."

"I'll be the judge of that when I hear what you have to say. You realize, if there's been illegal activity, I won't have a choice in the matter."

"Geez, Liv. You're acting like I'm a criminal."

"Are you?"

She pushed back in the sofa and crossed her arms. "No . . . just a fool who only wanted to help your dad's wishes come true."

At the mention of my father, my throat tightened. Was he really involved in this mess? I raised my chin and chose the words carefully. "I'm listening."

"First of all, you know the condition his mind was in toward the end. He rambled a lot . . . things I couldn't always understand." She shifted her weight and leaned on the arm of the sofa. "But there was one thing he said over and over, sometimes to himself, and then he'd look right at me and repeat the same thing."

"What did he say?"

"She's a real Modigliani." May nodded. "Yep, that's what he said, over and over."

The image of *The Girl in White*, the painting that had consumed my thoughts for the last several months, now danced across my mind in a hastened tempo. Could it be the same image that filled his confused mind? A piece of art that he was privy to?"

"Did you ask him why he said that . . . what that statement meant?"

"Of course, but he never explained. It was like a broken record, playing the same line from a song, again and again." May circled her finger in the air. "Especially if he'd been drinking."

"Which was often, I suspect."

"The man liked his whiskey."

"As do you." It was a petty jab, but the thought of May joining my father for too many drinks and cigarettes made my stomach churn. She was supposed to be his caregiver—not his party friend.

"What else do you want me to say, Liv? Thomas rambled nonsense . . . that's all I know."

"Tell me about the photos I found on your computer. The ones taken in the Richard Museum archives."

"How do you know they came from there?"

"For starters, I happen to be working on a Modigliani case for said museum." I couldn't contain my sarcasm. May knew full well I'd be familiar with the resources available at the museum. Her snarky attitude was wearing on me, and we'd only just begun. "And I didn't know you're a grad student at Georgetown University . . . impressive."

"Like I've said, there's a lot about me you don't know." May frowned.

"Apparently."

"Well, you do know I appreciate art history . . . wanted to learn more about French artists."

"Then why Modigliani? And, by the way, he was Italian, not French. I would have thought you learned that basic fact from all your art history research." *Touché.* I couldn't help myself. "It's too much of a coincidence that of all the artists you could have chosen to study, Amedeo Modigliani was your man. Don't you think?"

"I happen to like his work." May glared at me. "Does only Oliva Danford have the corner on the market of all things Modigliani?"

"Of course not. Apparently, so does Amy Green." The words seethed through my lips. Oh, how I hated deceit. "I find it hard to believe that you don't know what my father was talking about. Somehow, you have a connection to the case I've been working on, and we'll stay here all day until you explain."

"What if there's nothing else to tell you?"

"Then you can talk with the police."

May's protruding lower lip reminded me of how she used to pout as a young girl, and later, a sassy teenager. Maybe I did the same long ago, but now I'd put away childish emotions.

"All right, then. This is what happened." May stood and walked to the window. Her back was to me, and it felt uncomfortable not to see her face. As long as she talked, I'd have to rely on body language to determine whether she was telling the truth.

"Like I said, Thomas wouldn't stop talking about a real Modigliani. I began to wonder if there was something to it . . . some truth in what he was insistent in referring to. Maybe there was a piece of art. A sketch. Something he believed was a real Modigliani. Maybe in all his years of restoring art he stumbled upon, was gifted . . . maybe even bought something that could have been connected to the artist."

She continued to look out the window, although it appeared she was replaying in her mind the time spent with my father. "I admit, I looked high and low around the house. You know it was a hot mess in there, stacks of paper and junk everywhere." She turned and looked at me. "And that was not my fault . . . it's how he chose to live." She returned to staring out the window.

She was silent for a few minutes, and I was determined to wait.

May stepped away from the window. "Then one day, he said something else . . . like a clue."

I cocked my head, intent on hearing what she had to share.

"He said, endings are best left to surprise." May looked at me with sad eyes. "Just like your mother used to say."

"In her books. I haven't thought about her signature ending for years."

"Me either. That's why it was so surprising to hear him say that . . . and more than once."

"Help me with this, May." I shook my head, trying to clear the confusion. "What happened next?"

May stepped toward me, eyes cast downward. "Don't be mad at me, Liv. I know it wasn't my place. But I convinced Thomas to unlock the cottage so I could look around . . . see if there really was something to him constantly talking about a real Modigliani."

Slowly, I ran my finger along my mother's writing table, leaving a thin line in the dust. The stuffy smell of a room being closed up for some time still hung in the air—not overt, but enough that it was clear windows and the front door hadn't been opened regularly, inviting a refreshing breeze.

Was it that long ago, when I was a delicate, young teen, when Mother decided to leave the world? After the funeral, Father closed the cottage—removed the wilted flowers in the blue vase and locked the door. His voice cracking, I remember he said, "There's no reason for us to go there anymore."

Like a line cast onto a still pond, my mind drifted in the past for a few more moments until May's voice reeled me in. "Your mother and father hid it here for years . . . shortly after you were born."

"Hid what?" I moved to the edge of the chair.

"A portrait . . . *The Girl in White.*"

I knew before she spoke it. The first time I'd seen the painting, a deep stirring churned inside. Was it possible that I'd seen her when I was an infant, a subconscious image etched on my soul?

"It was hidden in the back of the closest, sealed in brown paper and stashed behind boxes of your mother's books. You know she never let us play in here, especially hide and seek or any game where we could have found it."

The chair I'd been sitting on became uncomfortable. It was my turn to stand and pace the room. "Why did they hide it? Why didn't I know about her?"

"Thomas was convinced the portrait was by Modigliani. Apparently, your mother came to possess it many years ago." May sat on the sofa and folded her hands. Now, she seemed the calm person in the room and I was frazzled. "But she made him promise to keep it a secret until, and if, she decided to share. Then, with your mother gone and Thomas's health failing, he decided to tell you about the painting . . . he never got the chance to do that."

"The unfinished letter I found from him . . . when we started cleaning up the house."

"Yeah, I remember you asking me about that."

I dug into my bag and retrieved my phone. "I took a photo of the letter. Didn't want to risk losing it, especially since he said how much . . . " A lump formed in my throat. Sadly, Father and I hadn't audibly shared the sentiment with each other enough over the years. Phone calls were too brief and visits were cut short for such words to be spoken. But we did love one another, and the letter confirmed my mother loved me as well.

I cleared my throat and read aloud, "Despite my shortcomings and the passage of too much time, there is no greater gift I can leave you—nothing else that will tell the entire story and show you how much your mother and I loved you."

"It's a beautiful letter, Liv."

Questions riddled my mind. "Then why didn't you tell me about the painting? How could you keep it a secret from your best friend?"

May's hands unfolded and her telltale finger began to twist her hair. She had more to say. I pulled up the chair and positioned it directly in front of May. It didn't matter that I would have preferred to pace—it was time to get to the bottom of this.

"Because . . . the painting wasn't complete. There were missing parts."

"What do you mean?"

"The face, hands, even the background were painted, but the dress was not."

The testing results and my discussions with Professor Barrett raced through my mind. Those details I would keep close to my chest, at least for now. May didn't need to know that I was aware that the painting had been altered at some point in its history.

May continued in a quiet voice. "I told Thomas that if a partially painted Modigliani would be worth a ton, then imagine what a completed painting by the master could be worth . . . perhaps tens of millions. Can you even begin to think what his gift to you could be worth?"

As if punched in the gut, I leaned back in the chair. Like connecting the dots, things were beginning to line up. "And it would be ethical to alter, or in my business, we say forge, an original painting?"

May's eyes widened as if she'd been falsely accused of a devious deed. "If Thomas was right and the portrait is real, then wouldn't it be at least half a truth?"

"Or more accurately, half a lie?"

Neither of us spoke as we were weighing the magnitude of what had happened.

Finally, May spoke. "It was Thomas's idea to finish the portrait. I doubted him at first, but he assured me he could pull it off to match Modigliani's style and brushwork. He was even convinced he could forge the signature. Your father definitely knew how to paint well, and his restoration work gave him a keen eye for details others would never notice."

"I'm struggling to believe any of this." I shook my head. "Thomas wouldn't have altered a painting if he knew it was an authentic masterpiece."

"Only if he knew it was ultimately for you . . . his only daughter."

May must have known she touched a nerve as I spotted a slight smirk.

"And if this seemingly nonsense is true, what was the end game? What was in it for you? Make lots of money. Maybe *fund* your own gallery?" I glared at May. "Or maybe you've had such a chip on your shoulder for all these years since I've gone on with my life—"

"And I haven't?" The crease in her forehead deepened, aging her before my eyes.

"Answer that for yourself, May."

She was quiet—either contemplating the answer or perhaps disgusted with her own plight.

May lifted her eyes to mine, and for a moment, I saw the childhood friend who once shared our deepest secrets and biggest dreams. "Liv, there was absolutely nothing in it for me, except what I told you earlier. To help Thomas's last wishes come true."

I wanted to believe her, but time has a way of tarnishing innocence. I pressed further. "With the help of Grant Richard? And tell me, did you enjoy your lunch with him at the George Town Club?" It was a slight stretch, but it was worth taking the next leap.

"Okay, I contacted him. There was an article in the *VOICE* art magazine about him being appointed as the new director of the Richard Museum—"

"And looking for new acquisitions. I know, I read the article."

"I figured he could take a look at the painting and give feedback on the chances it could be real."

"Strange, but that's what I do for my job. Oh, but I'm sure you know that."

May ignored my comment and instead pursed her lips. "But for obvious reasons, I couldn't show it to you. That was eventually your father's prerogative. But then he died."

"So, it was your prerogative to try to sell the painting to the museum?" The dagger was thrown. "And when sound provenance was needed to back your claim that *The Girl in White* was real, you snooped around in the museum archives and falsified an old receipt."

I leaned forward and took hold of May's forearm, squeezing firmly. "Tell me this . . . how much did Grant Richard know of the truth?"

May pulled away and stood. "Why don't you ask your boyfriend yourself. I mean *ex*-boyfriend. It sucks when they screw you over like that."

"That's enough! Sit down and let's finish this conversation."

May stomped toward the door. "The interrogation is done, Olivia. You're acting crazy, and I've told you everything I know." She opened the door and half stepped outside before glancing over her shoulder. "Last thing. Your father told me he was always worried one day you'd go crazy . . . just like your mom."

Like a boomerang, the invisible dagger I'd thrown at May spun around and pierced my heart.

CHAPTER THIRTY-NINE

Olivia ~ Smoking Gun

My mind and body felt equally numb as I slid boxes out of the cottage closet. There were heavy cardboard boxes filled with extra copies of her collections, when back in the day, she traveled to bookstores, libraries, and schools to do presentations and book signings. Each time, she was nervous to leave—trading her safe and secluded writing world to venture out where her publisher scheduled her to go. Anywhere else but home, Mother was out of her element. But, as I scanned around the small room, I doubted that she even fit in here.

I looked again in the mirror. I was nothing like her, except for our looks—tall, thin, with classic facial features. Though I appreciated the passing of those inherited genes, I preferred my lighter hair and eyes—not the dark, wavy locks and deep-set eyes that seemed to reflect what was going on in her soul.

It would be an arduous job to load much of her belongings into my car. Besides, I didn't want any of the furniture or sparse knickknacks. The house would be sold soon, and I'd let the realtor and new owners decide what to do with those items.

Her books, a few favorite classics from the bookshelf, Grandmother's quilt, and my mother's typewriter were all I needed—too personal to be left behind.

After enough trips to my car, I returned to the cottage for what I knew would be the last time. I stepped inside and slowly walked in a circle, imagining myself curled up on Mother's sofa as she tapped, tapped away. I breathed deeply and smiled—this time the memory wasn't scary and I didn't want to run away. "I love you, Mother," I whispered. "I'm so sorry you had such a hard life."

Before I walked out the door and locked it a final time, I carefully lifted the cobalt vase and held it close to my heart. "I'll keep this filled with fresh flowers for you."

*****

The drive back to the city was different this time. Somehow it felt disengaged, as if I was in cruise control and watching my life blur past. Before, I was anxious to get back to the office, dive headlong into whatever the current case would be. Now, something had changed and the magnetic field that once oriented me to what I thought was home had shifted.

Typical for the waning weekend, the traffic back to the city was heavy. The urbanites were slowly returning to prepare for the work week, and I was one of them. Replaying all that May had said to me, I was still trying to make sense of the far-fetched possibility Thomas would have been involved with any of this. The question that forced its way into my mind was not *could* Thomas pull off forging a painting, but *would* he partake in an unethical and dishonest scheme?

No doubt, he was a talented enough artist and had the restoration background to do it. Other famous forgers had the same modus operandi. But my father was a good and honest man . . . as were many of the others who for years pulled the wool over the eyes of art lovers and art experts alike.

There was only one way to find out. I picked up my phone and called Joel.

"Hey, Liv. I was about to send out a search party for you." Even though he tried to make light, I knew his voice too well and he was worried.

"It's all good. I'm fine. Lots to tell you, but first I need a big favor."

"What's up?"

The next exit was fast approaching and I turned on my signal. "I need you to go to my place and get something for me. Can you jump in your car and meet me at Winterthur in a few hours?"

"I'd need to cancel a date. Remember, I told you there's a lot about me you don't know . . . I have women waiting to go out with me."

"Well, whoever this one is, if she's a keeper, she'll understand your friend, Olivia, needs you right now. I promise I'll make it up to you."

"Olivia, I'm kidding. I don't have a date, and yes, I'm happy to help. I have your garage and security code in my phone. What's it you need?"

"My father's paint palette. It's in the living room on the display case. Next to the Matisse . . . the fake one." I couldn't ignore the irony of my statement. Was *The Girl in White* completed by my own father's hand?

"Now you really have me curious. I'm leaving right now."

Again, I merged back on to the highway heading to the Winterthur lab. "Joel, you're a gem. Thanks for helping me out. But please, don't drive too fast and get pulled over . . . we don't want any delays."

I ended the call and punched another contact number. "William, it's me, Olivia. I'm on my way back to Winterthur. Can you meet me?"

"Funny you should call. You were just on my mind."

"Genius minds think alike."

"I'll take that as a compliment."

"Intended." Butterflies were beginning to take flight in my stomach as I anticipated what could soon be discovered. I pressed the accelerator and passed a few slower cars—focused on getting to the lab and learning the truth.

*****

Joel arrived at Barrett's lab sooner than expected. Clearly, he ignored the speed limit.

"You made good time," I couldn't help giving him a stern parental look. "Glad you didn't get pulled over."

"Oh, they tried, but I was too fast to catch."

Professor Barrett chuckled. "Good to see you, Joel. And thanks for expediting the testing. This might take us a little while to run a full chemical analysis."

Joel handed the palette to the professor. "I don't know what's going on here, but I can't wait to find out."

While William calibrated and prepared the instruments, Joel and I huddled around the lab table. It was awkward, as if I was tattling on my father, but I told my colleagues all that had transpired with May.

Joel rubbed his head. "I can see why this is such a mystery. Never in the world would we imagine this case would loop back to you." He circled his finger in the air, coursing one way and then the other. "It's like a giant rollercoaster with twists and turns, and then it finally ends up where it began."

"No wonder I feel sick to my stomach."

"I'm sorry, Liv. It's been a rough time losing your father." He patted me on the back in a fatherly sort of way. Joel and I made a good team, regardless of our age difference.

The process was lengthy, but we agreed running multiple samples of paint from the palette was necessary. Only tiny extractions from each dollop of paint were needed. Since oil paints cure and solidify with time, all the colors appeared hardened. No colored pigment remained on my finger as I touched each hue. And, when pierced with the tiny scalpel to retrieve a minuscule sampling, the colors, though hardened as it had been several months since the palette was held in Thomas's hand, were slightly pliable. However, titanium white was unusually hardened, almost brittle.

"Look at the craquelure again from these close-up photos from the portrait." William laid a series of high-definition prints on the table. "These compare several areas of the painting . . . the background, the face, the dark hair . . . and now look at the dress."

"Noticeably different." Joel hovered over the photos.

I slid the palette under the high-powered Dino-Lite and adjusted the focus. "Now, look at the projection of the magnified palette."

Joel was silent as he studied the computer screen while I slowly moved the area of focus across the length and width of the palette. "Web-like cracks . . . similar to what's on the girl's dress." He stepped back and blinked. "This seems pretty conclusive to me."

"And I hate to say it . . . " William looked directly at me, his face expressionless as if he hesitated in what he was about to say. "The chemical results . . . they're incriminating." He motioned us to the output of a formidable piece of analytical equipment. A detailed analysis of numbers, percentage signs, and specific elements filled the screen.

"Give me a summary. I see the equation for a polymer, but I'm not sure I'm seeing what you're seeing."

"This segment here." He ran his finger along a code of numbers and words. "It's the exact chemical profile of the DuPont polymer found in the white paint on the dress. It perfectly matches the white paint on your father's palette." He lifted the palette from the table and tapped the hardened, white dollop. "This, I'm afraid, is the smoking gun."

CHAPTER FORTY

Olivia ~ Endings Are Best Left to Surprise

It was late when I finally pulled into my garage and turned off the engine. Joel had offered to follow me home and help unpack the items from my mother's cottage, but I told him to go home and get some rest. Tomorrow would be a busy day at the office as the report for Grant needed final tweaking, and surely, his forced patience was long since gone.

I decided to carry in the delicate vase and set it on the kitchen counter. On my way home from work tomorrow, I would stop and buy flowers. Fall mums, though not my favorite blossoms, would suffice to add color to the room—something that my father had always been able to do. Perhaps it was the nostalgia of the memory, but I decided to retrieve one box from the car. I hadn't read, or even thought of, my mother's books for years. But tonight, as the events

of the weekend subsided, I decided I needed to read myself a happily
ever after bedtime story.

I plopped the heavy box on the kitchen floor and opened the
top. The books rested on their sides, revealing spines with imprinted
titles, and the familiar scent of aged paper rose up. As I read the titles,
characters, settings, and plot lines from innocent and more simple
times filled my mind. Strange how those animals, people, and places
whisked me away to magical places when I was young. I thumbed
through the books, pausing at one in particular, and lifted it from
the rest.

"*The One-Eyed Bear.*" I read the title aloud. "My favorite." I held it
to my chest and squeezed the book tightly just as I did when May and
I would scurry down the hall and obediently climb into our twin beds.
Father's footsteps would follow, and soon, in his baritone voice, he read
us our nightly bedtime story, and then safely tucked us into bed.

Now in my queen-sized bed with smooth, Egyptian cotton
sheets and plump feather pillows, I propped the book on my lap and
ran my fingers over the cover. I remembered the story perfectly. A
stuffed teddy bear believed it was no longer loved because it had lost
one button eye. He set out on a journey, climbing high mountains
and sailing across stormy seas, becoming worn and tattered in an
effort to find his button eye. The bear eventually returns home empty
handed. And this is where my mother, in her signature manner, left
the story. I rested the book on my lap as the rest of the story, my story,
played across my mind.

The last printed page, customary in her highly successful *Endings
are Best Left to Surprise* series, asked the reader to make up his or her
own ending. *Now, dear reader, how does your story end? Remember,
endings are best left to surprise.* I remembered my mother's invitation
and popular sentiment, word for word. For this story in particular,

my ending never changed. Time after time, when it was my turn to talk, the bear returned home, and despite still missing an eye and no longer having fluffy and soft fur, he had been deeply missed by the little girl who loved him. And of course, as a child with a vivid imagination, the bear and the girl enjoyed all sorts of new adventures each time Father and I shared the book. *That was the happiest time in my life . . . sharing stories with Father.*

I opened the book and flipped through the colorful illustrations and oversized print. On the last authored page, before the invitation to finish the story, something out of the ordinary caught my eye. I blinked a few times, wondering if the day's events were truly making me go mad. A small illustration, one that had never been part of the story, had been added to the paper—a loose sketch of a painting on the little girl's bedroom wall—a miniature drawing of *The Girl in White.*

Most definitely, it was her. The tiny facial features, the manner in which she sat with petite hands resting on her lap, and wearing a dress. It was nearly impossible to read, but I could just make out the letters in the top right spelling Modigliani.

Quickly, I turned the page and read the familiar words aloud, "Now, dear reader, how does your story end? Remember, endings are best left to surprise . . . and truth." *Truth.* The last two words were handwritten, added to the printed page.

I flipped to the final page. Words, handwritten in pencil, filled what was the endsheet, a blank page necessary in the printing process. Immediately, I recognized the writing—the same scrawled and shaky strokes as in the unfinished letter from my father.

I slipped on my readers, intent on taking in all that my father had to say.

My dear, Olivia,

It was never my desire to hide the truth. Instead, it was your mother's wish that a long-held family secret would remain as such. Because I loved your mother, and she loved you, I made a promise to her long ago . . . on the day you were born.

You are a direct descendant of the master artist, Amedeus Modigliani. My daughter is . . . a real Modigliani! Imagine that! For me, that revelation has always been astounding—especially since you developed an intense interest for art. But for your mother, that lineage was the link to a curse—so awful that my precious wife, Anna, was determined to protect you at all cost.

Now, the backstory . . . Anna's mother, Rachel (the grandmother you never knew) was the only child of Amedeus Modigliani and his lover, Jeanne Hébuterne. Tragically, the brilliant, yet disturbed and addicted artist died an early death from tubercular meningitis (he was only 35). Severely depressed, Jeanne took her life in a most horrific way. The day after Modigliani died, she threw herself from the fifth-story balcony of her family's Parisian home. She and her unborn child were killed. Most likely, you have read about this story in your extensive art history research and case involvements, but would never in this lifetime think that it involved you.

After the deaths, Modigliani's aunt found a sketch and an unfinished portrait of a young girl in the artist's Montparnasse studio pinned to the wall (he had little money to own an easel and preferred to paint on canvas pinned to the wall). The story goes that the aunt recognized the toddler as Rachel, the only living child of Modigliani and Jeanne Hébuterne, and took the painting and sketch with her, along with little Rachel. The child was raised by grandparents and the aunt in Modigliani's hometown in Italy. Years later, the painting was passed on to Rachel, who also struggled with dark episodes. She eventually bequeathed the painting to Anna, your mother. But for your mother, who you are well aware struggled with her own demons, the family lineage of mental illness and brokenness were too much to bear. She was determined the "Modigliani curse" would end with her if you never were told of your true heritage.

The above might appear farfetched, but it is true. As much as I hoped and prayed that Anna would get better, there was no denying that she too had inherited the curse that took my wife, and your mother, to especially dark and depressing places.

But it's been many years since Anna's death and now I face my own mortality. You have never shown signs of the so-called curse, and I am forced to wonder if the family secret is warranted. It is not. Instead, the time has come for you to receive your rightful heritage—including a real Modigliani painting, possibly worth millions—especially if finished.

At first, I wrestled with the decision . . . whether it was the right thing to do. But, with much personal justification (and encouragement from sweet May) I completed the portrait. If a half-finished painting was worth millions, one can only imagine that a completed piece would be priceless. I'd like to think of it as a modern-day family member helping the past-century artist complete what was most likely his last work of art. Had he lived to complete the piece, I believe Modigliani would have painted the dress white. After all, I'm sure the child was his angel, and she resembles you.

So, now you know the truth . . . you are a real Modigliani.

My forever love,

Thomas

P.S. I made sure to do my very best work. I believe The Girl in White *is my final masterpiece.*

CHAPTER FORTY-ONE

Olivia ~ Seeking Liam

I awoke later than usual the next morning to a ray of sunshine cast across my bed. The picture book lay next to me, a reminder of how my life completely changed in just one night. Of course, I was still thirty-eight-year-old Olivia Danford, never married, a successful businesswoman, with a full life ahead of me. However, now I was the great-granddaughter of one the world's most revered, yet tragic artists. And my great-grandmother . . . so deeply depressed that she took her own life . . . as did my mother.

I pulled the covers higher, not sure I wanted, or was able, to get out of bed. Instead, remnants of a vivid dream—one that tossed me like a raging sea—trickled across my memory.

I dreamt that I wrestled with God. As in Alexandre-Louis Leloir's painting *Jacob Wrestling with the Angel*, a similar exhaustion overwhelmed me. I'd viewed the emotive oil painting at the Musée d'Art Roger-Quilliot while working on a case in Clermont-Ferrand, France several years ago. The piece had made quite an impression on me. The tension and conflict between Jacob and the angel were intense—their illuminated muscles against a sunless backdrop confirmed the existence of good and evil, and God's relentless pursuit of mankind.

My head sank farther into my pillow. In Leloir's painting, an angel had the upper hand. However, now with the revelation of my true identity, I was positive it was God who was getting my attention. Was Thomas fully aware of what he'd done? Did May pressure him . . . convinced they would both profit? And, if Father forged a portion of an authentic Modigliani, was it better to protect his reputation . . . never reveal the half-truth? I kicked the covers and slid out of bed. *Or was it a half-lie?*

When the phone rang, I considered not answering. However, when I saw it was Liam Elliot, I had to wonder if this omen was the conclusion to my dream.

"Hi, Liam."

"Good morning, Olivia. I hope it isn't too early."

"Oh, no . . . " I glanced at the mirror and quickly brushed my hair to the side. "I've been up for hours."

"Good, because you're going to want to have a clear head when I tell you what I found."

And you're going to need a pot of coffee when I tell you what I've found. "Well, you have me more than curious. What's up?"

"It's better if I show you, and if you're free, I'm actually in town." He paused. "It would probably sound better if I told you I was here on business or invited to present, but if I'm honest—"

"You came here to see me?"

"I did."

Neither one of us spoke for a moment. A sweet silence hung in the air.

"But I do have something to show you that's quite fascinating."

"Okay, then, how about if you meet me at my house at nine?"

"Nine it is. I'll bring along donuts and fresh coffee." He chuckled. "Because call me crazy, but I have a hunch you just got up."

I smiled and set down my phone. Perhaps the quiet and unassuming Modigliani expert knew me better than I thought.

*****

As promised, Liam arrived with a delicious assortment of donuts. I couldn't recall the last time I allowed myself the decadent treat. It seemed natural wiping extra sugar from our lips and laughing while sitting across from each another at the kitchen table.

Liam motioned around the room with his free hand. "I'll tell you what, it was worth the visit here to see all this art. It's like being on a museum field trip."

It was true. My three-story row house was its own sort of gallery. I preferred minimalism and order for my decor—no clutter or unnecessary items to collect dust and crowd my mind and space. Instead, each room hosted perfectly positioned paintings that told their own story—Matisse, Renoir, Picasso, Pollock, and even a Russian-forged Modigliani—all fakes, yet all stunningly beautiful.

"She's lovely." Liam stood and closely examined a woman wearing a purple robe and red pants, reclined on a green-striped couch of sorts. "Matisse's *Odalisque*. I would recognize her anywhere."

"Painted in the style of Matisse by the one and only, Elmyr de Hory, who passed in 1976. A good friend of mine, Mark Forgy, lived with the talented forger and became very close with him. This particular piece has always meant a great deal to me. I love it so much, I even have a copy of it in my office."

"Isn't it something that forgers are so good? I mean, many were and still are today highly talented artists in their own right but choose to copy and falsify the work of others." He turned and looked at me. "You've been in the art authentication business for years. What do you think leads them to do it?"

I took my time rinsing my sticky fingers at the sink. Finally, I turned to Liam and spoke. "I've been asking myself the same question . . . in fact, every moment the last several days." I dried my hands and motioned to the living room. "Let's go sit. We have lots to talk about."

*****

Liam was a good listener. As I told him the incredible sequence of events, he easily could have thought I'd lost my mind or deduced I was a pathological liar. Instead, he nodded on several occasions, tilted his head from side to side, and when I had finished, awkwardly gave me a hug. I didn't plan to cry, but the emotions finally spilled over, washing away any doubt that what I had learned was true.

"Everything your father shared is feasible, especially given an unexplained dead end in Modigliani's family tree. After Dedo and Jeanne Hébuterne's deaths, their child was raised in Italy. Apparently, she wasn't aware of who her parents were until much later in life, and it was assumed she never had children. That's where the lineage appears to end. The belief in a family curse must have been powerful enough to quietly let the family name pass away." Liam walked around the living room appearing in deep thought. "Interestingly, over the decades, references have surfaced regarding the last pieces found in his studio. In family letters, there is mention of a painting of a young girl, most likely the couple's daughter, Rachel."

"Then you believe all of this could be true?" I moved to the edge of the seat. Surely, confirmation from a well-known Modigliani expert would be welcomed. However, when I looked at Liam's gentle brown eyes, reminding me of his steadfast father, I yearned for the affirmation of a true friend.

"I do, Olivia. I absolutely do." For a moment, he disappeared into the foyer where he had hung his jacket and placed a brown leather attaché case.

This time, instead of sitting on the chair across from me, he gestured if he could share the sofa with me. I obliged.

"I told you I have something to share with you." He placed the case on the coffee table and opened the latches. "Ever since I was at Winterthur with you and Professor Barrett, I couldn't get the image out of my mind."

"Who? *The Girl in White?*"

"Well, of course her, too." He slipped a browned and worn piece of paper from his case. "No, I'm referring to the faint and very vague underlying pentimento that we thought we may have seen under the ultraviolet light."

"Yes, I know what you're talking about. We found nothing conclusive."

Gently, he placed the paper in front of me. "I have."

It was difficult to make out much of the faded, most likely charcoal lines. A curve of a small head, marks suggesting a petite nose and mouth, and folded hands. What seemed like quickly squiggled lines, though hard to say, could have indicated an item of clothing.

"I can't say for sure, but the style of the strokes is the same as Dedo's other sketches. His journal compilation is kept at the Georges Pompidou Museum in Paris. I've been in contact with them about this piece. They're waiting to see it in person until further comments are made. However, they believe the size and type of paper perfectly matches his sketchbook that he used up until the end. Even the perforated edge of the paper seems to align with his sketchbook, though that is still to be confirmed."

I narrowed my eyes and looked closer at the sketch. "I told you my father referenced the aunt . . . my great-aunt, maybe great-great?" It was so odd to make such a statement, but I continued my thoughts. "That she took not only the painting from the studio, but a sketch."

"This could be the one." Liam nodded.

"And how did you come upon it?"

"It surfaced at a book and print kiosk in Florence, Italy. The gentleman who owns the street shop said he'd had the sketch in a box with some others for years. An American art student who was on Semester at Sea saw the sketch, said it reminded her of a Modigliani and bought it."

"You've lost me. How did you ever find it?"

"Ah, social media isn't all bad after all." Liam smirked. "The college kid knows how to use Instagram and Twitter. She posted a picture of the sketch, bragging she'd discovered a priceless artifact. Fortunately, she knew how to use the right hashtags and her posting popped up on my feed. Of course, I didn't make much of it at first . . . a college kid buys beers, not pieces of art."

"I must have been an anomaly," I jested.

"That makes two of us." He nodded. "Anyway, I was able to connect with her, then convince her I wasn't a creep, and voilà—"

"You bought the paper?"

"No, she's actually a smart kid." He clicked his fingers. "I'm only borrowing it while I hope to confirm its authenticity. Turns out her father is a lawyer. He drew up a contract for me to sign that his daughter is the rightful owner and the sketch is only on loan."

"Hmm. She is a smart girl. Maybe I'll get to meet her one day."

"Of course, I'd like William to get his eyes on it as well. Would you be able to make a trip to Winterthur with me in the next few days?"

I stood and stretched. What I really needed was to get back to a Pilates class and get not only my body aligned, but my mind in order. "I can make that happen. Besides, as you know, I have an earful to share with William Barrett as well."

Liam now stood beside me. "That painting at the base of your stairs." He pointed at the forged Modigliani painting of the dark-haired, nude woman. Her downcast oval eyes and elongated face and torso were a convincing match to the master's work. "If I didn't know she was a fake, I would easily be fooled."

Approaching the painting, I gently touched the textured brushstrokes on the woman's body—layers of light and dark values creating depth and an illusion of life. Then, without hesitation, I ran my finger along his signature, and like melodic notes, the letters whispered my name, *MODIGLIANI.*

CHAPTER FORTY-TWO

Olivia ~ Cleaning House

efore I could allow myself to join Liam for a drive to Winterthur, I had business to complete. Surprisingly and to the best of my knowledge, Grant hadn't hounded my office for the report, even though it was close to noon.

Once again, Joel had arrived well before me at the office. A stack of new case files waited on my desk and the morning's pot of coffee was half gone.

"Good almost afternoon, Joel." I blew him a kiss as he walked in my door.

"Well, hello, sleepy head. Or I was starting to wonder if you'd fired yourself."

He held up a bag of donuts and shook them. "Thought I'd surprise you with the world's best junk food." He scratched his head. "It's odd, but I had a craving for chocolate glazed donuts when I woke this morning."

I couldn't help but giggle. "That is odd, Joel. Really odd. I had the same craving this morning. But seriously, I owe you big time for putting up with me the last few months. I'm the one who's been off."

"A little or a lot?" He laughed.

"Either way, you'll be happy to know the old Olivia is back." *At least the one on the surface who you've always known.* "I promise, after I deliver the final report to Grant Richard in less than an hour, this case is formally closed and then, we'll talk. You haven't heard from him, either?"

"Not a word." Joel set the bag of donuts aside and propped both hands on my desk. "I'm happy to take the report to the museum for you . . . save you the time—"

"You mean grief?"

"Yes, that, too."

"You're a good man, Joel. I appreciate you." I stood and tossed my bag over my shoulder. "But I'm a big girl. I can handle this."

"Not doubted for a minute." Joel handed me the envelope containing the revised and final report in which details of the polymer and falsified receipt were included. "However, I highly question if Mr. Richard can handle it." He smiled a devious smile, and I couldn't help but mimic him.

*****

When I arrived at Grant's office, I was greeted by Shirley's red-lipped smile.

"Good afternoon, Shirley. I hope all is well."

Her smile quickly turned upside down. "Apparently, you haven't heard the news." She leaned forward, pressing her chest into the desk. "I guess you wouldn't know as things went down only this morning."

I stepped closer. "And what would that be?"

"I probably shouldn't be telling you this . . . at least yet." She lowered her voice to a whisper. "Grant Richard has been fired . . . terminated perhaps is a kinder word."

She must have read the surprise in my wide-open eyes as she continued. "I don't know all the details, but it seems he took liberties with museum records and attempted to falsify the provenance of *The Girl in White.*" She pursed her lips. "Such a shame. Of all the Richard family members, he was the most fun."

Instantly, my mind began reeling. Of course, I hadn't said a word to anyone outside my close circle—Joel, Professor Barrett, and just recently, Liam. None of them would have any motive to break the news to the board members. The report was still sealed and not officially delivered as it was still inside my bag.

The only other person privy to the information was May. What benefit would she have to tattle on Grant?

I forced my voice to remain calm. "Shirley, I'm so sorry to hear that news. I enjoyed working with Mr. Richard. He was . . . fun." A quick flash of tender moments between Grant and me left a pang in my heart. He was charming, witty, and especially handsome. And, if I was completely honest with myself, there was more than merely a physical attraction. Albeit an unusual situation, Grant had stepped into my life when I realized there was more to be had from it— companionship, friendship, intimacy, and even love.

I started to pull the report from my bag but couldn't help but ask another question. "I'm curious, how did anyone know . . . that Mr. Richard was being unethical?"

Shirley motioned with her index finger for me to come closer. "My colleague, Bernie, she's worked in the archives for thirty-plus years. We're the old-timers in the museum . . . except for the artifacts, of course." Shirley's head moved in a slow nod. "She suspected something was up. Noticed too many files out of order, a sudden interest in the artist. I know her well, and she was doing her own research."

"And what did she find?" *Or didn't find is more accurate.*

"Well, the lady has the nose of a bloodhound, and she detected an important receipt was missing from the files."

"Really?" My voice was animated as I was actually having fun with this charade.

"Her suspicions were confirmed when a grad student from the university, who, by the way, had been on Bernie's suspect list, showed up again at the archives and said she had something to report."

"I'm riveted." *And eager to know that May would return to the scene of the crime.*

"She claimed the museum director had offered to pay her to steal an original receipt, falsify a copy, and make it out to be important provenance for *The Girl in White*."

"And Bernie believed her?" I tilted my head to one side.

"Yes, she said she was a darling woman. Gone back to school a little later in life and, unlike many younger people, knew right from wrong." Shirley shook her head. "Sounds like Grant picked the wrong partner in crime."

And so he did. I opened my bag and set the report on Shirley's desk. "In light of the news, I'm not sure who I should deliver—"

"You can put it right here. Mr. Richard is most likely back in California. When he called me this morning to say he wouldn't be in, I had a hunch he already had one foot in the Pacific Ocean." She tucked the report into her desk drawer. "When the board convenes this afternoon, I'll be sure they receive it."

"Thank you, Shirley. I'm sure I'll see you again soon. Always something exciting happening in the world of art." I turned and started toward the elevator when her sing-song voice called out to me.

"Now, tell me, Ms. Danford, because the suspense is killing me . . . is she real or not?"

I pressed the down button and nearly slipped away, but I couldn't help responding. "Well, Shirley, I'm sure you'll learn the results from the report in a few hours. However, I can tell you this . . . there is always more than meets the eye."

*****

One down, one more to go. I shut my office door and pulled up "favorites" on the phone and scrolled the short distance to May. How sad that the person I thought I could count on for the entirety of life changed.

After several tries, she didn't pick up. May was one to keep her phone in her pocket so I had a feeling she didn't want to talk with me. Understandably. I paused before dialing the shop number. What was it that I really had to say?

Perhaps it was best she didn't answer. I had resolved earlier in the day that the secret shared by my father would remain just that—at least from certain individuals. May was number one on the list. Even though it would have been satisfying to reveal to her what Father's rambling actually meant—beat her at her own game of attempting to pass off a real Modigliani—it was best to keep it to myself. The tender sentiments, handwritten at the dusk of Thomas's life. I'd forever hold tightly, and not among three, but only between my father and me.

After half-heartedly paging through a new case file, I admitted that I couldn't let it go. May needed to know that she was completely found out. Besides, I wanted her to know that it hadn't gone unnoticed that she'd stooped so low as to snitch on Grant. I shook my head in disgust. Although he deserved it.

I lifted the phone and called the store. Not knowing it was me on the line, she'd pick up.

After several rings, a familiar and ditzy voice answered. "Hey, this is Crystal. Oh, you've reached Triple A." A giggle followed. "How can I help you?"

"I'm calling for May . . . the manager. Is she available?"

"She's not here anymore."

"Oh." If I recollected right, and I'm sure I did, May still had a couple weeks before she planned to move. "New job in town?"

"No, nothing like that. She split yesterday. Said she was getting out of town. Ready to start a new life."

"Really? Did she day where she was going?"

"Nope. Came in, got her things." An audible puff of air came over the phone. "She was pissed off and said something about her computer being gone. I don't know. I never touched it. I kinda just stayed out of her way."

"Good idea." I blew out my own puff of air.

"Anyway, I'm the manager now. Do you need help with something?"

"No, thanks. You've helped already." I ended the call and set down my phone.

After all, some things are best kept a secret.

CHAPTER FORTY-THREE

Olivia ~ True North

On my way to meet Liam at his hotel, I took a few detours to avoid traffic and shorten the drive. Last night's dinner with Joel had gone longer than expected, and now I was running late. Plus, I was looking forward to our drive to Winterthur as there was something I couldn't quite define that made me breathe easier when I was with him.

After treating Joel to a much-deserved steak and lobster dinner at the George Town Club, the serendipitous happenings of the last several days were all told out. In Joel's turn-over-every-stone manner, he'd peppered me with every question imaginable until he personally felt he'd connected the dots. What kept the conversation particularly lively was Joel's saturation of British slang after enjoying a beer or two.

"Well, mate, it seems that both Grant Richard and your old friend, May, were cheeky. But the best part . . . you won. If it wouldn't create gossip in your fancy club, I'd lean across the table right now and give you a congratulatory snog. Imagine that, kissing a real Modigliani!"

I smiled. Joel was more than a faithful and reliable employee— he was a good friend. As new work came in each day to Axiom, most assuredly, we'd have many more adventures ahead.

Liam was waiting at the front door to his hotel when I pulled into the circle drive. He wore jeans and a plaid flannel shirt, and his hair was tussled in a boyish sort of way. I couldn't help but notice the stark contrast to the businessmen flowing in and out of the hotel door, dressed in dark suits, ties, and shiny loafers. Liam always seemed relaxed—perhaps confident, though not in a conceited way.

He opened the rear side door. "Hi, okay if I put my case on the seat back here?"

"Absolutely. I assume you still have precious cargo in there."

"Let's hope so."

We made small talk much of the way getting out of the city. He filled me in on his current research and teaching while we touched on the latest news in the art scene. Once we hit the interstate, I'd fill him in about Grant and May.

"By the way, I've been so consumed with everything going on, I haven't asked about your father. How is Marcus?"

"He's doing well. Slowing down a bit, but he'll never admit it."

"I like that about him."

"I do, too." He turned his head and looked out his window. "I've come to discover it's one of hardest things in this life."

Even though his statement wasn't definitive, I believe I understood what he was talking about. "It's difficult getting older."

"True," he said softly. "Especially if you're trying to do it alone."

How could I argue? Even if I wanted to, the reality of going through life alone wasn't as palatable as it seemed when my world revolved mostly around me.

Liam's dad lost his wife after many years together. My father was alone for the majority of his adult life. Grant, May . . . and so many others, either by choice or fate having its way, were alone. Though my eyes remained focused on the road, I imagined my great-grandmother, Jeanne Hébuterne. She wasn't merely another tragic character in an art history book, but instead, a broken-hearted and lonely young woman after her beloved died.

After I told him about Grant getting fired and May slipping out of town, he only shook his head and said nothing at first, most likely processing the oddity of the situation just as I earlier had to do.

"You told her you were calling the police. Did you ever do that?"

"No, and I'm not sure if I really could. Besides, no money, at least to my knowledge, was exchanged. The portrait wasn't passed off as real and sold to the museum." It was devious of me, but I couldn't help but smirk. "The threat sure made her nervous."

"You played your cards well, my friend."

"You know the worst?" I was surprised when my voice caught.

"What's that?"

"I think I might actually miss her. No doubt, there's lots of healing on my part that needs to happen because we were friends through really tough stuff." I paused and considered what I said. "But like you said, it's hard to go through life alone, including losing a best friend."

Liam lowered his window. The cool autumn air felt good. I took his lead and opened mine.

"Then, Olivia, here's to building our friendship."

I took a deep breath and lingered with the refreshing air. "Yes, Liam Elliot, I believe we already have a solid foundation."

*****

Professor Barrett was mesmerized by all that I had to tell him. He nodded and paced the laboratory, most likely computing all the facts and sequences in his logical and brilliant mind.

Finally, he stopped and beamed at me. "A real Modigliani. I always knew there was something extraordinary about you, Olivia."

However, the professor could hardly contain himself when he and Liam examined the aged sketch closer.

"It matches the pentimento we first found on the portrait." William tapped the screen of his computer displaying the ghostly fluorescing image gleaned from the first round of imaging.

"I agree." Liam was nearly as giddy. "That Modi most likely first made this sketch and then used it as his inspiration to lay the foundations for the painting is phenomenal."

William patted him on the back. "I've been in this business a hundred years and it never gets old when I'm in the presence of a piece of original art. Liam, you get extra points for finding this sketch. That college student—"

"And her father," Liam chimed in.

"Oh, yes, they'll both be over the moon when they find out this piece of what looks like scrap paper was created at the hand of Modigliani himself." William chortled. "And the value of this will easily exceed her college tuition."

"You know, Olivia, after hearing all of this, an idea has come to mind." William rubbed his chin. "Now, I'm no marketing genius . . . but this story, and of course, *The Girl in White*, could make for a fascinating exhibition here at Winterthur."

The thought of revealing my family secret to the public, especially risking the reputation of my father, made me pause. "Oh, I'd really need to think about that."

"I understand. When things are this personal, they take on an entirely new perspective." William hugged me in a fatherly way. "But think about it . . . the higher-ups at the museum would be thrilled if you'd curate another exhibit."

*****

The meeting with Barrett was worth every minute of the two-hour drive from D.C. It was agreed that *The Girl in White* would remain for the time being under the care of the conservation team until I was ready to bring her to my house . . . bring her home. Though the sketch would still undergo scrutiny at the Pompidou in Paris, it had received accolades from the professor—particularly promising.

"We should celebrate." Liam patted the top of the car as I searched in my bag for the keys. "How about I treat you to dinner. Someplace nice."

"You don't think that's premature? I mean, we think it's real, but it's not one- hundred-percent conclusive. At least not yet."

"Olivia," he laughed. "I'm not referring to the sketch's authenticity."

"Then what's there to celebrate?" I retrieved my keys and pushed the unlock.

We looked at each other across the top of the car. It was easier for Liam—tall and slender—a fit build. Though he told me he'd recently turned forty, each time I looked at him, I felt a little awkward, in a high school girl sort of way.

"You and me . . . friends, of course."

I thought his face flushed. I opened the door and slid into the driver's seat. A quick glance in the rearview mirror confirmed my face had reddened.

"If it's all right with you, I need to first stop by my father's house. It's not even fifteen minutes away. The realtor is ready to show it and there's one more item I need to figure out how to move."

"Your childhood home." Liam squinted. "That must be hard to sell, especially since your parents loved you so much."

How sweet it is to be loved by you. The lyric of my favorite James Taylor song played across my mind like a beautiful melody. "You're right, Liam. There's nothing sweeter than to be loved."

*****

It took some muscle, but Liam and I lifted the old garage door. Obviously, it hadn't been oiled in years and it moaned as if it were an old man being ousted from his rocking chair.

"Well, here it is." I motioned to the canvas tarp. "Thomas's pride and joy . . . his '63 convertible Bug."

"You've got to be kidding." Liam reached for the tarp and then looked at me. "Can I see it?"

"Of course. I have to decide how to get it out of here. And, more importantly, where it will go. I doubt it's been started in years." I shrugged. "But then who knows. Lately, my father was up to all sorts of antics."

With the vehicle uncovered and the tarp set aside, Liam circled the iconic car, staring at it as if he'd unearthed a treasure. "My first car was a 1973 Beetle . . . banana yellow. She was my first love." He ran his hand over the hood. "But this one is a beauty. Seafoam green, the perfect vintage color."

I laughed. "I've never understood people's love affairs with cars. Thomas felt the same way about this one." I leaned over and pressed the steering wheel . . . *honk!* "Well, she still talks."

"How about we see if she runs." Liam raised an eyebrow. The supposedly shy and reserved academic most definitely had a mischievous side.

I shrugged my shoulders. "Give it a try. Clearly, Thomas never worried about anyone stealing it . . . he always left the key in the ignition."

"Ha. Smart man. No time to be bothered with such details as to where one left one's keys." Liam settled in the driver's seat and patted the passenger side. "Let's go for a ride."

He turned the ignition a few times. Silent, except for a slight clicking sound as if the car was waking up from a long slumber. Liam got out and opened rear hood. He tinkered for a few minutes, and then called up to me. "Slide to the driver's side and try it now."

"Ready?"

"Yep, give her a go."

I turned the key and gave the pedal pressure. The engine began its distinctive, *Slug Bug, click, clack* dance. Liam let out a yelp of excitement and I followed suit. I don't recall whooping and hollering like that since I was on a roller coaster—it felt so good to laugh.

With Liam at the wheel, we slowly pulled on to the drive. The afternoon was waning and a chill was in the air.

"Hey, stop for a sec. I need to grab something." I trotted to my car and opened the trunk. Grandmother's quilt, along with the few other items from Mother's cottage, still hadn't made their way into my house. I gathered the quilt in my arms and climbed back in the convertible.

"We might need this, especially with the top down." I smoothed the soft fabric over my legs, imagining all the time and dedication it took my grandmother to sew the many squares together by hand. Did she understand something about life as her fingers ached and her eyes grew weary? Something that I was now only figuring out? If so, I think she would have told me a patchwork life is a good life . . . family, friends, work, play, pain, comfort, love, and faith.

"So, which way do you want to go?" Liam smiled a big smile.

I thoughtfully considered the question, looking both right and left. "There's only one way to go, Liam. True north."

About the Author

Loosening the reins and leaning into a creative life—that's Jayme's sweet spot as an author, artist, and educator. Speaking at book clubs and interest groups, teaching the writing craft, and guiding others in their artistic pursuits at her longtime art studio, Piggy Toes, is the icing on the cake.

The transformative power of art and faith are common threads in her award-winning historical novels, *Chasing the Butterfly* and *RUSH*. Her contemporary novel, *Seasoned: A Vintage Love with Modern-Day Flavor*, delivers the same. *RUSH* won several awards, including the Gold Medal Illumination Award for Enduring Christian Fiction, Selah Finalist, Excellence in Editing, two prestigious Colorado Book of the Year awards, and finalist for the Chanticleer Laramie Award for Excellence in Western Fiction. *RUSH* was named the 2019 Village Read and celebrated throughout Colorado. Her bold floral paintings and imaginative landscapes blend luscious color and playful texture—a testimony to what is acclaimed as "joyful and hopeful" art.

Jayme lives at the base of the Colorado Rocky Mountains where she and her husband have survived raising three hungry hockey-playing sons. Currently, two very needy Golden Retrievers run the roost.

Visit jaymehmansfield.com for books, art, and creative inspiration.

P.S. - Insights and Information

Readers often ask what inspires an author to write a particular book. For me a story begins with a seed, takes root, develops in spurts, and finally when it is ready . . . blooms. *Portrait of Deceit* was a patient story—steadily growing over the course of several years, nourished by a unique friendship with a shared love for art, sprinkled with story-related travel and solid research, and soaked with imagination.

The story seed for *Portrait of Deceit* landed on fertile ground when I heard Dr. Colette Loll, founder of Art Fraud Insights, lecture in Colorado about art forgery. I listened to her share about notorious art forgers and her unique specialization to investigate, prevent, and educate about these prolific criminal entrepreneurs. To say I was interested would be an understatement. I was captivated—so much that I introduced myself to Colette after the presentation, told her I was a fiction writer and was already composing a story in my head, and suggested we could talk further.

Two years later, with her business card coaxing me from my bulletin board next to my writing desk, I picked up the phone and called. The initial discussion confirmed that Colette is not only passionate about her work, but the crème de la crème in the world of art fraud . . . on the good side that is!

To learn more about Dr. Colette Loll's work, lectures, and exhibitions, visit: https://artfraudinsights.com/colette_loll/

Be sure to visit my website for all things Modigliani—photos, facts, artwork, reader's discussion questions, behind-the-scenes insights, additional resources, and much more: www.jaymehmansfield.com.

FOLLOW JAYME H. MANSFIELD

Follow and enjoy Jayme's other historical and contemporary novels, *Chasing the Butterfly, RUSH*, and *Seasoned*

———————

https://www.bookbub.com/authors/jayme-h-mansfield

Website & Newsletter Sign-up ~ www.JaymeHMansfield.com

Facebook ~ https://www.facebook.com/JaymeHMansfieldAuthor/

Visit Goodreads, Amazon, and BookBub!
Reviews are appreciated!